Precious Jewel

by

Lisa Chablis Gardner

DORRANCE PUBLISHING CO., INC.

PITTSBURGH, PENNSYLVANIA 15222

ISBN # 0-8059-5404-X
Printed in the United States of America

First Printing

For information or to order additional books, please write:
Dorrance Publishing Co., Inc.
643 Smithfield Street
Pittsburgh, Pennsylvania 15222
U.S.A.
1-800-788-7654
Or visit our web site and on-line catalog at
www.dorrancepublishing.com

Dedicated to my family with all my love and respect. To my co-author and sister, Rose, thanks for helping. This story wouldn't have been completed without you. And last but not least, this book is dedicated to all those without soulmates.
LOVE AND JOY LIVES JUST AROUND THE CORNER...
IF YOU PATIENTLY WAIT.

In loving memory of my sister (Mikki) Pauline Gardner Young. You started me on the road to words. I know you're up there celebrating with angels.

There's a light that lingers within us all, guiding us through our lives on a path of righteousness. Unfortunately some of us choose mentally to turn it out, going through life in a state of darkness and treating others wrong. It is the light of conscience and in many of us it goes astray. But in some of us it never burns out or goes away. It will be the power that has led and will continue to lead us until our dying day. So honor your light within, that even with lost innocence will shine just like the golden rule. And hold onto its overwhelming power and beauty, just like a precious jewel.

Introduction
1987
Detroit, Michigan

Julian stripped off his black denim jeans and white shirt. He wore no underwear and was now totally nude. His excitement was evident in the hardness of his young, masculine body. The sight of his nude body hypnotized Myra. She was seated on the hotel bed, feeling a little nervous and a whole lot giddy. "I...I really shouldn't be here," she said. "My mother would kill me if she knew I skipped science to come to a hotel with you, of all people." She folded her arms, feeling a little insecure, as Julian breathed deeply. He rolled his eyes in disgust at her statement.

He walked over to the bed and gently caressed her cheek. He then tilted her chin slightly so that her face looked up at his. "Baby, you know you want me. I've seen you checking me out for months now," he said. He then shook his head, slinging his long black hair away from his eyes. He pushed her back on the bed. "I don't care about your mama. I want you," he said in a deep, seductive tone. He then caressed her breast and said, "Let's get in bed."

Myra quickly and willingly took off her lime green shell. "Oh...you know, Julian, I want you so much. I've wanted you since the first time I saw you," she said softly. She licked her lips and stood up from the bed, which Julian had gotten into. A naïve Myra, after stepping out of her flowered flared skirt, followed. He lifted her bra off of her small pouty breast and teasingly caressed and kissed it. She sighed, "You're wonderful, Julian." He didn't comment. He just moaned as he continued to kiss her soft body. Myra then said excitedly, "I knew you would be. You're so sexy and smart...and so...talented."

Julian, who was still kissing her firm body, moaned in ecstasy. He breathed deeply as he caressed her curvy hips and thighs. "Mmm, baby you feel so good," he murmured.

She chuckled, running her fingers through her black shoulder-length hair wildly as she said, "Well, yes. I'm much better than that blonde tramp, Shelly. She's nothing but a tease. Like I said, you're better off with me."

Julian's thrusts were earth shattering and dynamic. However the more he made love to Myra, the more she raved on about...everything. "You know what's wrong with our high school?" she asked. Julian didn't comment. He was still enjoying the pleasures of her body. Agitatedly, she snapped, "Julian! are you listen...."

"Will you shut the hell up?" he yelled angrily. "Do you want to do it or not?" he asked, his eyes wide with passion and anger.

"Of course, you're sensational, Julian. I'm just glad you haven't been with that Shelly Nohl slut. She's such a...." He rolled his eyes disgustedly at her constant talking. He again made love to her fervently, wickedly, as only he could. He spasmed physically, letting out a horrifying "Uhm!" then rolled over and sat up on the side of bed. He got up and gathered his clothes.

Myra, looking slightly angry, said, "Wait, what about me? We're not done yet." Julian looked at her and nonchalantly said, "I'm done," then headed toward the bathroom as he said coldly, "I have to get back to school." He frowned and said, "You need a shrink, baby. You obviously get off on talking and you need to sex someone who gets off on listening to that bull." He went into the bathroom and closed the door.

As he washed up, Myra swore angrily and loudly. But Julian had the water running and didn't hear a bit of her furor. "Fag! No wonder they say you're a weirdo! You creep! You...you jerk!" she shouted. He opened the bathroom door, was now fully dressed. As he stepped out of the bathroom, Myra started silently putting on her clothes. She sat on the bed and said nothing to him. He smiled at her as he opened the motel room door and said to her, "It's been fun. You've got a great ass." He left the room as a stunned Myra just sat there and watched him leave.

Chapter One
September 1, 1969

Rachel reached over for Steven as she lay in their king-sized bed. But Steven Parr, Rachel's husband, had already awoken. He was out of bed, dressed, and putting on his jacket when she woke up. "Where are you going, love?" she asked. She rubbed her tired eyes and said in a groggy voice, "I thought we were going to stay in bed all day, Steve. Where are you going?" He zipped up his jacket and smiled slightly at her. She continued, "After all, Tracy is staying with my mom this weekend."

He lifted the hood of his jacket over his head and said, "Sorry dear, I have to go out to the lawnhouse."

She frowned as she looked over at the window. Rain was falling heavily. Looking puzzled she said, "Steven...."

He interrupted her, saying, "I have an idea for a song. I have to go get my guitar." Rachel gazed at him without commenting. He walked over to the bed and kissed his wife on the cheek, then said, "You don't want to be teaching music at that lousy high school forever, do you?" He caressed her cheek playfully and said, "You can make it big, kid. With your voice and my managing and writing for you...we can reach the top!" His face seemed to glow as he spoke of entering the entertainment business again.

"...Past the top, baby. We can reach the stairs, Rach." He then shouted, "You can be a star, baby!"

Rachel rolled her eyes, then sat upon the side of bed and said, "Yeah, Steve, it sounds good. But, this is Saturday." She then sternly said, "I know fame is your dream. But I don't want to think about music, work, or becoming famous. Not today. I just want to stay home with my husband and make lo...."

Steven again interrupted her. In a musical voice he sang, "We can make love anytime, baby. But a hot song will leave you, if you don't care for it as soon as it comes to you."

She rolled her eyes again, then angrily stood up. "Forget it, Steve. Just forget it," she spat. "You're about as romantic this morning as that song you just sang." Steven's guilty conscience was getting the best of him as he saw and heard Rachel's disappointment in him and the way the day was turning out. Rachel smacked her lips and stomped into the bathroom.

She took a shower and decided to make the best of her Saturday. Stepping out of the shower, she sat down at her vanity table in the bathroom and brushed her long, black, wavy hair. As she brushed, she again thought about the perfect Saturday that she wasn't having. It's a cloudy day. Our daughter is at her grandma's and...I'm just going to sit here watching Steven write a song all day, she thought to herself. She threw the brush down on the vanity table and yelled, "What a fun day!"

She applied her lipstick quickly, then headed out the bathroom, still miffed.

She was still nude as she entered the bedroom again.

Steven was still in the room. He was staring out of the window at the rain that had started falling heavily. Rachel took her clothes from the closet without saying a word to him. She started to dress and calm down. Steven, feeling the presence of his wife in the room, turned from looking out of the window. He watched her petite, shapely body as she put on her tight-fitting dark corduroy pants.

Steven was captivated by his wife's beauty. He and Rachel had been married for five years and the sight of her still turned him on. He walked over to her, put his arms around her, and breathlessly said, "Ooh doll, I would love to get back into that bed with you and make love with you forever." Rachel's eyes held the look of love in them as her husband held her in his firm and strong arms. His deep voice ravished her soul and senses as usual. They kissed passionately for several minutes. A now-flushed looking Steven pulled away from her, and he smiled and cleared his throat as he stared longingly at her. "I'd better go before I change my mind about spending the day in bed with you again." Steven spoke in a deep and still raspy voice. He breathed deeply and said, "Well, you know how it is when inspirations hit, honey...You have to go with it." His eyes were wide with optimism as he spoke. She glanced at the window. The rain was pouring on the window harshly and, it seemed, with no end.

"You can't go out there, Steve!" she shouted. "It's raining cats and dogs." She ran her fingers through her slightly damp hair.

Steven chuckled. "Come on now, Rachel. A little rain has never killed anyone," he said patronizingly. He winked his eye at Rachel and said, "I've got to go." He left the room.

Rachel stood there spellbound as she heard his footsteps heading down the stairs. Now startled, she yelled, "Steven!" But there was no answer. She quickly put on her white, oversized shirt and ran after him. Running down the stairs, she yelled, "Are you crazy? Don't you dare go out to that shed in this weather!" But it was too late.

By the time she reached the bottom of the stairs, she heard the back door close. She swore. "Damn you, Steve." She then quickly went into the kitchen. She was about to open the door and yell some more, but through the door's window, she saw him tracking through the yard. Lightning and thunder seemed to surround him. But his determination was fervent as he walked through the large muddy yard to get to the shed. A helpless Rachel sighed. 'Steven...that guitar is going to be the death of you. It almost was when I met you back then and it surely will be now," she whispered to herself. She kept him in sight as he headed toward the lawn shed.

Steven's sight had become impaired by the pouring rain and lightning, however, although he still headed for the big white lawn shed to get his guitar.

He hadn't played or thought about playing his guitar since he married Rachel. He had gotten a steady job at the local television station and was now a sound engineer. When Rachel told him that she was expecting a child, he decided to put away his guitar for good and become a responsible husband and father. He had always intended to get back into the music business, but when his daughter entered the world and his life, the idea of becoming a rock musician left his thoughts. That is, until he awoke with the idea of a love song that would be perfect for his ever-complaining-about-her-job wife.

Steven unlocked the lawn shed. The lightning was fierce and Rachel stood in the kitchen door, squinting her eyes to see him with crossed fingers, hoping he would be all right. Steven pulled open the large door and stepped inside. The lawn mower and chairs filled the shed. He stepped carefully and stumbled over objects until he reached the back shelves. He had stored his guitar on the very top shelf, where it had been for a few years and was now probably weather worn and dusty. He reached up on the high shelf, patting around wildly since it was up high on the wall and he hadn't got his ladder. He suddenly felt the wooden, hollow-sounding instrument.

He grabbed the guitar and headed out of the old, damp shed. Once outside, he closed the big aluminum door. He then fumbled with his keys, trying to find the correct key to lock the double doors. The wind cut through his skin like a knife, while the rain whipped his skin like a switch from a tree.

As Steven stood out in the pouring rain, thunder, and lightning, the more disheveled he became mentally and physically. His long black hair was limp and hung down lifeless against his face. The cold, cutting rain stung his face from its wind-blown contact. "Steve, just leave the damn thing unlocked," yelled Rachel out of the back door, but he didn't hear her. He continued to search for the key, even though the rain made visibility zero that morning. The lightning lit up the dark, cloud-ridden sky. With each streak, Rachel could see her husband still standing out in the storm. "The best sound and light show ever put on!" he yelled as he finally locked the shed door. He turned, looked up at the stormy sky, and said, astonished and a little disoriented, "A light show...and God, you don't even need plugs or cords either!"

Streaks of lightning lit up the sky in a dramatic fashion. The sky seemed to turn shades of green, orange, and purple. At the same time the thunder seemed to be directing the colorful laser show. He gripped his guitar and started back to his house. He made his first step toward the house as a loud horrendous sound of thunder clouded his ears, making him flinch in startled surprise.

Just then, a bolt of lightning struck the worn, rust-covered shed. A strong bolt then ricocheted off the shed and hit Steven, knocking him to the ground. Rachel, who was watching from the kitchen window, instantly swung open the kitchen door. "Steven! My God, oh my God!" she screamed. She ran out of the house and across the large muddy yard. After many slips and falls, she finally reached him. He was unconscious and his face was pale. She got down on her knees and put her ear to his chest area after unzipping his jacket. She heard a very faint heartbeat and began slapping both sides of his face. "Steven, no!" she yelled. "Wake up, honey! Please, don't leave me, Steve, come on!" She again put her head down to his chest, listening to his heart for a regular beat. After not hearing anything, she broke down and cried. "Oh my God, why? I knew that darn guitar was going to be the death of you, one way or the other." She put her forehead on his chest and cried for several minutes. The rain continued to fall but the lightning, after completing its apparent mission, had stopped. Rachel's crying continued until she heard, "Hello, beautiful. Why are you crying?"

Steven's eyes opened and he spoke.

Rachel sighed. "Oh Steve, I thought you were...." She paused and chuckled, then said, "It doesn't matter what I thought. Let's just get you to a hospital."

He sat up looking dazed. He then said, "I...I was struck by lightning. It hit the shed and ricocheted off of it."

She gasped, "Oh dear Lord, you could have died." She had a shocked look in her eyes. She then said to him, "Can you stand up?" She put her arms around him to assist him, but he pulled away.

"Hush woman," he demanded. "Of course I can stand. I'm fine, just fine." He gently caressed her cheek and said jokingly, "Thank God you're not a doctor."

Rachel said, "What?" sounding a little confused.

"I saw you trying to hear my heartbeat. I was going to tell you a little to the left, but I just enjoyed having your head on my chest," said an exhausted-sounding Steven. He then stood up. He felt slightly nauseous but he didn't let Rachel know, thinking that it would pass. She stood beside him, holding his hand, and said, "I'd make a great doctor. That is, if all of my patients wouldn't try to pretend they're dead."

Rachel and Steven walked up toward their house holding hands lovingly. He laughed. "Your patients wouldn't have to pretend, my love." He paused and said, "With you not knowing where to listen to their heartbeat, you'll pronounce them dead yourself."

"Ha, ha...very funny," said Rachel. They both laughed and continued walking up to the house.

Chapter Two

Steven lay in bed at Rachel's insistence after his near fatality. She poured him a cup of tea as she sat in the chair beside their bed. He said, "My guitar! It's probably totally ruined now."

She handed him his cup of tea and furiously said, "Steven! Who cares about that old guitar?" She rolled her eyes and said, touching his arm sympathetically, "Baby, you could have been killed."

Steven grimaced and said, "You worry to much, Rach. Now I have to go see if I can salvage my guitar."

She objected, "No way, Steve. You are going to emergency at the city hospital so I'll know for sure that you're all right." He complied with his wife's command.

The doctor examined him with a positive report. "You're as healthy as a horse...no harm done." He wrote Steven a prescription for nerve pills and said curiously, "What on earth was it that sent you out to that shed in this weather?" Steven didn't answer and the doctor then said, "You're a bit shaken up. That's what the medication's for, but lightning should be taken seriously." He frowned at him and said, "You could be dead right now, son. You were lucky." Steven got up off of the examining table quickly. The doctor's question made him remember his guitar and the song that had come to his mind earlier that morning.

"My instrument's still out there on the ground!" he yelled excitedly. He looked at Rachel and exclaimed coyly, "I almost forgot about it with all this hospital nonsense."

Rachel, helping him put on his jacket, said sounding puzzled, "I thought you said it was probably ruined, Steve."

He zipped his jacket and asked, "What do you think repair shops are for?" He then balled up the prescription and tossed it in the trash can. "I don't believe in taking anything stronger than aspirin."

Soothing his now tense mood, she said, "My music crazy husband." She looked at the doctor and smiled. "Thanks doc. I'm glad he's all right."

Steven said, looking anxious, "Yeah, thanks. Gotta bolt." He opened the examining room door, and Rachel walked out with Steven following.

The doctor had stood to see his patient out of the room. He looked at Steven, raised his snow-white thick eyebrows, and said, "A guitar, huh?"

Steven said, looking back at the middle-aged doctor, "I was the best player in town." He then closed the door behind him and left the hospital.

Going out to the car, Rachel folded her arms and said, "When we get home, that darn thing's going in the trash."

Steven retorted, "No way. I'll put it in the shop tomorrow and it'll be as good as new. And then fame and fortune, here we come."

She sighed and got into the car next to him and said, "Whatever you say, dear." They then drove away.

Steven pulled up in front of their house about twenty minutes after leaving the hospital. They got out of the car, and he yawned while closing his car door. He complained, "I am exhausted."

Rachel replied, "Go on up to bed darling. I'll be in shortly to start dinner." He was about to comment, but she beat him to it saying, "I'll go get your guitar from in the back yard."

He smiled at his wife and said, "You're a jewel honey. Hurry on upstairs, I'll be waiting."

She rolled her eyes and agitatedly stated, "Go on in, now," as she gently pushed her husband toward their house. She then quickly went around the house to the back yard. She walked out toward the shed and picked up the old broken guitar. Looking at the worn, ragged guitar, Rachel quietly said, "Hmm....you and the damn band nearly broke us up before." She paused and glared at the tattered instrument, saying angrily, "You and my husband attracted more whores than a john, and you are not entering our life again!"

She took her keys out of her purse, and with the extra key to the shed, she went and unlocked it. She then hid the guitar under several thick quilts on the floor under the shelves and left the shed. Thinking quickly, she looked around at the alley. The garbage truck was at the other end of the alley and had already gotten their garbage out of the alley. She smiled, cleverly thinking of a more than believable lie and headed back to the house. She entered the house and took a beef roast out of the refrigerator for dinner, then called her mother to check on Tracy. Soon after her quick chat with her happy daughter on the phone, she headed upstairs to check on Steven. He was already lying in bed. As soon as she approached the bed, he grabbed her and gently pulled her over, forcing her to sit on him. She giggled and touched her husband's bare chest, saying, "Steven...please!"

With passion in his eyes, he looked at Rachel and said, "Baby...we missed the morning, but let's spend the rest of the day in bed."

Feeling blissfully in agreement with his idea, she sighed and caressed her husband's cheek, then said, "I have to prepare dinner, love. We've missed breakfast and lunch already today, my love, due to that...." She didn't finish her sentence, instead kicking off her shoes and joining her husband under the covers.

Holding Rachel close, Steven moaned, then said, "That's better." He kissed her neck and said in a deep, sexy tone, "I think I'll have my breakfast, lunch, and dinner right now, in bed with my sexy wife."

She replied, "Oh Steven, you were almost killed this morning and you still...." Finishing her statement, he said in his deep, seductive voice, "Want to do it...every day, all day...with you, my beautiful wife."

She smiled. She then said, feeling uneasy, "Uh.... Steve...the garbage man must have taken your guitar. The truck was down the alley when I went in the yard to get it." She shrugged her shoulders and said, "But it wasn't there."

He ran his fingers through her soft wavy hair. Surprisingly to Rachel, he wasn't upset about the guitar at all. He just looked gazingly at her and said, "I want you. Forget that guitar. I can get another one."

She breathed a sigh of relief at her husband's calmness over her guitar tale. She then chuckled as she ran her hands through his thick, black, curly hair.

Steven was already undressing his wife and throwing her clothes wildly around the room. He kissed her while caressing her nude body, and Rachel's breathing deepened and quickened. "I want to love you forever," he moaned.

"As you wish dear," she said giddily.

He made mad, passionate love to her for hours. When she looked around it was dark outside and the clock read 12:00. "It's midnight, Steven!" she exclaimed. "We haven't had dinner."

He reached over for the phone and said, "I'll order pizza. We can make love until they get here."

She giggled and again caressed his hairy chest. She then said, "I love you, baby."

He kissed her and said, "I love you, too." The guitar issue wasn't brought up again...not then.

A few weeks later, she walked into the house and said, "I'm going to have a baby. Congratulations, Daddy." He ecstatically jumped up from the couch. He held Tracy up to the ceiling and yelled, "You hear that, Trace, you're gonna have a brother or sister!" He then sat Tracy down on the couch. He and Rachel held and kissed each other intensely over her good news.

Chapter Three
1970
St. Margaret's Hospital

"Oh my God...uhn...uhn, please...oh, please...uhn!" exclaimed Rachel loudly. "Steven...you!" She swallowed hard and let out another passionate sounding cry. Breathlessly she laid her head back on the pillow. Her eyes fixed straight ahead, and she saw it. The doctor slapped her baby's bottom and the baby let out a horrendous cry. The happy nurses laughed with joy.

"You did it Rachel. You did it!" said one of the nurses. The doctor then said, "You have a healthy baby boy, Rachel, congratulations." Rachel, who was exhausted, laughed a tired but happy laugh as she gazed at her son.

Steven paced the lobby floor nervously. The nurse finally came out of the delivery room and informed him of the good news. "You have a son, Mr. Parr," said the young blonde nurse excitedly. "Your wife will be back in her room shortly. We'll bring the baby in for both of you then," exclaimed the nurse.

"Yes!" he shouted when the nurse left the lobby. He jumped up excitedly and yelled, "I have a son! I have a basketball player!" He then chuckled happily and after a few minutes, Rachel was rolled back into her hospital room. He soon joined her. "You did it, Mom," said Steven as he looked at his wife lovingly.

Rachel, a little tired and a lot exhausted, smiled and said, "I...I didn't do it alone. Remember...I think you had something to do with it."

He kissed her and said, "Yeah, baby we did it, we made a son. A healthy...son."

She smiled at her husband and said, "Now we have the perfect family, Steve. We have a son and a daughter."

He also smiled and said, "Yeah...the perfect family." A nurse entered the room, carrying in her arms Steven and Rachel's bundle of joy. She handed the baby to Rachel, smiled, and said, "Here you are, Mommy, all clean and beautiful." She then gazed back at Steven and smiled. His eyes were filled with tears and love as he bent over and kissed his son. "Julian, Julian Philan Parr," Rachel whispered as she looked at her son. She cuddled baby Julian, then looked up at Steven, saying, "A fitting name for him, don't you think, honey?"

Steven smiled and said, "Julian, my father's name; and Philan, your dad's name...is perfect!" He then looked down at his son.

Rachel said joyously, "Fits him like a glove."

He smiled at his wife and son, then jokingly said, "Thank you, Mommy, for giving me what I've always wanted...a son." He cleared his throat and said, "Well, you two lovely people of my life, I have papers to sign and fill out. So, is it possible for a daddy to hold his son?"

Rachel chuckled and replied, "Oh darling, of course you can hold your son."

He went over to the sink and washed his hands, then the nurse handed him his son. She warned him to watch the head. He held Julian carefully and lovingly, saying, "Hi, fella, welcome to the world." Rachel smiled as she watched them. Steven spoke softly, looking into his son's face, "Yeah...your sister's gonna love you just as much as your mom and I do." Tears filled Steven's eyes as he said, "Well, Julian. I guess I'll go home and start making the basketball court for us." He again gazed at Rachel lovingly and winked his eye at her, then looked back down at Julian. "We'll leave the cooking to your mom and your sister," Steven said in a joking tone. He sighed loudly and again said, "Oh, your sister's going to love you."

The nurse chuckled and said sternly, "Okay...okay you two. Time to let Mommy rest."

She went over to Steven and gently took the baby away from him, but not before Steven kissed his son, saying, "Goodbye for now."

The nurse smiled and said, looking at baby Julian. "Time for bed for you, too, little one." After Rachel held the baby once more the nurse took him away to the nursery. Steven and Rachel kissed, joyously celebrating their little bundle of joy. A tired Rachel caressed Steven's cheek and said groggily, "You really love him, don't you?"

His eyes widened as he said, "What's not to love? He's my son. My healthy basketball player son," Stated Steven proudly.

Another nurse then entered the room. The plump, gray-haired nurse announced loudly, "Okay, Mr. Parr. Your wife needs her rest!" The nurse went over and touched his arm and said gently, "You can come back in a few hours." Standing by the side of the bed, he bent over and kissed Rachel goodbye. He then went, as planned, out to the desk and filled out the designated hospital papers, after which he left the hospital. The rain sprinkled lightly and a gray mist filed the atmosphere on this dreary afternoon of June 7, 1970.

Chapter Four
Three Years Later

The wind blew fiercely outside. It was a cool and drafty March day in Detroit, Michigan. The wind blew so strongly that it shook parked and passing cars. It had been a bad day for women wearing skirts or dresses. And hair styling on this day was a waste of time for people venturing outside. March again was proving true to form in Detroit, Michigan on this windy March 9, 1973.

Inside the medium-sized colonial house, Rachel was in the kitchen ironing clothes. She carefully watched three-year-old Julian and seven-year-old Tracy. They were in the adjoining family room. Tracy threw her brother the big round beach ball. He caught the ball, saying happily, "Throw it harder, Tracy, harder. This game is too easy." He then laughed. But she continued her normal throw to her little brother. Steven had brought him the new ball on the previous day. Tracy received only a kiss on the cheek and a warning to watch her ball play with her little brother.

Steven worked as assistant sound engineer at the television station. Rachel had been a music teacher, but since having Julian, Steven had forbidden her to work. "You raise the kids, I'll raise the money," he told his wife jokingly. But he had meant every word that he had said. This arrangement pleased Rachel because she loved her children and her husband. She hated being away from them for any long period of time.

Rachel would now play the family piano and sing to Tracy and Julian. She always prompted her children to sing along. "Music is the language of love, children, sing," she would tell them happily. She would then laugh and wipe the tears that would start to fall from her eyes.

Tracy noticed how sad her mother now got when playing music and singing for Julian and her, how sad she got about everything lately. She also noticed how her mother had started drinking the booze from the in-home bar that sat in the corner of the living room. When the bottles were empty and Rachel was a lot happier, Tracy would have to baby-sit her little brother while her mom went down to the corner liquor store and bought more booze to replace the empty bottles on the bar. Rachel would come home and set the bar up to look as it had once looked, then put Julian to bed and send Tracy to go and study or do homework. Rachel then slept for hours.

Tracy silently watched Rachel's new routine each day. Steven, however, was none the wiser. Each night when he came home from work, he was unaware of Rachel's now almost daily ritual. He just he had a very happy and loving...overly loving wife. Life is good, thought Steven to himself, and it'll only get better.

Rachel, meanwhile, would cover her tracks well with mouthwash and anything that would erase the fact that drinking was a new hobby she had undertaken. This arrangement worked well for awhile until one day, lightning struck again or just maybe a drunk Rachel walked under a ladder.

Precious Jewel

It was now March 31, 1973. It was a cool, gray day. The wind blew mildly and the naked branches on the trees gave an eerie look to Station Street.

Tracy had just came home from school. Once again she had to baby-sit her baby brother because her mother had gone to the corner store to buy more booze. The bottles on their in-home bar were empty as usual during that time of the day. So...Rachel had to buy new bottles of the beverages. She did this to keep her husband from knowing that she was drinking. The only way she could now make it through the day was by getting loaded.

Chapter Five

Once again playing catch as usual, Tracy unhappily threw the ball to Julian. She thought of her mother's constant drinking and the fact that her dad knew nothing about it. Rachel had sworn her children to secrecy about her, so mum was the word.

Julian was enjoying catch with his sister. He laughed and shouted, "Come on Tracy! Throw harder. You throw like a girl!" He laughed again.

Tracy rolled her eyes in disgust and said, "I am a girl, you idiot." Julian continued to laugh. She then said, "I'll show you how a girl throws." She was going to throw her brother a swift, strong ball just to show him just what she was made of. However looking at her baby brother's happy stance, she smiled and took a deep breath, then said, "You're right, Julian. You're just a better catcher and thrower than I am."

Tracy's thoughts traveled again to her mother. She looked at her brother, whom she knew wasn't getting their mother's attention like he should and sighed sorrowfully. She threw the ball to Julian once more. The ball bounced off of his chest, and he had a blank expression on his face. He then passed out on the floor.

"Oh my God!" she exclaimed. She ran over to him feeling terrified as she yelled, "Julian, Julian! What is it? Are you okay?" Julian just continued to lay there, then his body started jerking and shaking out of control. Kneeling beside her brother, Tracy started crying. "Help! Help!" she screamed. "Somebody help my brother, please!" His convulsions were getting worse as he lay there on the floor. She stood and ran to the front door. She hesitated, suddenly wondering what to do next. She burst out of the screen door. She ran across the yard to go to the neighbor's for help, then saw her mother walking up the street, singing and smiling. She yelled frantically, "Mom...Mom, Julian's sick! He needs a doctor!"

Rachel's happy tune and smile quickly ceased. She immediately took off running toward her house. "Baby! My baby!" she screamed as she entered the house. "Oh my God!" yelled a hysterical Rachel when she saw Julian. She quickly went to him. He was still convulsing horrifyingly. She kneeled down beside Julian's body and lifted him slightly, holding Julian's small, shaking, out-of-control body in her arms. She cried, "Oh my boy! My sweet boy, what is it? What hap...." Rachel caressed his small face, then quickly jumped up from the floor.

Feeling helpless, she went over to the phone, screaming, "My God...oh my God, help!" as she dialed the phone for an ambulance. When the operator answered the phone, Rachel yelled, "My son...he's...he's sick. ...Please, he needs a doctor! He's only a child." Tears were pouring like a constant stream down her face. After briefing the operator on Julian's condition, she hung up the phone. She went back to the couch, where Julian still laid shaking profusely and looking as helpless as Rachel felt. She held his body the best that she could while saying silent prayers and making promises to God.

After a few minutes, Tracy ran to the front door and the sounds of sirens flooded the house. "They're here, Mom, they're here!" she yelled, now relieved.

The paramedics entered the house swiftly. They stuck a flatboard into Julian's mouth, telling Rachel, "So he won't bite his tongue. Looks like he's had a seizure, ma'am." He asked her, "Has anything like this happened before?"

Feeling as if she was in a hypnotic nightmare, Rachel quickly snapped at the paramedic, "No, never! He's a healthy baby." Tears filled her eyes. She frowned and said, "He's my son...my only son." Feeling panic, she urged the paramedic, "Faster...come on! We've got to get him to the hospital."

The ambulance soon took Julian to the hospital. Rachel stayed by his side in the ambulance all the way there. Before leaving the house, however, she sent Tracy to the neighbor's home. Their neighbor's daughter, Jolelle Wilks, loved Rachel's children. She had been sitting on the porch observing the ambulance come and take Julian out of the Parrs' house. She told Rachel that her parents were at work, but she would be happy to look after Tracy.

The doctor replied, "Well, he definitely had a seizure. I'm going to give him more tests. But I'm pretty sure that we may be looking at a case of epilepsy." The doctor gave him a shot that somewhat calmed the seizure. Julian became drowsy and almost fell asleep in the examining room.

"Epilepsy," sighed a puzzled and stunned Rachel. She frowned and asked the doctor, "But...but how? Is this a permanent condition? You can cure him, right?"

The doctor stared at her, then said, "Well...if it is epilepsy, it can be controlled in a variety of ways. Medication or perhaps bio-feedback is an option." He patted a troubled looking Rachel on the shoulder, then said assuringly, "We'll discuss all of your options later, after we run tests."

Rachel anxiously asked, "Are you gonna keep him?"

"Yes, I think we'll keep him tonight for observation. We'll then run a series of tests on him tomorrow."

Afterwards, Julian was in his hospital room sleeping safe and sound. Rachel called Steven at his job. She told him of Julian's terrible incident. Steven was distraught. He left his job early that evening, got in his car, and rushed over to St. Margaret's hospital to see his son. Speeding above the limit, he was sure he would get a ticket, however, his rapid and disturbed drive to the hospital was not interrupted.

He ran in the hospital. "My son, Julian Parr, was brought in today! What's his room number?" shouted Steven to the receptionist. After a quick glance the receptionist told him Julian's room number. Steven hurried down the hall to the room, practically before the receptionist had finished telling him the room number.

Julian was in the children's ward. Steven burst into his room and spotted Rachel. "Rachel is he alr...!" Before finishing his question, he noticed his son's small body laying across from where she was sitting. He stopped in mid-sentence and went over to his son's bed.

She stood and walked over to stand by her husband's side. "Yes...yes, he's all right for now," she said. She spoke in a low tone. "I think I'll stay with him tonight, though," she added.

Steven kissed his wife on the cheek, then protested, "No love. You look like you're about to drop." He then bent over and kissed Julian on the cheek, then told Rachel, "Go home, baby, and rest. I'll stay with him tonight." He said firmly,

"Go...take care of Tracy. We'll be fine." He looked at Julian, who was sound asleep, as she yawned.

She stretched out her arms and hugged Steven. "I am pretty beat, honey," she whispered. She stepped back from him looking worried, then continued, "But what about Julian, sweetheart?" Pausing, she added, "Epilepsy, Steven! What are we going to do? He's just a child."

Steven sighed. He caressed her flushed cheek and said sternly, "He'll beat it, dear. He's a Parr. No one in my family is sickly and it isn't going to start now. We're strong, us Parrs. We all are!"

Rachel folded her arms. "But...." She started to speak, but Steven interrupted her. "Look! I heard you when you told me over the phone, and I'm hearing you now," he hissed. "My son will get well! He'll get beyond this," shouted an angry but determined Steven.

Rachel sighed, running her fingers through her hair. She whispered, "I hope you're right, dear. I hope you're right."

"Oh ye of little faith," said Steven to Rachel. He stared at his lovely wife, then at his ailing son. He hugged her again, then said, looking somewhat desperate and emotional, "He's got to beat this, baby. He's got to.... He's just got to." Rachel felt her husband's fear as he held her. She remained silent. All she could do was hope and pray. Julian still lay there in his hospital bed sleeping peacefully as divine wishes were being sent toward the heavens for him.

Chapter Six

The next afternoon, Julian was back at home. He was still a happy, active three-year-old boy. It appeared that after his illness and overnight hospital stay, he had developed an extra sparkle to his eyes and an overwhelming zest about himself. He seemed more aware and energetic than ever, and some would call him spoiled.

The doctor had earlier given Rachel and Steven the diagnosis of Julian's condition. It was, in fact, epilepsy. Rachel cried as Steven held her in his arms. Still the voice of optimism, he breathed deeply and said, "He'll beat this, dammit!" Before they left the hospital, the doctor gave them pamphlets on how to deal with and treat epilepsy. He also prescribed a special diet and medication for Julian.

However Julian didn't have another seizure for a couple of years. Life resumed, pretty much back to normal for the Parr family. Tracy attended elementary school as usual. And a wide-eyed Julian waited at home anxiously for her to return. When she did, they often played ball.

It was now May of 1975. The day was warm and sunny. Five-year-old Julian was a cute little boy. He had green eyes and a light complexion. His hair was long, black, and straight and accented his very big eyes. Despite the horrible illness that kept him somewhat subdued and from playing like the other kids, he remained happy and spoiled.

It was Friday, May twentieth, and Julian went to school as usual, a half-day. He was in kindergarten and hated school a lot, but he went with no fuss. Most of the teachers at his school loved him as everyone seemed to love this cocky and cute little boy. When Rachel took him and Tracy with her to the supermarket, ladies would go out of their way to compliment her on how cute her son was. She would just smile and say thank you. Julian, on the other hand, would just roll his eyes from both arrogance and embarrassment. Tracy, once more being overlooked, would just walk away.

On Saturday, May 31, 1975, Steven came home from work after pulling an overtime shift at the television station the night before. He entered the house carrying a big flat box. Inside it was a guitar for Julian. "Here, son," he said to him as he took the guitar out of the box. Julian and Tracy were seated on the floor in the family room, watching television. As soon as Julian saw the guitar, he shouted excitedly, "Oh boy, Daddy! A guitar, like Bootsy's! I'll be like the Parliament Funkadelics!" He jumped up and ran over to his father and grabbed the guitar. He started stroking the strings and singing, "Flashlight, neon lights...stoplight...."

Steven said, "Hold on, hold on!" He had a pleased look on his face, admiring his son's enthusiasm. "We got to get you some lessons first, my boy. Then you will be...." He paused, then excitedly said, "Bigger than Hendrix was." Looking somewhat puzzled, he continued, "You know, I had a guitar." Julian and Tracy were surprised by their father's omission. They hadn't heard a whole lot about their father's musician days due to Rachel's insistence on burying Steven's wild musician's past. Julian and Tracy didn't even know their father had owned or played a guitar.

"Really, Daddy. You had a guitar?" asked Julian excitedly. Rachel, who was in the kitchen preparing lunch, looked over the counter of the adjoining television room at Steven. She held a look of disbelief on her face, disbelief in the fact that he was breaking their silence about a past rule. She also couldn't believe he had bought Julian a guitar.

Noticing his wife's disapproving gaze, Steven said, "What the hell." Distracted by Rachel's stare, he cleared his voice and continued, "Ye...yeah, Jewel, I play guitar." He added, "I was lead guitar player in my ba...." As Rachel walked into the TV room, his conversation quickly ended as he saw the cold look in his wife's eyes.

Tracy sat there with a slightly sad smile on her face. Looking at her dad and brother's enjoyment, she was feeling somewhat sorry for herself. She sat there thinking to herself, He didn't give me anything, again.

Julian excitedly shouted, "What! What else, Daddy? You were a lead guitar player in a band, was that what you were saying?" he whined. He then urgently said, "Tell me, Daddy, tell me?"

"Oh, Steven, you didn't. Julian's too young for a guitar," Rachel stated firmly. She then sat down on the floor beside Tracy and put her arm around her shoulder, caressing her daughter's cheek as she smiled.

Rachel was only too aware of Tracy's sad demeanor, which was starting to diminish with her mother's loving touch. Rachel then reached out her hand. "Give me that thing, Steven," she said somewhat angrily to her husband. He rolled his eyes and handed her the guitar, which she examined closely. Julian was having a small tantrum as his mother looked the plain but adequate object over.

"It's mine, Mom. Give it to me! Give it to me now!" he shouted. Rachel frowned as he pulled on the instrument, trying to take it from her. Stunned, she said, "Steven, my God, this is a real guitar! Julian's too young for this. It will be broken before the day is over." Tracy smiled. She was enjoying her brother's tantrum over not getting the guitar from his mom. Rachel agitatedly said, "Julian, would you be quiet and sit down! You're not keeping this."

"Aw man, Mom. Why?" once again whined Julian. He walked over to his dad. "Daddy, can I keep it, please?" he asked Steven.

After sitting down on the pullout couch, Steven picked him up, placed him on his lap, and said, "Of course you're gonna keep it, son."

Rachel stood up suddenly, folding her arms. "Steven, we talked about this! You know that we agreed not to force the music thing down their throats." She continued, "If they want to get into playing music when they're older, fine. But I'm not gonna force playing the piano on Tracy, the way my mom did me." She glanced at Steven and said, "And you shouldn't force the guitar on Julian either, just because you like to play the guitar. Right now, he's too young to know what he wants to do or play."

Julian yelled, "But Mom, I do want...." he stopped talking when Steven stood up from the couch.

Looking at Rachel somewhat angrily, he blurted out, "You're talking nonsense! You know as well as I do that the younger they learn to play the better." With a smirk on his face, he added, "Why, he can almost play the piano better than...." Rachel sighed in disgust from what he was about to say, but he didn't finished his comment. He chuckled slightly and so did Rachel. She then said, somewhat humorously, "I guess he does have some inherited talent."

Steven said excitedly, "My rocker, Precious Jewel, is gonna be a big star."

Rachel questioned, "Precious Jewel?"

"Yeah baby, he's gonna be a big star...the musician I never was." Hearing the tone of Steven's insistent voice, Rachel saw that she was arguing a losing argument. Steven ruffled Julian's black hair, then smiled at him as he picked up the guitar again. "Now, on Monday, Rachel, you look in the phone book and find our boy the best darn guitar instructor around," said Steven.

Rachel walked toward the kitchen, saying, "Whatever you say, dear."

Tracy rolled her eyes and smacked her lips, then said in disgust, "Figures."

Julian jumped up from the couch excitedly. "All right!" he yelled joyously. He struck the guitar strings again. The guitar made a blaring sound that was heard throughout the house. "All right!" he shouted again.

The day was clear and warm. After his parents' discussion, he placed the guitar back in the box as Steven went to his room and changed into sweats. Feeling energetic, he yelled, "Come on son," as he passed through the kitchen on his way to the basketball court. "Let's go out and play some b-ball!"

Rachel, who was still preparing lunch, shouted, "No! Steven, no!" She stared at him and said, "Let him watch his cartoons." She frowned. "Besides, Steven, it's dangerous...you know that." She gave Steven an evil look that would break glass.

Steven said, "Nothing's wrong with the boy, Rachel. Nothing but he needs some exercise and he needs for you to stop smothering him."

She curtly replied, "I'm his mother, Steven. It's called mothering him." She then said, sounding concerned, "I don't want him to have another seizure."

Steven grabbed ahold of his wife, who was quickly preparing plates, and whispered in Rachel's ear, "You're gonna make him a sissy, dear. He hasn't had a seizure in years now, and he won't have one." He then said nonchalantly, "The boy's cured." Rachel slammed the prepared plates on the counter harshly as she listened to him.

Tracy and Julian had been hearing their parents fuss, even though their eyes were watching television. When the plates clanked loudly on the counter, Tracy jumped up and ran into the kitchen, saying excitedly, "I'll play, Daddy! Can I play?"

"Naw...go play with your Barbie dolls. You're a girl," said Steven. He then yelled, "Come on, son!"

Julian and Steven headed out of the back door with the basketball in Steven's hand. Before walking out the door, he kissed his wife on the cheek. "You worry too much, love," he stated.

"Well, I guess I'll watch," said a somewhat heartbroken Tracy.

"Sorry dear," said Rachel sorrowfully. "You know how your father is. He's old-fashioned and thinks girls should bake cookies or play dress up." She caressed Tracy's cheek, then said, "Make sure your dad doesn't work your brother too hard for me."

Tracy shrugged her shoulders. "He just doesn't love me, that's all," she said. "I bet he wishes he had two sons instead of a dumb girl." She walked out the door, her braided pigtails bouncing lively.

Steven was dribbling the ball on the gray pavement. "Take the ball! Take it!" Steven taunted Julian, dribbling the ball from side to side. Julian was running and panting, trying to steal the ball. Steven suddenly jumped up and made a basket. "Yeah!" Steven shouted. "You're too slow, son. We've got to work on that."

Tracy observed from the edge of the backyard lawn, never being noticed. The smell of apple and pears blossoming on the trees soothed her senses, letting her know that summer was on the way. "Here, take a shot!" Steven said to Julian. He then threw the ball to a blue-tinged Julian, who just stared straight ahead as ball hit him in the chest. Tracy frowned as she observed her brother. Just as quickly, Julian fainted, hitting the cement of the driveway with a hard force. He was having another seizure. Tracy yelled, "Daddy! He's sick again!"

Steven ran to his son, who was once again jerking out of control. His body was hitting the pavement harshly. "God, no!" he yelled. He was startled by the sight of his son's illness. He then tried holding Julian's small body so that he wouldn't hurt himself on the pavement. "Go get help!" he yelled.

But Tracy had already gone and was returning quickly with Rachel, who held in her hand a glass of water and Julian's medicine. Steven's light brown complexion had turned gray, and his eyes were teary as he watched her administer to Julian. She placed an object in Julian's mouth to stop him from injuring himself and applied cold compresses to his forehead, acting like a real pro, thought Steven. The only thing he did was sit next to Julian's body with tears streaming down his face, feeling just as helpless as Tracy during this situation.

When the seizure stopped, he carried Julian to his bedroom. Steven hadn't uttered a word since his son's attack. Rachel called the doctor, who in this instance made a house call. He examined Julian and told them that he would be fine. The doctor also told them to keep him calm and let him rest.

When the doctor left, the grits really hit the fan. "How could you?" shouted Rachel. Steven just sat dumbfounded, looking at and listening to her. They were gathered in the cozily decorated white and black livingroom. Steven was seated in the black chair in front of the fireplace while Rachel paced the floor. "I told you, he's sick. He's a sick little boy. You can't have him out there hustling after some ball. He's got to take it easy, and he's got to be careful," she said.

Steven calmly and sadly stated, "My God, I almost killed him." He then frowned, and broke down and cried.

Rachel went over and put her arms around him. She ran her fingers through his black curly hair. "Oh, my dear, Steven...I'm sorry. It's been a long day and those attacks take a lot out of me. I didn't mean to blame you. I'm...I'm just so afraid." She began crying.

Steven pulled her down on his lap. "Don't cry, baby. He's fine now," he said soothingly.

"What if he hurts himself...or dies?" she hysterically asked. "I...I don't know what I'd do." She wiped her tears and rested her head on Steven's shoulder.

He said, "It's all right. He's our son. We love him and we'll get through this." He caressed her long black hair. He frowned as his mind pondered his son's condition, and he looked as if he was a million miles away.

Chapter Seven
One Year Later

It was now 1976. The Parr household was still the same. Steven worked and Rachel wanted and needed to work. Tracy and Julian attended school regularly. Julian's illness continued, but fortunately his seizures were few and far apart. The Memorial Day holiday was coming, and the Parrs decided to have a cookout.

At the Memorial Day gathering Rachel had arranged, about thirty people showed up. The packed crowd was in the Parrs' backyard. The smell of barbeque filled the air along with laughter and talking. Steven cooked constantly while chatting with his guests. Rachel, seated in one of the many lawn chairs that filled the yard, gossiped with her guests as well. Included among the guests were neighbors from down the street as well as friends from a few streets over.

A strange but lovely woman, Corina Charles, attended the affair along with her five-year-old daughter, Brandie. Corina had moved on Station Street the same year the Parrs had. She had met Rachel at a nightclub Rachel used to work at. Corina had driven her home many nights after Rachel had one too many drinks and was too tipsy to drive home herself. She would drive Rachel's car, then would give her the keys and walk the few streets over to her own house. Steven, who usually was at work when Rachel came home, was still none the wiser, or so Rachel thought.

A few of Steven's co-workers were at the barbeque as well as a few of the teachers with whom Rachel had once worked. Rachel had always tried to impress her snooty, uppity co-workers. This barbeque was another chance for her to try again. Her co-workers had never accepted her as a legitimate music teacher, a fact that disturbed her terribly. She had been a nightclub singer before she started teaching music at the school and didn't have M.A.'s in teaching like her former co-workers. Steven couldn't care less what Rachel's rude arrogant coworkers thought. He had told her so often.

Still, Rachel had to always prove herself equal to the other teachers, not less. By giving the barbeque they were proving to friends they were the perfect family and not a dysfunctional one.

The flies and butterflies flew around the yard. Happy people chattered and drank beer and punch.

Steven looked up on the large back porch after turning the ribs. He frowned as he saw Julian up on the porch, plugging in his guitar and small amplifier through the back door. "Julian, what the hell!" he yelled, but unfortunately his voice was drowned out by Julian's exceptional guitar playing.

Rachel put her hand to her mouth, astonished. She then said, "Oh...my God!" as he played a mean version of "Purple Haze" and JB's "Cold Sweat." He gyrated his hips, stripped himself of his holiday T-shirt, and screamed a musical, "I don't need anything, baby but your love!" He struck the ending cords of the guitar and looked up exhaustedly at the sky.

Corina Charles yelled, "Yeah baby! More! Bravo! More!" There were more cheers and whistles from the crowd, as well as a few chuckles.

Steven ran up on the porch and said jokingly, "I hope you all enjoyed my ham of a son's musical talent, but the show's over." He swept a bare-chested Julian up in his right arm and took him into the house. There were more chuckles, laughter, and applause from the guests. An embarrassed but proud Rachel just shook her head saying, "Oh my God! Oh my God!"

Inside the house, in the family room, a laughing hysterically Tracy said, "I told him not to do it, Dad. But you know how bullheaded he is when he gets his mind on something."

Steven exhaustedly said, "Tracy, go out and join your mother. I have to talk to Julian." His face held a stern expression on it. Julian's eyes were wide as he sat on the couch looking at his father. He was wondering what kind of punishment he was in for. Tracy smiled wickedly as she walked to the back door. She looked back at Julian and burst out laughing as she headed out the door.

Still standing, Steven looked seriously at Julian and frowned. He then shouted, "Baby, you're a star! I got myself a real, natural-born star." His gray eyes sparkled as he spoke to his son.

Julian, looking confused, said, "Huh?" scratching his head.

Steven sat down on the couch next to him then said, "What you just did shows that you have guts.... Not just guts, talent! You have talent."

Julian shyly asked, "You aren't mad at me?"

Steven hugged him slightly and yelled, "Hell no! Why should I be mad?"

Julian then said lowly, as he shrugged his shoulders, "Because I did my James Brown and Elvis imitations. You know, and I took off my shirt."

Steven chuckled and said, "Oh...that." He hesitated and said, "Here." He handed Julian his shirt. He then patted his son on the back and said, "Well your mother might be mad, but I think it shows character. It shows that you aren't afraid to be you." He added, "So...your mom is trying to be Mrs. Cleaver in front of her former coworkers and a few stuffed shirt neighbors—who cares? Everyone loved it, especially that nutcase, Mrs. Charles."

Julian kept a serious look on his face. Shaking his butt and taking off his clothes might not mean beans to his dad, but to his mom, Oh Boy! he thought.

Surprisingly though, all Rachel said when he went back out to the yard was, "Well, my son, the rock star." She smiled and then said, "It's time for you guys to eat. Go find Tracy." Steven gave him an assuring wink and Julian ran to find his sister.

Chapter Eight

Weeks passed with life continuing pretty much as normal in the medium-size colonial home of the Parrs. Julian and Tracy attended Blake Elementary school. Steven still worked. And Rachel had pulled down a part-time job playing piano and singing three nights a week at Zemis Restaurant in the heart of downtown Detroit. Julian's illness seemed to cease and Tracy busied herself with her school friends. She was still being over looked and shoved aside for her brother by her father, but she was used to this treatment. However hanging out with her friends, she didn't seem to mind as much.

Julian had begun taking guitar lessons, but his unorthodox way of playing made the male instructor nervous. He had taken lessons for two months, with his last lesson ending when he angrily told the instructor, "Mister, I need to teach you how to play!" He then grabbed his guitar and said, "Come on, Mom, let's go home."

It was now 1977. A year had passed since Julian's last attack. "Tracy has a play at the school tonight," Rachel told Steven while they all were gathered at the dining room table eating. She had prepared her famous spaghetti and meatball dinner, along with a tossed salad. They all were eating heartily. Steven wiped his mouth with his napkin as Rachel said, "Are you going with me tonight, dear?"

"Nope, sorry, Honey. The big game between Detroit and Boston is on tonight. Can't miss it." He was an avid basketball fan.

Rachel then said, "Good, dear. Julian needs to rest tonight. He had a long day with going on that field trip and all with the school. You can stay and look after him until we get back." She smiled at Julian, knowing how he hated to be fussed over and treated like a kid.

Tracy rolled her eyes in disgust. "Why don't we all just stay home. We can watch the...." She smiled sarcastically as her voice rose in pitch. "Oh, we love you so much, Julian. You're the only important show!" Angrily she got up and went to her room.

Rachel was furious at her behavior as Steven just shook his head and Julian lowered his eyes sorrowfully. "I don't know what's gotten into that girl," exclaimed Rachel as she got up from the table and headed for Tracy's room.

Julian said sadly, "What's she mad at me for? I wish I could go see her play tonight." He had a sad look on his face.

Steven ran his hand through Julian's hair, frustratedly saying, "She's not mad at you son. She's mad at...at circumstances...situations, the damn situation!" He slammed his glass of iced tea on the table and said, "She's not the only one angry in the house." He stood up, clearing the dishes from the table. Julian sat there silently. A tear dropped from his eye. Steven then said, looking at Julian uneasily, "It's not your fault, son. It's not your fault." He touched the top of Julian's head, ruffling his hair again. Steven tried to smile, but it failed him. He just patted Julian on the back lightly and headed toward the kitchen with the dirty dinner dishes.

"Young lady, what's wrong with you?" Rachel asked angrily. She was looking at Tracy, who in turn was sitting on her bed. Rachel had a frown on her face, but her eyes had the look of concern. Tracy again shrugged her shoulders.

She was now eleven years old and in the sixth grade. She had gorgeous black hair, which she still wore in braided pigtails. She was smart and semi-quiet, but loved music and dancing. Rachel had enrolled both Julian and Tracy in a piano course a year before. Tracy loved it and was taking lessons every Friday at seven o'clock. She never missed a class. Julian, on the other hand, loved music but hated taking any musical lessons. Just like guitar lessons, Julian stopped going, but this time after his third week.

"I hate it," he told Rachel. "Can't nobody teach me music, that's dumb." Rachel and Steven didn't argue with him and let the lessons go. Julian, however, would go in the living room some evenings, turn on the radio, and sit at the family piano. He played all the songs that came on the radio true to form without any mistakes. This feat astounded and amazed Steven and Rachel.

Tracy would comment, "Just dumb luck. He still should take lessons, like me." She loved her brother, and they were close, but...she hated the fact that music came so easy for him. She practically had to bend over backwards, study, practice, and practice again.

Rachel and Steven noted their son's natural knack for music. Not showing off, Julian always let his talent show. At home he would play the piano like a monster and the guitar like a demon. At seven years old, his voice was a match for any professional singer. Rachel never treated either of her children better than the other. Sure, even though sickly Julian had a gift, Tracy was smart and talented as well, thought Rachel. She knew this about her children, and Steven believed all these things about his kids, too...hopefully.

Tracy, looking at her mom, then said, "Daddy doesn't love me. It's always Julian this, Julian that...both of you!" Her face and voice looked and sounded angry.

Rachel sat on the bed. "Now Tracy, you know...." Her voice was sympathetic and understanding.

Tracy interrupted her, saying, "I know that whenever I have or do something important, it gets overlooked because of Julian."

Rachel continued, "Honey...that's not fair. You know your brother is...."

"Is a spoiled brat!" screamed Tracy. "If Julian brings home an E on his school work, you guys are ready to celebrate." Rachel frowned and looked at her as she continued, "Oh, I forgot. Julian doesn't get E's. He's perfect." She stood up and said angrily, "And now, Daddy says no, I can't go see Tracy's stupid play. Julian and I got to stay at home and watch a stupid basketball game."

Rachel tried to quiet her rage, saying, "Tracy, baby, you know it wasn't like that.... Please."

Tracy then said, nastily, "I don't know anything. Julian can't play basketball. You know what happened to him before."

Rachel jumped up from the bed ferociously. She went over and grabbed her by the shoulders. She shook her harshly, saying, "Shut up! That's mean. Don't you talk so cruelly about your brother! What if he di...." Before the words were completely out of her mouth, she broke down crying. She then sat back on Tracy's bed with her hands covering her face. She was crying and saying, "Oh

God, why? Why?"

Tracy walked over and sat by her mother. She put her arm around her, saying, "I'm sorry, Mom. I love Julian, too. I didn't mean it. I didn't."

Rachel, regaining her strength, wiped her eyes. She hugged Tracy, saying, "Oh sweetie, you're our baby, our firstborn. Your daddy and I love you so much. We'll always love you." She continued, "Honey, your brother is ill. We don't know if he'll be with us always or...God forbid, he'll be taken away from us tomorrow." She took her arms from around Tracy, took a deep breath, and said, "Yes, we may pamper him a little too much, but...it's because he's sick. He needs our attention." She stared at Tracy and said, "All of our attention, Tracy." Tracy nodded. Rachel added, "You've looked after him pretty good every since he was a baby...don't stop now, please."

Tracy replied, "I do love him, Mom. I'm sorry for being...being...."

"A little jealous," Rachel swiftly helped her out with her statement.

Tracy said, "Yeah, I guess I was. I'm sorry."

Rachel hugged her daughter again and said, "Forget about it, sweetie. You have a play to get ready for. Get your things. I'll drive you to school." She left the room.

"Everything's fine," Rachel told Steven as she was getting her purse to drive Tracy to school. Steven, seated in the white recliner in the living room, said, "That's great." He then yawned and said, "Julian's in his room, I guess you can hear him." The guitar blasted as usual from Julian's room.

Rachel smiled and hung her purse on her shoulder. She then checked her hair in the mirror on the wall. She fluffed a few curls and said, "Yeah honey, that's great, but you're gonna have to start taking a little time out to notice your daughter." Steven grunted. Rachel licked her rouge-colored lips. She walked over and sat sideways on his lap, then said, "Yes, honey...and your son, too. Lately, you've neglected us all."

Steven, sounding a little agitated said, "Aw honey...it's just that...I have a lot of work to do. And when I get home, I'm tired. I barely find time to eat except on my days off."

"Well, you'd better make time," said Rachel as she caressed his cheek. "Or the next time, it'll be me and Julian complaining that Daddy doesn't love us." She kissed him and then stood up. He playfully gave her a swat on the bottom. "Later, when I get back," she promised. He laughed wickedly.

Tracy then came from her room. She said goodbye to her father and went to Julian's room and peeped in on him. His guitar was laying on top of him and he was sleeping soundly. Tracy closed the door headed for the front door.

"We won't be long," Rachel told Steven.

He replied, "Take your time. My precious jewel and I will be just fine." He got up and walked Rachel to her car. Before pulling off, she smiled at him. She rolled down the window on the driver's side. After opening and closing the door for his wife, Steven stood in the street next to his car. He told Tracy, talking through Rachel's rolled down window, "Have a nice play, baby. Break a leg."

"Thanks, Daddy. Say goodbye to Julian for me," said a cheerful Tracy. Rachel smiled at her husband and started the car. Before pulling off she said to Steven, "Goodbye, love."

Chapter Nine

"Slam dunk, baby, yeah!" yelled Steven excitedly. He was watching the basketball game between Detroit and Boston. Popcorn was scattered all over the gray carpet, and beer and Pepsi cans cluttered the coffee table in the living room of the house. Julian sat near his father, drinking Diet Pepsi and eating popcorn. This was a familiar scene in the Parr home, since Steven and Julian watched sports together on television religiously. Even though seven-year-old Julian wasn't allowed to play many sports, he knew as much about basketball and football as the players. He and Steven would spend countless hours shouting at the TV screen during a game. This night was no different.

Julian yelled, "Steal the ball! Steal the ball! He's right there. Ahh, the other guy made a basket. They're gonna blow this game!"

His father agreed. 'Here, son, you want some more popcorn?" asked Steven. Julian didn't respond. "Son...son are you feeling all right?" asked Steven.

Julian got up, saying, "I need some water." He walked to the kitchen with Steven following behind him.

"Did you take your medicine?" asked Steven.

"I got a headache," answered Julian. He wasn't aware of Steven's question and didn't answer.

Steven headed to Julian's room to get his medicine but it was too late. As he walked back to give him his medication, he heard a loud thump. Horrified, Steven ran back to the kitchen screaming, "Julian! Jewel! Son!" When he reached the kitchen, Julian was having another seizure. He was sprawled out on the kitchen floor, jerking wildly and intractably. Steven went through the necessary procedures of giving him his medication and making sure he was out of harm's way, however, Julian's demon continued to haunt him for several minutes.

Julian's head brutally struck the kitchen table leg and was now bleeding. Steven yelled, "Oh Julian, please! Stop! I can't...son! I can't do!..." Bent down beside Julian, he now stood up. He had a distant look on his face as he murmured, "No! I can't, not anymore. I can't deal with it." He ran upstairs, leaving Julian in an helpless state of uncontrollable spasms.

A while later, he ran back down the stairs and passed through the kitchen and headed out of the door like a bat out of hell. He acted as if he wasn't aware that Julian was laying there on the floor. Julian's eyes stared blankly at his father, inwardly crying out as Steven left the house, slamming the door behind him. Steven held a small overnight bag as he walked outside, jumped in his car, and pulled off.

Chapter Ten

Rachel and Tracy entered the house at 9:00 P.M. "Steven, we're back," yelled Rachel. No one answered. Tracy headed for the kitchen to find a snack as Rachel put her purse in the closet and closed the door.

"Mom, come quick!" yelled Tracy frantically.

Rachel just then heard a bumping sound coming from the kitchen and ran back. When she got there Julian was lying on the floor, totally pale and still convulsing harshly. "Oh my God!" she screamed. "Where's Steven?" She bent down, holding a just starting to calm Julian. "What the hell is going on here!" she yelled angrily. "Where's Steven? Why did he leave you alone, anyway?" She thought Steven might have gone to the store or something because the basketball game was still playing on the television.

Tracy then said, "I'll help you get him to the couch, Mom."

"Thank you, baby, but I think I can manage," said Rachel. She lifted Julian with a little trouble, but she nonetheless lifted him. She then exclaimed, "I could kill your father for doing this. What could he have been thinking?" She laid Julian on the couch, and Tracy skillfully gave him his medicine. Just like every other seizure, he was exhausted, but his eyes and face held a certain peaceful glow uncharacteristic of epilepsy victims, noticed Rachel.

Tracy sat on one of their beanbags silently. Rachel got a cloth and cleaned the nasty cut on the side of Julian's forehead, then brought him a cup of juice. Soon, after several swallows, Julian started to calm. "Darn, I knew they were gonna lose," he said disappointedly. He was referring to the basketball game on TV that had just ended, 105-99.

Rachel laughed and hugged Julian. She then said, "Julian, where is your father?"

He's...he's...." Julian thought of seeing him leave with a duffle bag. "Gone." Rachel had an uneasy feeling as he spoke.

Tracy spoke up. "Gone? We know he's gone, stupid. Gone where?" She folded her arms.

Julian replied, "No...I saw him leave when I had the seizure."

Tracy laughed. "You saw him? When you have those things, you don't even know who you are. You might be looking but you don't see anything."

"Tracy!" her mother yelled.

"It's all right, Mom," said Julian. "I saw him go out the door, then I saw the bright light."

Rachel, a little disoriented herself, asked, "What?"

Julian replied, "The light. It's the light I usually see before I get sick. But this time, I saw it after. That's funny, huh?"

Rachel said, "Yes, baby, very." She was looking a little concerned and confused. She then said, "Tracy, watch your brother. I'm going upstairs for a minute."

"Sure, Mom," Tracy exclaimed.

When Rachel entered her bedroom, she saw the dresser drawers open. She walked over and saw that all of Steven's socks and underwear were gone. "Oh my God!" she said. The words came out before she realized she had spoken. Her eyes were quickly becoming glazed.

She walked over to the bed and picked the white paper up from Steven's pillow. She read it carefully: "Dear Rachel, I just can't take it anymore. You're good with the kids, so you raise them. My son's disabled and there's nothing I can do about it but leave. Goodbye. P.S. I love all of you. Steven.

She balled up the letter and threw it on the floor, then laid across the bed swearing angrily. "Bastard! Bastard!" she yelled. "He's our son! Not just my son, our son! Whatever happened to, 'We'll get through this, Rachel!' You chickenshit bastard!" yelled Rachel again. She cried until it seemed she had no more tears to cry, then thought of her life with Steven, remembering how she had met him.

Rachel had met Steven when she was eighteen years old. She was in her first year of college then, and had been a reckless groupie and drinker since the age of fourteen. Her parents were both lawyers and were more interested in their law careers than their own daughter. That's why, after feeling and being constantly ignored by them, Rachel developed her own adolescent lifestyle. She became an avid concert and after-party goer. That in turn led to her obsession with meeting and trying to have affairs with flamboyant rock stars.

By age eighteen, she had developed a taste for booze and had slept with more musicians than she wanted to remember. In college, a now somewhat mature Rachel, along with her college girlfriends, went to an all-night club. That was when she first laid eyes on the club's house band guitar player. It was love at first sight for the both of them. Steven Parr, the medium height and well-built musician, jumped off the stage during their first break that night. He walked over to the table where Rachel was seated with her friends and introduced himself to her, then handed her his card. His name, address, and phone number were printed on it. Months later, Rachel Bently and Steven Parr were married and starting a life of happiness. He didn't drink and convinced her to give up the sauce. Now, after two kids and a happy marriage, she laid there still not believing he had walked out on them. "What am I gonna do? What am I gonna do?" she cried.

Chapter Eleven
Three Years Later

It was March 1980. The Parr household had gone through a drastic change after Steven left. Rachel had tried to find him many times. She called her in-laws in Flint, Michigan, and a few of his close friends. His mother, who didn't particularly like Rachel, just said, "If he left you, it was for the best. But I haven't seen him since that travesty of a wedding the two of you had." Rachel's parents had moved to Miami, Florida, shortly after Julian was born. Steven's friends were no more sympathetic then his mother was, and no more helpful.

Julian was now ten years old and in the fifth grade. He attended Blake Elementary School, the school at which his mother had formerly worked.

Tracy was now a high school freshman at Clarkston High School. She was pretty and popular, very popular. Her life no longer revolved around her family, now that she was in high school, and she was a knock-out, a beauty. All she wanted to do was hang out with her friends, party, and get as many boyfriends as she could. Taking after her mom in more ways than one, Tracy matured early. Her curvaceous body made even older men take a second glance. This had been going on since the seventh grade and she loved it and encouraged it. She had started wearing lots of make-up and dressing to look like a freshman—not in high school, but in college. In seventh grade she was dating high school boys. And in high school...well, the not-into-school crowd. She was a trend setter for all of her friends and the majority of the girls in her class. She studied hard, but also partied hard. She got straight As in class, but to her friends she was a grade A party girl. Guys, drinking, and having fun were her new interests after Steven left home.

Julian walked into his classroom. He was a little late due to having another epileptic seizure before leaving home. He now wore his hair long to hide the scar that remained on his forehead. He slung his long black hair back as he entered the classroom. "Sorry I'm late, Mrs. Sheers," he told the middle-aged teacher. He then sat at his desk.

Lance Hamilton, a small-framed, semi-muscular student was seated in the desk beside him. He taunted, "What happened, Parr? Did you have to curl your hair some more? I know how you girls are about your hair." He then batted his eyes at Julian. The class laughed.

"Class...class...be quiet. Be quiet!" ordered Mrs. Sheers as she stood up. The unruly students didn't pay any attention to her order and continued to laugh. Julian sat there, trying not to lose his cool.

"Quiet!" shouted Brandie Charles, the strange girl with a big voice. Brandie lived a few streets over from Julian. She and her mom had admired the Parrs dearly ever since they had been invited to the Parrs' Memorial Day cookout years ago. Brandie had long, reddish-brown hair and big brown eyes. Her clear complexion radiated. The class's laughter quieted somewhat after her outburst. She again shouted, "Shut up, you guys!" as she looked around the room at the hysterical class. She then looked over at Julian, who held a placid, nonchalant demeanor.

"Oh, I know, he's started his period this morning. Didn't you, Parr?" Lance continued to taunt. Julian yawned, then got up from his desk and grabbed Lance by the collar, standing him up. Julian then punched him in the face, and Lance fell to the floor.

"Come on, weak-ass punk...talk all your big talk now," Julian said angrily. Lance laid there on the floor dazed and in pain. The class had all gathered around Julian and the laid-out Lance.

Mrs. Sheers swiftly and anxiously went over to help Lance up and back in his seat. "See what happens!" she shouted. "See what happens when you bully someone to the limit!" She looked up at Julian as she was assisting Lance up off the floor. She was amazed at how his small stature could lift up Lance from his seat and knock him down afterwards. After all, Lance had a somewhat husky build.

Most of the students booed Julian's action, but a few of them cheered. Mrs. Sheers then angrily shouted, "Now that you all have seen big time wrestling, maybe you'll finish your math assignment." The students calmed down and all went back to their seats.

Lance looked over at Julian and mouthed the words, "I'll get you, sissy." Julian chuckled.

Mrs. Sheers, knowing about Julian's epilepsy, asked, "Are you okay, Julian?"

"Yeah, I'm fine, Mrs. Sheers. Thanks for asking." The students, only some of them having seen Julian have a seizure on the school grounds, weren't concerned one bit.

Shelly Nohl, a blonde-haired, beautiful girl said jokingly, "You should have asked Lance that question, Mrs. Sheers. After all, Julian floored him." The class again laughed. Lance looked back at Shelly and scowled. She sat a few rows over from Lance, and said, "Take it easy, Lance." Lance and Shelly had been puppy lovemates since kindergarten. Their whole class, however, knew that she also had a crush on Julian. Lance also knew it.

Julian was now working on his math assignment. His guitar, which he carried everywhere he went, was positioned on the floor next to his desk. Lance looked over at him and said in a threatening low tone, "You're dead, you faggot sucker. I'll see you in the lunch room."

Julian finished his school work. He chuckled and said, "You just don't learn, do you, Hamilton? I'll mop up the damn cafeteria floor with your ass." He was suddenly blinded by a bright light. He grabbed his head and yelled, "Oh no! Oh no!" He fell out of his seat and onto the floor. "My eyes! My eyes!" he yelled in pain.

Once again, his classmates were gathering around him. Mrs. Sheers, the teacher, quickly called the principal's office on the intercom. "Please, Principal Mannard, I need help. It's Julian Parr. He needs a doctor, and you'd better call his mother. I think he's having another seizure," said a panicking Mrs. Sheers.

Julian groggily sat up. He rubbed his right hand over his face. "No...no, Mrs. Sheers. I'm fine," he excitedly said. "It wasn't a seizure. It...it...." he jumped up from the floor. He looked at the students who had gathered around him, spellbound. Thinking quickly, he said, "It was...just a...just a small seizure, no problem. It happens all the time." He didn't dare tell them that it was a light...his own light...his own blinding light, that no one else could see.

"I don't care, young man. Big or small, a seizure is a seizure and you're going home," said Mrs. Sheers. "The principal has probably already called your mom. Go...go sit back down students. It's all over," instructed Mrs. Sheers.

As the students headed back to their seats, Lance whispered, "Freak, he's gonna die anyway. I'm gone kill him." He spoke so only Shelly could hear him.

A little later, Julian was in the principal's office waiting for his mother to pick him up. Rachel came into the office, where he was sitting in one of the waiting room chairs. "I'm fine, Mom. No jerking or anything. It was just a small one," he said.

Rachel frowned and said, "I don't know, Julian. They told me you had a little altercation with another student this morning. Maybe you should go home and rest."

Julian chuckled, then said, "Mom, I clobbered the fool. He's the one who should be going home."

Rachel laughed. She then looked at the principal and Mrs. Sheers. "Well, what do you think? It is lunch time, and he seems fine now." She was looking a little unsure of herself and what to do.

Julian looked at her, touched her arm, and said, "Mom, I'm fine. Go home, relax."

Rachel laughed. "All right, all right!" she said, surrendering to Julian's green eyes and charm. She then said sternly, "All right, but no playing around at lunch. I'll be back to get you after school."

Julian rolled his eyes and said, "Okay, whatever you say." After briefly chatting with Rachel, they sent him back to class.

Afterwards, in class, Julian was talking with his few friends. The other students were talking and preparing to go to lunch as well. Mrs. Sheers was grading papers. She also kept a close watch on Julian Philan Parr.

At twelve P.M. the lunch bell rang. The students headed out the classroom. Brandie Charles caught up with Julian as he was headed out of the classroom. "Julian, I'm glad you're okay," said the petite redhead. Julian frowned. He looked Brandie up and down and then looked away. She then said shyly, "Well, if you ever need anything, I'm here."

Shelly pushed Brandie and said, "Get lost, El Crippo. What can you do for anyone—you can't even walk."

Brandie lowered her head in embarrassment, then speaking lowly said, "Goodbye, Julian." Still looking at her, he didn't comment. She walked down the hall to the lunchroom.

Shelly, walking beside Julian, said happily, "So, Julian, don't worry about Lance. He's all ta...."

Julian interrupted her, yelling, "Who said I was worried?" He then walked away from her swiftly. She just chuckled.

Chapter Twelve

Lance walked into the crowded cafeteria and sat at the table across from Julian's. Lance looked over at Julian, who was seated at the table on the side of the cafeteria and writing a song. He hadn't noticed Lance had entered the cafeteria. Lance then shouted loudly, with a smirk on his face, "Hey, Parr! What's the matter? Did your mother want a girl? That's what it looks like you're trying to be with all that long hair." Lance laughed nonstop as Julian ignored him and continued to write. Lance then said, "Hey, uh, Parr, why don't you show us that new dance you were doing on the floor yesterday? What is it called, the floor jerk?" The students in the cafeteria all began to laugh at his taunting of Julian. Julian had also had a seizure the day before in school.

He looked back at Lance and the laughing cafeteria crowd, then stood up on his cafeteria chair holding his guitar. As soon as Julian played a few cords, the students in the cafeteria seemed to quiet down. He then belted out the song he had been writing while sitting in the cafeteria. The laughter was completely gone now and the students were clapping and dancing.

Lance, looking agitated, still tried to provoke him saying loudly, "He's just a...he's just a fag." However his words were drowned out by the cheering students and Julian's dynamic voice. Lance continued, "That fool can't sing! He's a punk."

Brandie Charles, who was seated at the table next to Lance, looked at him and said, "Lance, you're stupid! You can't even spell punk! So don't you dare call Julian one."

Julian was finishing his song at the request of the lunchroom attendants. The students in the cafeteria laughed at Lance and Brandie's comment. He then said, "Well, I guess all you freaks look after one another."

Julian, now paying attention to Lance badgering Brandie, said, "Go to hell, Lance. If you don't know the way, I'll show you!" He then stood and approached Lance. The crowd started oohing and ahhing, but Julian turned, heading out the cafeteria and saying, "He isn't even worth it." As he passed by Brandie, he said, "Thanks, kid, for standing up for me. Even though it wasn't necessary."

He didn't like Brandie or anybody else trying to fight his battles for him. As he headed out of the cafeteria, Shelly ran, trying to catch up with him. As she passed Brandie, she yelled, "Take your peace sign and get the hell out of here. Julian doesn't like you. You crip!"

Brandie had been born with a slight case of polio, which occasionally impaired her walking somewhat. Her humiliation showed on her face after Shelly's cruel words. But as usual she ignored her words of hate. Brandie was a little girl with a style of her own. She wore faded jeans, peace signs, and flowers in her hair. She was used to the comments of the students at Blake Elementary School's. So Shelly's comment didn't phase her too much, and neither did Julian's passing words.

Julian walked into the house, returning home from school. Rachel had started drinking again since Steven's departure from her life. "Mom, I'm home. I'm back," said Julian. He threw his books on the couch and walked into the kitchen. Rachel was standing by the counter. She poured herself a glass of scotch and drank it. He sat down at the kitchen table and said, "What's for dinner? I'm starving."

Rachel turned toward him with her glass of scotch in hand and blurted out, "I...I'm so t...tired of you coming in here...lo...looking for food after school. D...don't you eat your lunch at school, dammit!" Her words were slurred from the alcohol she had been consuming all afternoon.

"Mom, you're drunk again!" shouted Julian disgustedly.

"Mi...mind your da...damn business," she drawled. "Go do your homework!" she shouted, she then burped. "Yo...you kids are...s...so ungrateful." She burped again. Angrily she shouted, "You brats! Go to your...bedroom!"

Tears filled Julian's eyes. He jumped up from his chair and shouted, "But Mom...." He then saw his mother's drunken disorientation and smacked his lips. He rolled his eyes and disgustedly ran to his room.

"Go on! Go on!" shouted Rachel. "You're the...the rea...reason Steven le...."

He slammed the door before her statement was through, accusing him for being the reason Steven had left.

Tracy walked into the kitchen through the open side door. She had heard her mother's shouts from outside on the steps. "Mom! You're at it again!" she shouted angrily.

The guitar sound blared out of Julian's room. The raggedy-sounding cords of the past had been replaced with smooth-sounding, mellow cords. The practice had finally helped. Julian had mastered the guitar at age ten.

"I'm tired of all this, Mother. Your drinking and everything has to go!" shouted Tracy. "I can't take this! Daddy's gone and you're a drunk!"

Rachel stood up and stumbled over to Tracy, who was standing by the refrigerator. Rachel said, "A dr...drunk! How dare you!" She slapped her face.

A startled Tracy looked shocked, then yelled, "I hate you, Mom! I hate you!" With tears in her eyes, she ran to her room.

These events occurred several times during the next several years, each time getting worse and worse. The drinking, the family fights, they just kept getting worse.

It was now September 2, 1984. The day was hot and sunny in Detroit, though the streets were quiet. Sure signs of school starting soon. Julian, now fourteen years old, woke up and dressed in his jeans and T-shirt. He went into the living room and sat down on the couch. He waited for his mom to drive him to the doctor. After a few minutes, Rachel emerged from her room. She was fully dressed and ready to go. Julian stood and walked to the front door with Rachel behind him. As he unlocked the front door, she ran her hands over his long hair, then said, "It's time to get this cut, I think. You'll be in high school soon."

He opened the door and angrily said, looking back at her, "Naw, Mama, uhn-uhn. I don't care if I'm going to high school. My hair is who I am. It is a part of me. And besides, it hides my scar, remember?"

Rachel then said, "But Julian...." She didn't continue her statement. After seeing how strongly he felt about his hair remaining long, she let it go. She then said, "Okay let's go, but I think that hair is going to give you hell, and a lot more problems in high school." Julian and his mother walked to the car, got in, and drove off.

After being examined, the doctor told them Julian was as healthy as a horse. The signs of epilepsy had seemed to diminish just as strongly as they seemed to occur. Rachel was overjoyed. Julian, who had been feeling like a charged battery lately said, "I knew I was well, I knew it."

The doctor had called the cessation of the epilepsy nothing more than a miracle. When Julian brought up the bright light that appeared during his epileptic seizures, the doctor sarcastically talked it off, saying in a patronizing tone, "Sure, son, sure. Let's just hope all the ugliness is behind you now." The doctor still gave him a healthy diet to follow along with a prescription for milder medication.

When they got home, Julian told his mom he wouldn't be needing the medicine and to throw the prescription away. Rachel refused the request, however she told him that she had thrown it away. She kept the prescription in a secret hiding place just in case his seizures reoccurred.

Julian told Tracy the good news. She was just as thrilled as he was. He then spoke to her about the light he had seen the night Steven had left. She laughed wildly, but Julian continued to explain to her about the light, the blinding light he had seen before most of his seizures. Tracy, still laughing hysterically, said, "You're crazy."

He then said, still trying to explain, "Tracy...You see, it might have been a sign."

Irritatedly, Tracy replied, "So what? You used to see a light before your attacks. Who cares? It doesn't mean anything. So why do you keep talking about it? You were sick. Do you hear me? You weren't well. It doesn't mean that you have any miraculous power," said Tracy disgustedly. Tracy twirled her long hair that was hanging down the side of her face. She then said, "And that bright light that you saw after your last fit...was probably Daddy's car lights getting the hell away from you as quickly as he could!" Tracy then laughed.

Rachel stood. "Tracy!" she shouted. "I'll kick your fast butt out of here if you don't sit down and shut up!"

Tracy said, whining, "But, Mom, he's always trying to act like he's some bigshot." She frowned. "Like those fits made him, like some sort of super hero or something." She paused. "He was sick, tell him—he was sick!" Tracy then turned to Julian. "You're no better than anybody else!" she shouted. She again rolled her eyes in disgust.

Rachel then said, "That will be enough, young lady."

Julian, taking the whole thing in stride, just said, "You're right Tracy, you're right. Just call me Julian Clark Kent."

Chapter Thirteen

On September 7, 1984, Julian went to Clarkston High School on the east side of Detroit. The older girls, having seen him on the previous day, swooned as he walked into the school. Many of them tried to meet and talk to him, however, he was only interested in his guitar, which he still carried with him everywhere he went.

Rachel woke up and poured herself a drink as usual. She didn't have to work until noon. The money she and Steven had saved in their account was more than enough to keep her and the kids secure for awhile. But she worried the money would run out. That fear kept her teaching piano and voice lessons. But the drinking was slowly putting a halt to that. She was no longer obligated to stay at home with the children since Julian wasn't ill anymore and Tracy was now in senior high and would soon be starting college. She no longer had to stay sober, she thought as she poured herself another drink. "Here I am, separated, with a reformed sick kid and a smart-ass mouthy daughter....It's time for me to have some fun." She sat back on the black couch and took a drink from her bottle.

Julian walked down the hall, heading to his gym class. This being high school, the class was filled with students from ninth to twelfth grade. "Hi.... Hello.... Isn't he cute.... I know who I'm taking to the dance.... Look at his hair, isn't it long and pretty.... He's probably gay." Julian walked down the hall as the girls ranted and raved over him. Shelly, who was already hanging in the halls with her high school friends, was among the swooning girls. Her attraction for Julian seemed to triple when she got into high school. He carried himself like a student in a higher grade than ninth.

As he continued toward the gym class, three guys stopped him. "Where do you think you're going?" said one of the three guys roughly.

Julian just disgustedly replied, "What, man! What is it? I've got to go!" The African-American student placed his hand on Julian's chest and pushed him backwards. The rest of the boys laughed.

The other, a Caucasian student, punched his fist into his hand and said, "Later. We'll deal with him later." They then went into the gym class.

Julian was somewhat disgruntled. He shook his hair and entered the class as well, walking over to the gym teacher, to whom he handed his doctor's excuse. Mr. Lyons said, "So, no strenuous exercises for you, huh? Well, my boy, you can do the warm up exercises with us. Anything that's too strenuous for you, just tell me. I'll have you assisting the other students and helping me to keep them in line."

Help him to keep them in line, thought Julian. The words of death to a ninth grader. He just said, "Yes, sir."

He then went to the locker room with the other boys to suit up. "Look! We've got a girl in our class!" said the white muscular student. The rest of the boys laughed.

"Yeah," shouted another boy. "Where are your ribbons and barrettes?" They were two of the other boys who were taunting Julian as he entered the gym room. The students again laughed.

Julian placed his gym bag on the long wooden bar that served as a seat and said, "I've got your barrettes, punk!" He then went over and punched the boy in the eye. The boy swung a weak punch, hitting him on the shoulder. Julian then said, "I think you're the girl, sissy." He went over to the other boy who was taunting him, Lance, and punched him in the stomach.

"Fight...fight!" yelled a medium-complexioned black kid, the third boy who was previously taunting Julian. He went over to him, exclaiming, "Shut up, punk, or you'll be next."

The stunned spectators shouted, "Ooh!" as they watched the prince who was quickly becoming king.

The gym teacher entered the locker room. "What's going on in here, fellas?" the man shouted.

Lance, who was now straightening up from holding his stomach, said anxiously, "Man...he pun...." Julian's big green eyes glared at Lance hauntingly, daring him to say anything. Lance shuttered, "Uh...uh...we...were playing around and Julian accidentally hit me in the stomach." The coach looked around the locker room at the students and then at Julian. "Uh...ain't that right, man?" Lance asked.

Julian was now taking off his shirt to put on his gym shirt. He said, "Yeah, Mr. Lyons, I'm sorry. We just got carried away." His face and eyes held a look of sincerity as he spoke.

"Well, all right, you guys. Hurry up out of here. You've got one minute and I want you all in the gym." The burly gym teacher left the room and most of the boys followed.

"He whipped your ass, man," one of the boys yelled to Lance.

The other boy Julian had threatened just said, "Aw, forget that fag...I'll get him. You just wait, I'll get him."

In the gym, the boys all warmed up and played basketball. Julian headed out onto the court. Mr. Lyons called, "Hey Parr! Maybe you should sit this one out!" The teacher hadn't told the other students of his fragile condition. He just told the boys, "Parr can't get too exhausted guys. He's under a doctor's care, so be careful."

Julian rolled his eyes, thinking, Thanks a lot. Now they'll think I'm a punk. "Naw, Coach, I'm fine, I can play." And play he did. He won three games straight out of five. He impressed both Coach Lyons and his classmates. Lance hated him all the more now. The cute kid with the long hair was now proving true to form.

As he was walking home, Brandie Charles, one of his ninth grade classmates and a self-proclaimed hippie, caught up with him. "Hi, Julian, I guess you really made a big impression around the high school for your first two days, huh?" said an always happy Brandie. He didn't comment, he just kept walking. She then said, "I have two classes with Lance. Man, he's talking about kicking your butt. He thinks that you want his girlfriend, Shelly Nohl. He's always thought that, every since elementary school." He cleared his throat and still did not say anything. She tagged along, prompting him to talk. "You don't like her, do you Julian? I told him that you didn't....I told him...."

He interrupted her rapping, saying harshly, "Yes, I want to get laid by Shelly, and I want Lance to kill me."

Her eyes widened. She then said devastatedly, "Oh my God! You can't mean that! Are you crazy? Do you really want to die?" He again was silent. He looked at her, still not commenting, then looked away. She felt a little uneasy about his comment and asked again, "Do you really want to die?"

He looked at her, his green eyes sparkling. He was thinking, I don't need a common tramp like Shelly. He then glanced at Brandie. You're kinda cute. I just wish you would shut up sometimes, thought Julian as his mind drifted wildly.

Brandie, getting nervous at his silence, nervously ran her fingers through her long, reddish-brown, curly hair. She then rambled on, "Well, anyway, you can't like that flake, Shelly. Do you, Julian?"

Julian quietly asked, "Why do you wear those tie-dyed jeans?"

Caught off guard, she said, "Huh?" sounding surprised that he had changed the subject and had asked her...that.

Shelly, who had been walking a few feet behind them, came up and pushed Brandie slightly forward, knocking her away from Julian. Shelly grabbed his arm and exclaimed, "Julian, hi! I've been trying to catch up with you." She slung her long blonde hair to the back. Brandie was now walking a few steps behind Julian and Shelly, the way Shelly wanted it. Shelly then yelled to her, "Why don't you go on! Julian doesn't like you. You crippled freak, hippie want-to-be!" Tears filled Brandie's eyes. She looked back at Julian as she hobbled ahead of him. She shook her head remorsefully and ran off ahead. Shelly laughed. She then said happily, "What's up, Julian?"

He shook her off of his arm and said nastily, "Why don't you get away from me? Go find Lance or something." He then increased his pace, leaving her looking dumbfounded. Brandie had already turned and was walking up her street, feeling awful. She didn't see his departure from Shelly.

Nine months passed. It was now June 10, 1985. Things were still going pretty bad for Julian, both at school and at home. Fifteen-year-old Julian walked into the house.

Chapter Fourteen

"Why is you as...so late?" said Rachel with a slurred voice from alcohol. "Ya...you don't care about me." She stumbled clumsily over to the door where Julian was standing.

"I care about you, Ma, I love you. Why don't you go get some sleep," he stated tiredly and sympathetically.

"Sla...sleep!" she shouted. "I can't sleep!" Julian sat down on the couch as she staggered over and sat down beside him, saying, "You want to kn...know why I...can't sleep?"

Frustratedly Julian said, "Naw, Ma. Just go to bed, will you?" Rachel again stood up. The strap on her black nightgown slid down her right shoulder, exposing her breast. She sloppily pulled the strap back up. He pretended not to notice his mother's clothes dislodging.

"I'm...I am na...not going to that bed, because...because it's lonely, and I don't choose to be alone." She walked over to the bar and poured another drink. She then said, "You kn...know what?" She continued, "Your sister's pregnant. Can ya believe that, huh?"

Julian said, "What?" Looking confused, he pushed his long hair off of his shoulders.

"Yeah!" exclaimed Rachel. "I...I'm barely making ends meet with you two, and...and now, here comes another one. How'd ya like that, huh?"

He exclaimed, "Man, oh man." He was an innocent, but Rachel made sure she told him the facts of life. "You don't have a father to tell you these things, so I guess I'll have to," she told him on one of her sober days.

Tracy came out of her room, having heard her mom's remarks. Her eyes were red and swollen from crying. Not knowing exactly what to say, Julian just sat silently. Tracy said, "And how does good old Mom congratulate me?" She walked over and stood by the bar. "She told me that my life is ruined and so is my baby's." Tears fell from her eyes again.

"Congratulate you?" Rachel yelled. "Damn it...Tracy, ya...you've got no man...no job, and you haven't even graduated high school yet! Now you're telling me, you're...you're, pregnant and I'm supposed to congratulate you...young lady? You've got a lot to learn...." She took another drink. Julian just sat there observing.

Tracy then said angrily, "Right, Mom, and I guess you're supposed to teach me." She looked at her mother, who was still drinking from her glass of vodka, and said, "Damn you, Mother! The only thing I'll ever learn living with you is how to be a drunk." She ran down the hall and went back into her bedroom.

Sympathetically Julian touched his mom's arm and said, "Oh Mom, you're not a dr...."

Before he could get the word out an angry Rachel harshly knocked his hand away from her arm. "You smart alek, self-righteous faggot. Look at you...with your long hair. Don't you dare patronize me! I changed your damn diapers, wiped your snotty nose...do...don't you dare act like...."

Before she could say, "You're better than me," he jumped up from the couch while she remained seated. He shouted, "I was just trying to be nice to you.... You're my mother and I love you, but I want my daddy. I need my dad!"

Rachel jumped up and slapped his face saying, "Ungrateful brat! Yo...your father doesn't give a...a damn about you. You're the reason he left so...so don't cry you want your daddy to me!"

He quietly walked to his room, then looked back at his mother, who had flopped down on the couch and was sobbing uncontrollably.

Two weeks passed. Tracy had decided to drop out of Clarkston High School. Things pretty much remained the same in the Parr home. Fifteen-year-old Julian went to school and Rachel taught her music lessons from the house. She also had got another job singing at night at a club called Travis Alley. Her drinking eased a little. She had also started dating again, a fact that didn't please Julian or Tracy, but Mom was happy, or so they thought. Night after night Rachel went out with a different man or came home with one. The school year was close to ending.

Julian constantly got into fights at school, usually with some girl's jealous boyfriend. He stood at his locker. Shelly, who was down the hall from him, exclaimed, "Julian! Julian, the dance is Friday and I would love to go with you, if you haven't got a date." She was now a cheerleader. She and Lance were still dating and had always been neighbors and childhood sweethearts. Lance was now on the ninth grade football team, but Shelly didn't care. Julian was so good looking, and she had always had a crush on him. So she was going to try her luck. She would be the envy of all the girls at Clarkston High School, even more than she already was. She was a beautiful Caucasian with blue eyes and a smooth clear complexion. She had long strawberry blond hair that hung down her back. Shelly was now standing next to Julian at his locker.

"Uhm, Shelly," he commented, "I think your boyfriend would ob...." He changed his approach and said, "I mean, don't you go with Lance Hamilton?" His big green eyes looked her over seductively. It was just something he found himself doing.

"No...yes...well...it doesn't matter. Lance isn't my husband, and you're so cute." She caressed Julian's cheek and said, "Besides he's going out of town tonight and you're so cute."

He blushed, then looked into her blue eyes, commenting, "I think you're kinda cute yourself."

Shelly smiled and said, "Thank you." She then ran her fingers through her blond hair. "So, Julian, what about the dance? We could meet here tonight, say about 8:30."

He said, "Okay, but are you sure your boyfriend is gonna be out of town?"

She smiled and said, "You don't have to worry about him, he's not gonna be here.

He frowned, then said, "Who said I was worried?" His voice was sounding deeper than usual. "I'll meet you at the dance," he exclaimed and left, closing his locker door behind him.

When he got home, Tracy was sitting on the couch crying. Rachel, as usual, was at the bar pouring herself a drink. Julian entered the house with a forced,

"Tracy, what's the matter?" She didn't answer him, she just kept crying.

"The damn fool went and got an abortion, that's what's wrong," Rachel blurted out. "She had it done yesterday. She didn't go to work, then or today. She left the house and circled back around and climbed through the window. If her job wouldn't have called here today, I would have thought everything was just fine." She took a drink and said sorrowfully, "Oh Tracy, how could you?"

Tracy stood up. "'I would have thought everything was just fine.'" She mimicked Rachel's earlier words, then said angrily, "No, Mom, everything's not just fine around here. It hasn't been for a long time!"

Rachel ran her hand over her face, then said, feeling a little guilty, "But honey, an abortion? I think we could have come up with a better solution than that."

Tracy rolled her eyes. "Oh, Mom, please. It's my body, and besides, now this uneducated, manless dummy can resume her life, and you can resume yours without another mouth to feed." Tracy sighed, then said, "And all it cost you was a few hundred dollars, which I swear I'll replace in your drawer as soon as I get my first pay. I just got another job today."

Julian stood up and once again headed for his bedroom. He said frustratedly, "Damn, I can't take this."

As he was leaving the living room, Rachel yelled, "Hey...watch your mouth."

Inside his room, he slammed his school books on the table, exclaiming, "Damn crazy house." He laid on his bed, thinking about his mother and Tracy, and then his father. How different life around here would be if Dad were here, he thought. He rubbed the scar on his forehead. Was his mother right? Was he the reason his father left he wondered. He rolled his eyes and stared at the ceiling. He already knew the answers to those questions. He remembered hearing his father say, "I can't deal with it," as he left him lying helpless on the kitchen floor. Tears filled his eyes as he thought of his father and of his own illness that had come and seemed to have gone. He thought of the blinding light that would enrapture the atmosphere before and after his attacks occurred.

He turned sideways as he lay in the bed. His eyes spotted the English books he had brought home from school. He had always been an excellent student, but this assignment scared the pants off of him. His English teacher had told the class to write a poem about something or someone special that had a profound impact on their life. His head began to spin. He had never seriously written a poem for credit. He would dibble and dabble in class at songwriting, usually during a boring lecture. At home when he was bored, he would dibble and dabble at poetry, but it was scribble. He didn't take his writing seriously. "I can't write poetry!" he shouted. He sat up on the side of the bed. "Skip it. I'll just go shoot some hoops and then get ready for the stupid dance." He grabbed his ball and went out of the room.

"Hey, baby, where you going?" shouted his mother. Tracy had a glass of vodka in her hand, and Rachel was drinking also. Julian observed this touching mother daughter moment. He then said, "I'll be back later. I'm just gonna play a little basketball. I'll be back."

"Sure hon, don't tire yourself out now," shouted his mother. Her voice was slurred from the alcohol.

"Damn crazy house," he said lowly after he was out of the house and standing on the porch.

Jolelle Wilks was getting out of her car. The shapely twenty-five-year-old was gorgeous. She had been the object of Julian's desires for many of his younger years. He walked off of his porch and called to her as she was taking her shopping bag full of clothes out of the back seat. "Jolelle, do you need some help?" he yelled.

She took the shopping bag out of the back seat and yelled to him, "No thanks, cutie, I only have one bag." She then closed the car door.

He started across the street, and looking back at her, he yelled, "Hey, Jolelle, I'm gonna make love to you, baby!" He headed across the field toward the basketball court. Jolelle rolled her eyes and chuckled. She was use to his harmless comments.

Chapter Fifteen

The community center court was full of people, mostly teenage boys. Julian knew or was familiar with them all. "Game!" he shouted after sinking the last basket in the game. "Twenty-two points, guys, I win." He added, "Well, I won't press my luck. Winning two games will do it for me for awhile."

The boys all taunted, 'Aw...faggot, we let that sissy beat us. Yeah, he won't play another game because he knows I'll burn him the next time."

Used to all the name calling by now, he just looked back and yelled, "Burn me? Yeah, right, in your dreams."

He headed over to the spot by the swing set where he had placed his basketball. He didn't need it since one of the other guys had brought his to the court. He sat on the grass and laid back, resting his head on the basketball. He closed his eyes, thinking about how much he hated going back home. That house isn't a home, it's a damn crazy house, he thought. Mama's drinking her life away, and Tracy soon will be following in her footsteps. But he had to go and get ready for the dance. "Why the hell did I ever agree to do a damn thing like that?" he murmured.

He then opened his eyes. Brandie Charles was walking in his direction. "Oh no," he grunted. He closed his eyes again. Brandie was a lovely and lively girl with reddish-brown hair and a light complexion. She had a mild case of polio, which would now and then have her walking with a limp, and she was often teased humiliatingly in school. Damn kids could be so cruel. She would always come to the defense of Julian when they were in class. If a kid didn't know the answer to an easy question asked by the teacher, an energetic and restless Julian would often remark, "Dummy, you should have known that." This in turn resulted in arguments or threats made to him by other students to Julian.

Brandie would remark, "Look, he didn't mean it. You just took too long and he got tired," or some remark like that.

He would then snap, "Look, Red, if I want your help I'll ask for it, all right!" Then his eyes would look at her seductively. It was just something he did in a one-on-one encounter with a girl.

Back on the playground, Brandie limped over to the swing beside where Julian was laying. "Hello...hello," said a wide-eyed Brandie. "Julian, hello...wake up. It's me, Brandie."

He then opened his green eyes slowly. "I wasn't sleep," he said sternly.

"Oh, all right," said a happy-go-lucky Brandie. The girl's always cheerful mood irritated the life out of him. "So...have you started on your poem for Ms. Lichem's class?" she asked.

He sat up. His eyes had an angry look about them as he said, "Poems are dumb. I'll probably just write a few lines that rhyme about a goldfish I used to have." He paused, bending his knee up toward his chest. "I hated the damn thing. It went away just like my...." He didn't finish his sentence. Instead, angrily he said, "What's it like to be you anyway, Ms. Smartypants? I bet yours is all done with pink little ribbons attached to it."

She stared at him point blank and said, "Yes, I'm done, and it's not a sticky sweet poem about flowers and sugarplums, if that's what you were implying?"

Julian stood up. His gray jogging suit top was drenched with sweat. He said, "I ain't implying anything, girl. I really don't care." He bounced his basketball on the grass.

She continued, "I could help you, if you want." Still bouncing the ball, he frowned at her. She still held her delightful nature, even when dealing with this...massive state of confusion named Julian Parr. "I have seen the poems you scribbled in class when it gets boring." She rolled her eyes. "And boy, does it get boring." Still bouncing the ball, he didn't comment. She raised her eyebrows and said, "I know I shouldn't have, but I took a couple of your writings that you balled up and threw in the garbage home with me."

"Ugh! What did you do that for? You went in the garbage and took them out?"

She retorted, "It wasn't so bad. You're not that good a shot." She saw his expression change to angry after her comment. She then noted, "Most of your writings were balled up on the floor, anyway. And the baskets that you did make, I just went to the ladies room and washed my hands after I took them out of the garbage. It's no big deal."

He then said, "For some dumb words, you went through all that." Sounding puzzled, but snide, he cracked, "I'll give you words; 'She likes me, but it's such a pity, all I want to do is suck her....'"

She interrupted his so-called poem, snapping, "Julian, you're disgusting!" She rolled her eyes and countered, "Not those words, these...." She licked her lips, swallowed, and said, "'One more hour, then I will be free, from the prison known as school that for seven hours, five days a week, seems to capture me.'"

He frowned again and asserted, "That ain't no poem. That's what I wrote when I got finished with my work early and you bozos were still working."

She then said, "It's poetry. Some of them are beautiful. Do you want to hear 'em?"

He angrily shouted, "No I don't want to hear them! I know what they say and they're stupid, just like you!" He paused, calming down, then said, "Besides, I write songs, not poems."

She chuckled and said, "That's what songs are, silly, poems put to music." She stood up and touched her hair, which was pulled to one side in a ponytail puff that hung to her shoulders. She observed, "It's all right here," pointing to Julian's heart. "Julian, write what you feel right here." She smiled as she pointed at his chest. "I think you have a lot to say...from the heart."

He knocked her hand away angrily and exclaimed, "You don't know nothing! You're just a girl, a stupid cripple!"

Her face lost all vibrance. She looked and felt as if someone had just punched her in the guts. Tears filled her eyes as she sorrowfully said, "I only wanted to help." She then stumbled away.

He heard her sobbing as she crossed the community center playground. Guilt took him over immediately. He rolled his eyes and said, disgusted with himself, "Damn...oh damn." He then yelled, "Red! Brandie, come back! Brandie!

He ran across the playground after her. He reached out and grabbed her arm. She stopped, pulling her arm away from his grip, then crossed her arms in front of her chest. He walked around her and stood facing her. "I...I'm sorry, Red. I didn't...I mean, that was mean of me. I'm sorry," he stammered.

She took a deep breath and smiled, then said, "Apology accepted, I guess."

He offered, "Let me walk you home, all right?"

"Okay," she agreed. They walked to Reynolds Street with Brandie still talking to and coaxing Julian about his writing. However he wasn't interested and made jokes all the while she was talking. When they were finally in front of Brandie's house, she said, "Wait a minute, Julian." She ran into her house. A little while later she returned with her phone number written down on a piece of paper. 'Give me a call if you have trouble with the poem," she suggested. "But, I doubt that you will."

He hesitantly said, "All right." He then headed for home. Brandie stood on the sidewalk watching him until he was out of her view.

Chapter Sixteen

Julian entered the house. His mother was in the kitchen cooking and singing. He didn't see Tracy anywhere. So he figured she had gone out with one of her loser boyfriends. He ran up the stairs, showered, and dressed in his brown dress pants and a beige silk shirt. When he returned downstairs, he went into the kitchen and told his mom he was going to the school dance. He also told her he would be back around 10:30 that night. "Sure, have a nice time. You look great, Jewel," exclaimed Rachel. She was still a little tanked.

He left the house at 8:15 and headed for Clarkston High School and Shelly. When he entered the gymnasium, the music was blaring out of the speakers. The gym was half-full. Shelly spotted him as soon as he stepped into the decorated room. Wearing a plain blue dress that buttoned up entirely in the front, she headed over to him. "Hello, Julian. Don't you look incredible," said a smiling Shelly.

He stared at her seductively as his eyes lowered and lifted, checking her out from head to toe. "Hey, Shelly, you look nice, too," he responded. Her eyes sparkled as she then shook her hair and said, "Let's dance, Julian, all right?" He didn't answer, but she grabbed his hand and led him onto the dance floor.

They danced to almost every song, then Shelly led Julian out to her mother's car. Although only fourteen years old, she had received her license early because of her mom's Parkinson's disease. She was allowed to drive in case her mother took ill and her dad was at work.

She opened up the passenger door and got in. Julian went around to the other side and also got into the car. They made small talk for a while, then she unbuttoned her dress. His eyes were in a fixed stare at her naked body, concealed only by her bra and panties. She moved forward on her seat, then removed the opened dress. Her car was parked in a dark spot in the field in back of the school, so her body was exposed for Julian's eyes only. She reached over and kissed him very hotly and passionately. Despite being his first kiss, this didn't boggle him one bit. He handled it and Shelly like an old pro, squeezing her nipples and fondling her breast wholeheartedly. "Get in the back," he said in a husky and hoarse voice. She crawled over the seat as he took off his shirt and joined her. He removed his pants and his innocence was made history while Shelly moaned in ecstasy and he learned a new lesson.

They kissed and hugged for several minutes afterwards. "Mmm, Julian you're absolutely perfect. Let's do it again," she whispered.

Looking a little perturbed and confused, he picked up his pants from the floor of the car. "I...I've got to go. Drop me off at home, will you?" he asked.

She caressed his chest and said pleadingly, "Aw, come on. We're good together. Let's f...."

He pushed a very aggressive Shelly away. "Would you give it a rest?" he snapped, sounding agitated and angry. "Yeah, I'm good and you're okay, but it's over. We did it, and it's over, all right?" He then frowned, rolled his eyes, and said, "Damn!" He crawled over the seat and put on his shirt that was lying on the front seat. "I've gotta go," he continued.

Shelly sighed. She looked at him somewhat angrily as she put back on her bra and panties. "I can't believe you're treating me so cold. I just gave myself to you, for God's sake," she said heatedly. She reached over the seat, picked up her dress, and put it on, still arguing. "You just made love to me! You could have least acted like it." She then began crawling back over the seat.

He rolled his eyes and in a huff, said sternly, "I didn't make love to you, baby. We were both hot and we fucked. No big deal, all right?"

She turned on the car engine and said through gritted teeth, "Fine, just fine, Julian."

She drove him home without any conversation. Her pride was becoming more and more wounded with each mile that she drove as he sat there on the passenger side, happy and singing every song that came on the radio. She had to admit to herself he sang better than the artists on the radio, even if he was a freaking jerk.

She finally pulled up in front of his house. "Here we are," she said happily.

He looked at her as he nonchalantly said, "Hey Shell, it was fun, huh? See you around."

He started to open the car door, but before he got the chance to, however, Shelly was caressing his thigh. "Come on, baby. Let's do it once more for the road," she enticed.

He removed her hand from his thigh harshly. "Get a grip, huh?" he said coldly.

"I think that's what I was trying to do," she said teasingly. He rolled his eyes in disgust, opened the door, and quickly got out of the car as she just looked at him. He slammed the door of the car and headed up to his house. Shelly pulled off quickly, burning rubber.

Jolelle Wilks, his next-door neighbor, was sitting on her porch when he pulled up with Shelly. As he began walking up to his house, he hadn't noticed Jolelle sitting there. "Julian, Julian, sweetie, can I talk to you for a minute?"

He stopped in his tracks, hearing the call in the darkness. "Who is it?" yelled a semi-deep voiced Julian.

Jolelle Wilks quietly said, "Come over here. I need to speak to you."

He realized the voice was coming from the Wilks's house next door. He frowned, looking in that direction. "Who is it?" he asked again. "Jolelle, is that you?" He began crossing the lawn, heading over to his neighbor's house. "Boy oh boy, what did I do now?" he whispered to himself as he approached the Wilks's yard. He could barely see Jolelle, who was sitting on the bottom step of the porch.

She then said, "Come on over and have a seat. I have to talk to you."

He swallowed hard, thinking, I might as well get it over with, whatever it is I've done. I'm about to be told off.

He finally reached the porch where Jolelle was seated. "Sit down, Julian, please sit," said a pleasant-voiced Jolelle.

He flopped down on the stairs of the Wilks's porch. "What did I do now?" he asked. He didn't even look at her as he spoke. "Did I leave my ten-speed too close to your father's car again? I know he thinks I'm gonna do damage to his perfect paint job," he said sarcastically.

She laughed. "No...no, not at all Julian," she said. She looked up at the star-filled sky. "It's such a beautiful night."

He quietly sighed. "Yeah, yeah. What do you want?" he angrily asked her. She didn't answer him. The few moments of silence were quite unnerving for him. He had always had a secret crush on Jolelle Wilks; half of the guys on the block did, both young and old. "Uh, if you didn't want anything, I have to be going," he declared.

She then asked abruptly, "How old are you, Julian?"

He stood up and replied, "I'm fifteen. I'll be sixteen next June."

She grabbed his hand, pulling him back down onto the porch step. "You are very mature. You could easily pass for a nineteen- or twenty-year-old guy," she remarked.

Julian, after being prompted back on the porch by Jolelle, now looked at her. She had on a yellow sundress and sandals, no stockings. Her hair was in a upswept style. He breathed deeply and commented, "Oh baby, you really look great tonight."

She looked over at him and said happily, "Hey, I baked a cake today. Come on in. I'll get you some." She stood quickly and went up the porch stairs.

He was right behind her. He said lowly, "Are you sure that's all you called me over here to get some of?" She chuckled, then entered the house, as did Julian. She went into the kitchen, and as she stood at the counter slicing the cake, he slipped up in back of her and kissed her on the neck. "Where are your parents?" he whispered in her ear.

Jolelle jumped in astonishment. She was unaware he had entered the kitchen. "Julian," she sighed in a surprising tone. She breathed deeply and smiled. "They're visiting my aunt in New York, for a couple of weeks." she said joyously.

Julian countered, "Then I'm planning on having desert twice tonight." He picked up the two plates off the counter and took them into the livingroom.

Jolelle stood there with her thoughts racing. She poured herself and Julian a glass of milk, then joined him in the living room. She set the two glasses of milk on the coffee table, and he then swiftly pulled her down on the couch. "Baby, you know I've wanted you for so long," he said in a husky voice. He gently laid on top of her, kissing her eagerly.

Jolelle, after several seconds said, "Julian, I'm too old for you. I'm twenty-five."

Julian lowered the dress straps off of her shoulders with his teeth. "Isn't this why you called me over here?" he asked sensuously. He kissed her again as he felt her breast gently.

"Yes...no...wait a minute," she said, sounding confused.

He caressed her now naked body, which he had already exposed, taking off her dress completely, saying, "Don't talk, just do me, baby. Please...do me." He caressed her curvaceous hips. "Mmm, mmm, baby," he moaned. "My brown sugar."

She said breathlessly, "I must be crazy," as her body began moving uncontrollably under Julian's. She moaned, "I want you honey...want me."

"Let's do it," said a very virile Julian.

He and Jolelle made love for hours. "Julian, I'm ten years older than you are," she said, out of breath. They were lying on the couch naked and holding each other close.

He ran his hand through her hair and said, "I don't care, this is right. I've wanted you for so long."

She quickly pushed him away, sitting up on the side of couch and nervously saying, "I...I must be crazy. This can never get out, Julian. You're a kid. I could go to jail."

He chuckled. "No one will ever know, baby."

She didn't comment, she just kept putting on her clothes. He started dressing also. Jolelle, panicking, then said, "Besides, I'm engaged to be married. I should not be here with you."

Now fully dressed, he stood up and said, "A fling before the wedding ring, huh, mama?" He headed for the door with Jolelle behind him.

"You really are a terrific lover, Julian. You seem much older than you really are," she observed. He opened the door, looking back at her as he smiled slightly without commenting. She then said, "I'm sure that you have many girlfriends, so you'll forget about me."

Surprisingly, Shelly's and Brandie's faces quickly flashed before Julian. He walked out of the door, but on the porch he yelled back to Jolelle, "I'm a musician. I don't have time for girlfriends." He headed home. Jolelle was quickly becoming a faint memory to him.

Chapter Seventeen
June 22, 1985

It was midnight when Julian arrived home. Tracy had been standing in the doorway and was returning to her seat on the couch. She had a drink in her hand. "Hey Tracy, what's up?" he asked as he came in and sat on the couch.

"Oh, yes, Mark! Mmm, you're wonderful!" The words came from their mother's room upstairs. "Uhn! Uhn!" a man's voice grunted. Rachel's laughter was next. "Don't stop! You're great!" she screamed.

Julian frowned. He then looked over at Tracy, who took a drink from her glass of vodka. The bottle sat on the coffee table in front of her. "What the he...."

Before Julian could get the word out, Tracy said nastily, "She's a fucking whore, that's all."

Julian responded, "Well, sis, what does that make you?" He got up and went into his bedroom. When he sat on his bed, it was like lightning had struck him. A bright light, like the bright beams of a car, shone brightly into his eyes. The light was so bright, his eyes ached with pain. "Ugh!" he shouted, covering his face. He leaned back on the bed, trying to escape the bright lights, but there was no relief from the beams that seemed to be only for him. "What is it?" shouted Julian. "Why are you attacking me? What do you want?" He didn't feel like he was about to have another seizure, though. As soon as he stopped shouting, the light, or presumed light that had blinded him for a few minutes left.

"What are you shouting about?" Tracy asked as she opened his bedroom door.

An exhausted Julian stammered, "The...the li...." He looked into his sister's eyes and didn't finish his reply. He just said, "Oh...noth...nothing. I just...fell asleep and had a bad dream."

Tracy then snapped, "Well, shut up all that screaming. One crazy person screaming in this house tonight is enough." She closed his door.

He got up off the bed, walked over to his homework table, sat down, and picked up his pen. He thought about Shelly. What a joke, he thought to himself. He smiled, thinking, Great tits, though. She had dropped him off at home and was trying to have sex with him again before he got out of the car. "Aw man," he said as he thought back to the blonde shapely girl. "Little tramp," he then murmured.

His thoughts then traveled to Jolelle Wilks. Great body, he thought. But the lady needs help. He then thought of Brandie. "Me write poems, yeah right," he said sarcastically. He then scribbled on his scratch pad: I have a light that comes to me at night. I don't know if it's a light of good or evil. All I know is that it's bright. And no one else can see it. And so I guess I can't confide my sights...to my family or to my friends. So, all I can do is say goodnight.

It was Monday, and only two weeks were left in the school year. Julian avoided Shelly like the plague. Lance had gotten word of Julian and Shelly being at the dance on Friday and confronted him. Heading toward his last class of the day, Julian stopped at his locker and took out his guitar he had brought with him. "Hey punk! I heard you left the dance with my girl Friday night," shouted Lance. He was getting his football gear from his locker and slammed the door closed, then headed toward Julian. Lance was a medium-built black guy with brown hair and brown eyes. He walked up to Julian and said, "So what do you have to say for yourself, sissy? You trying to move in on my girl, eh?" He pushed him against the locker.

Julian's eyes widened. His stomach muscles tightened. Anger was building inside of him, but he knew he had a class to attend and couldn't afford to get kicked out of school for fighting this dumb ox. He had been kicked out once before because some jealous student confronting him in the hallway about his girl. As he thought back, that guy's girlfriend was trying to hit on him. The guy had called him a pretty faggot, and Julian jawed him. He was suspended from school for a day, which didn't bother him because he got a chance to play his guitar all day instead of sitting in class, bored as hell. However what he didn't need was to be stuck at home with his mother, who was usually drunk, and his sister, who had quit school and was becoming a drunk like his mom.

Julian's green eyes glared into Lance's brown eyes as if he was staring straight through him. Julian smiled and kindly stated, "Naw, man, she drove me home, that's all." Then he roughly shoved the guitar case under Lance's neck, forcing him back against the lockers opposite them. The halls were empty and the rest of the students were in their classroom. The bell rang announcing to the boys that classes had started and they were late.

"Ma...ma...man, I'll be late for gym," stammered Lance.

Julian, still holding him pinned to the locker with his guitar case, angrily said, "Chump, I don't want your dumb girlfriend." He paused, shoving the curved end of the guitar case harder under Lance's neck.

Lance pleaded, "I...man, I...know, man. I...I was just kidding around. Please...please, man, let me go."

Julian, squinting his green eyes, said, "If I wanted her, I could have her right now." His eyes were filled with anger as he said, "Do you hear me, loser?

"Yeah man, whatever...just let me go!" said a panicked Lance. Lance was a football player and a lot more rugged-looking than Julian. But for the life of him, he didn't know why this light-complected pretty boy scared the hell out of him. And being pinned to the lockers, not able to move a muscle, by Julian's medium-framed body, made no sense. Julian had always felt that there was a force helping him when he would get in uncompromising positions. He was strong, but some of the things he had been able to do scared the hell out of him, too.

Julian backed up and, still holding his guitar, dropped it to the side of him. Lance, still looking terrified, said anxiously, "You're a damn demon...a weirdo...a lunatic.... Stay the hell away from me." He then ran down the stairs and to his class.

An exhausted Julian leaned back against the locker. Angrily he murmured, "Dumb spineless whimp." How on earth did I pin big Lance to the locker? he thought to himself. "Ugh, Ugh!" shouted Julian. Flashes of light were again blinding him. He dropped the guitar, which swung down beside his leg, completely to the floor. He grabbed his eyes in pain.

A teacher, whose classroom was next to where he was standing, opened her classroom door. "Young man, don't you have a class to go to?" the teacher tartly asked.

He looked at the tall, blonde teacher and said, "Uh, yeah...I...I just dropped my guitar.... Sorry about the noise." He then walked to his English class.

The blonde teacher said, as Julian was walking away, "What a cute young man.... A damn musician." The teacher then closed her door.

Finally in class, Julian sat listening to his classmates recite poems. He wasn't chastised for his lateness, so he said to his teacher, before he lost his nerve, "I'll go next. Might as well get it over with."

He stood in front of the class with his guitar in his hand. Mrs. Lichems asked him, "What's all this, Mr. Parr?" She then frowned.

Julian then said, "I,...Uh, I don't write poems."

Mrs. Lichem said, sounding puzzled, "Well, this isn't Soul Train, Mr. Parr." The class laughed.

He plugged in his guitar and said, "Uh...you didn't let me finish." He then said directly, "I wrote a poem last night called, 'I Have a Light', but...it was kinda personal, ya know, and I didn't want anyone to hear it, so...so I wrote a song this morning when I woke up. And since a friend of mine told me that songs are just poems put to music..." he then looked at Brandie, who was seated in the desk beside his. She smiled excitedly, sitting up on the edge of her chair. She was enthusiastically anticipating Julian's next feat. He fascinated her to no end. He continued, "Well, here is my poem."

He played a few cords and then began singing along with a soft, slower cord. "If I were to go away today, would you kiss me? Would anyone really care? And if I said I'll come back to you someday, would someday, you be there...awaiting my arrival with a loving heart to share. I need to know the answer. I need to know that you love me. And that the love you feel for me is rare. Because if the love I've felt from you, enrapturing me like clothes is a fallacy, then I have to go shopping...because I'm walking around bare."

The students clapped after Julian finished his song. Mrs. Lichem looking over her wire-framed specs, said, "Very impressive, Julian. That was indeed a poem, made much better with music."

That was the beginning of Julian's green eyes really being opened. He now knew what he wanted to do—make music. He had a message for people and through his music he could convey it.

He walked home from school satisfied with himself. Brandie caught up with him when he was nearing her street. "Julian...Julian! That song was terrific!" she said excitedly. "And...and your singing is awesome, just like the stars on TV and radio." She paused and said, "Aw, you're a natural. I knew you were special."

Julian hadn't looked at her and just said a cocky, "Well, yeah thanks." He increased his pace and walked on home. Brandie turned, looking sad and confused from Julian's cold behavior. She then went home also.

Chapter Eighteen
Two Years Later

It was now May 22, 1987. Julian was almost seventeen years old and very hand-some. He was a mature young man, and the girls swarmed around him like bees to honey.

It was 3:30 in the afternoon. The high school hall was crowded with stu-dents preparing to leave for the day. It was a rainy, cloudy Monday. Julian, head-ing for home, passed Shelly Nohl and Myra Evers standing at their lockers. They were pulling their raincoats and umbrella out as he was approaching.

Shelly exclaimed, "Oh, my God!"

Myra said, "What is it Shelly?" She had a puzzled look on her face.

Shelly replied, "I just...love Julian Parr. I went out with him when I was in the ninth grade and here he comes right now."

Myra looked down the hall and saw Julian walking toward where she and Shelly were standing. She nonchalantly said, "Well, if it isn't Mr. Rock Star him-self." She frowned. She didn't care for Julian Parr very much. She continued, "He doesn't give a damn about anyone or anything except that stupid guitar. He's so weird. He walks around with that thing like Linus with his security blan-ket." She laughed.

Shelly, feeling a little tense, said, "Shh, here he comes now." Julian was now on the opposite side of the hall from the two girls. He adjusted his cap and jack-et before venturing out in the rain. Shelly, still aggressive and spirited, said, "Myra, watch this. I'm going over there."

Myra smacked her lips and looked at her, then said, "He acts as if he does-n't even know or care that you're alive." She looked at Shelly strangely and said, "You've been going with the hottest jock in school for years now." Sounding dis-gusted, she continued, "I don't know why a smart chick like you still has the hots for that weirdo creep."

Shelly waved her hand at her in an I-don't-care fashion. She then headed over to him, calling "Julian! Julian! I'm glad I ran into you."

Julian, with his usual very serious expression, just said sternly, "What?"

Anxiously, Shelly ran her fingers through her hair and excitedly said, "I...uh...I'm having trouble in my math class." Her eyes were wide with enthusi-asm and happiness.

"So?" Julian replied coldly.

She chuckled, then said, "Aw, come on, sweetheart. I'll be at home by myself tonight."

He sighed, and looking nonplused said, "I'll be there at seven."

Shelly looked over at Myra with a smile on her face. Myra was already lis-tening to their conversation as Shelly winked at her mischievously. She then told Julian, "Seven's fine. My mom leaves for work at five."

Julian then said, "First house on Dawn Street, right?" as he walked out of the door. He didn't mention Lance and neither did Shelly. She wasn't given a chance to answer Julian's question, either.

She went back over to her locker, where Myra was still standing, shaking her head sorrowfully in disbelief. "I guess he is kinda cute, in a weird sort of way," she told Shelly. She closed her locker door and said, "You really love him, huh?"

Shelly closed her locker, put on her raincoat, and said to Myra, "Ha! I don't love him. He's a jerk. Besides, like you said...I go with a cute hunk, Lance Hamilton." She declared, "But nobody makes a fool out of Shelly Nohl, the way Julian did to me when we were in the ninth grade." Myra frowned at her as she continued, "Besides, if he's still as good as I remember, I'm gonna have fun tonight—big fun."

Myra thought, You slut! She didn't tell her friend that, just saying, "Oh...okay," happily.

Julian walked home once again, catching up with Brandie. He thought, She must have been walking slower just so I could catch up with her, because she left the school an hour before I did. "Hi Jewel. I was hoping that you would catch up with me," exclaimed a happy Brandie.

He rolled his eyes and said, "It's raining, Red, don't you think you'd better put a rush on?"

She replied, "Nah, I love the rain." She chuckled and continued, "I hope the man who falls in love with me will make love to me in the rain every times it falls." She held her head back and let a few drops sprinkle on her face.

Julian sighed and said, "Brandie, go home. You're losing your mind." He then swung his guitar case wildly forward.

She lifted the hood of her jacket back over her head and said, "Just because I'm disabled doesn't mean I don't dream and have desires just like you, Julian." She then turned up Reynolds Street and headed for her house.

Julian licked his lips and said, "Chicks, they're all horny toads." He then headed for home.

As Julian returned to his home, the rain was letting up some. Tracy was sitting in the living room with one of her numerous loser boyfriends. She told Julian their mother was in the kitchen cooking, so he walked straight to the kitchen. He completely ignored his sister's boyfriend, who was kissing Tracy on the neck while she giggled on the couch. The dark living room smelled of booze, and seeing the half-empty booze bottles on the table in front of them, he knew why.

"Hey Mom!" he yelled to Rachel as he entered the kitchen. He lifted the lid off of the pot that was cooking on the stove, and the aroma of spaghetti hit his nose immediately. "Mmm," said Julian as he replaced the lid on the pot.

"I know it's your favorite. And since I've been neglecting you guys lately," Rachel paused, then continued, "well, it's the least I can do for you." She was slightly hung over.

He sat down at the kitchen table, getting ready to have a somewhat civilized conversation with his mom, who for once wasn't drunk. "Uh, Mom, since I'll be graduating soon...." he paused then resumed uneasily, "I was...thinking of trying to find Dad." He rubbed the scar on his forehead.

She turned from the sink and frowned at him. "What?" she said in a low voice. "What!" She then yelled at him.

Looking puzzled, he said, "Well, you guys aren't divorced and if he sees that

I'm well now...maybe he'll come back." He ran his fingers through his hair.

Rachel exploded, "You're always talking about your daddy! I break my neck for you preparing this good meal and all you can talk about is your damn daddy!" Her eyes held a look of fury in them, her voice was loud and angry.

"No...no, Mom, I meant...."

Rachel interrupted Julian's comment and said, "I know what you meant— you meant I'm not enough. You need your daddy! Well, you're wrong. Your daddy doesn't want you. All he's gonna do is tell you that you're not enough and run out on you again!" Julian's eyes filled with tears. She shouted, "Wake up, will you! The man doesn't give a damn about your sick ass! He doesn't give a damn about me either!"

Julian got up from the table angrily. He nearly knocked down the chair as he was standing, then headed for his room. "Damn...damn, I hate her, damn her," he said as he entered his room. His eyes filled with tears, but they didn't fall. He again played his guitar, letting go of all his hate and anger...for his mother, his father, and his sister.

Hours passed and his mother called him. "Julian...Julian, come eat, son!"

He frowned, murmuring, "When does she quit? She insults me and now she wants me to come eat." He left his room and ate his spaghetti dinner whole-heartedly, along with orange soda pop, his favorite. His mother was drinking and again playing the piano. He frowned and said, "I can't take it anymore." He got up, put away his dinner dishes, and went upstairs to change clothes. He had a meeting with Shelly to get to.

Julian prepared for his date, then left the house. Before he left the house, he called to Rachel and told her he'd be back soon. His mother was still playing the piano, so he wasn't sure if she heard him.

Shelly opened the door at exactly seven o'clock on the dot. Julian was standing on her porch. His handsome face and build caught her eyes immediately. "Please, come in," she said. He entered the house looking unsure of his actions. "My room's upstairs," pointed out an anxious Shelly. She headed upstairs, almost taking them two at a time, and he followed behind her. In her room, he stood by the open door as she went and pounced excitedly down on her mattress. "So...how do you like," she said, opening her arms to show off the fuchsia camisole that she was wearing. She also had on tight-fitting mini jeans that came to around five inches above her ankles.

Julian looked at her and frowned, then said sternly, "Where are your books? I thought you wanted me to help you study your math."

Shelly replied, "Julian...I asked you...how do you like?" Julian still didn't answer. He rolled his eyes with an angry expression on his face that fooled neither himself or Shelly. Knowing math help wasn't the reason he was there or her reasons for inviting him, he smiled slightly. She smiled also and said, "Look, I'm as good at math as you are, Julian. You know that. The only math that I need you to help me with is...." She shook her curly hair out of the loose bow that held it in place. Her long hair fell to her shoulders. He breathed deeply as he watched her. She then continued, saying, "Maybe subtracting my clothes from my body." He held a slight frown on his face watching and listening to her. She confidently went on, "Or dividing my legs to suit you, of course." She stretched her arms out behind her and laid back, bracing herself by her arms.

"Enough of this stupid game," said Julian as he walked over to the bed and caressed her cheek. Her brown eyes stared up at him seductively. He said, "You know what I like, baby." Her breathing quickened at his rough touch.

"I bet I'll please you better than you've ever been pleased before," she said. Julian then lifted Shelly, who was seated on the side of the bed. He laid her at the head of the bed, then pulled the bed clothes back and placed her on the mattress and laid on top of her. He kissed her hotly, lowering her jeans as they tasted each other hungrily.

At the same time, Shelly was unbuttoning and pulling down Julian's gray tight-fitting jeans that hugged his curvaceous buttocks enticingly. Her hands then traveled under his black frilled T-shirt, caressing his hard and semi-hairy chest. "God, I want you," she said breathlessly as he pulled off his shirt completely. He kicked off his shoes as he was kissing and caressing Shelly's body, while at the same time she felt his firm buttocks. "Oh, Julian," she cried in ecstasy. His touches and thrusts were both gentle and rough. "You like it rough, baby. So do I, come on, make love to me," said a lustful Shelly.

He breathlessly lifted his head and, looking into Shelly's eyes, assertedly, "I like it, baby, whichever way I feel like doing it."

They rolled around in the bed for hours, kissing and releasing every bit of energy that got them into Shelly's bed. Julian's climax was earth shattering. He then got up out of bed and said, "Where's the john? I got to get out of here." Shelly snidely remarked, "Ha! Love 'em and leave 'em, huh, pretty boy?

Julian, still naked, held his clothes as he frowned, then said, running his fingers through his black hair, "I have a lot of tension to work off. So, I came to the gym and now I'm going to take a shower." He remembered passing a bathroom on his way down the hall. He remarked, "I don't love 'em, so how could I love 'em and leave 'em?"

Shelly was still lying in bed, propped up on her elbows. She breathed out disgustedly after hearing Julian's comment. She then rolled her eyes and chuckled as he murmured something that sounded like, "Bore," and left the bedroom. She heard the bathroom door down the hall close, then heard the water from the shower running. She yelled angrily, "Freakin' faggot! You're lousy in the sack anyway." But she knew that was a lie. He was an exquisite lover and anyone who thought he was gay was crazy. "Damn you, Julian...I'll get you one way or the other, you'll see," she said.

"See you around, Shell!" shouted Julian. She heard his footsteps heading down the stairs and jumped out of bed, still naked. She ran down the hall and stopped at the top of the stairway as Julian was about to walk out front door.

As he grabbed the knob Shelly barked, "You just screwed me and now you're just gonna leave without saying goodbye! And oh yeah, I'm not a whore."

He looked up the stairs and laughed. "I gotta go Shelly. I just had a workout, and you were my exercise equipment."

She shouted furiously, "Get out of here right now, you dog! You damn dog!"

He chuckled, then said, "Put some clothes on, Shell. You look like a whore." he opened the door and left.

Shelly was furious. "Grrr!" she growled.

Chapter Nineteen

Julian went home to once again find Tracy drunk. His mom had gone to work after several cups of coffee. The night club where she played the piano and sang could hardly care less about the state of Rachel's condition when she came to work, they just wanted her to entertain the dinner crowd. And that's exactly what she did, with no complaints. Out of everything she was, she was a professional. Her musical talent never failed.

Tracy greeted Julian a little too happily when he came in the house. He knew she had been drinking. "Hello there, my handsome playboy brother." She giggled and said, "How many girls have you been with tonight?"

He sat there on the couch, then said calmly, "Shut up, Tracy, and sober up." He was kidding, but he meant every word that he spoke.

"Ahh, come on, lover boy. We know you aren't our little virgin boy anymore."

Julian yawned, then got up saying, "Well, I guess living in this house, being a virgin would make me a misfit, now wouldn't it, sis?" He looked directly at her as she just laughed.

He rolled his eyes and headed toward his bedroom. The guitar had to wait that night, he was too tired. He dozed off as soon as his head hit the pillow. However a disturbing dream woke him up. In the dream, the blinding light he now considered the after-effects of a recovering epileptic was following him constantly down a deserted road. He didn't know where he was or where he was going, all he knew was that the light shone brightly beside him, forcing him to keep walking in the direction he was headed. He couldn't look back or around him for the light was too bright and blinding. All he could do was walk forward and look straight ahead. But Julian being Julian turned his head after a while. He was wondering why this bright light had surrounded him and was guiding him to God knew where. As soon as he looked back, the light shone brightly in his eyes with such a blinding force he fell down immediately. The pain in his eyes was like no other pain he had felt in his life.

Julian awoke screaming in pain. He held his hands over his eyes tightly, then jumped up and ran into the bathroom. While there, he thought long and hard about his dream and about Shelly. "That slut," he exclaimed. He got into the shower and turned the water to hot. As the water washed away the filth from his day, he lathered up and closed his eyes. The steaming hot water fell upon him as he thought of his dysfunctional family and his dysfunctional life. Tears filled his eyes and fell down his face on his chest and the basin of the tub. Mixing with the water, they all went down the drain.

The next day, he went to school carrying his guitar case as usual. In any other instance, the guitar would have been confiscated so fast that your head would spin. But at Clarkston High School Julian, being so smart and really somewhat of a gifted student, was allowed to keep the guitar on school grounds. He would play it on his lunch breaks or when he was outside waiting for the bell to ring.

He was often approached by Mr. Sullan, the jazz band instructor, who had been trying to talk him into trying out for the band since he had started high school. He had heard Julian's exceptional playing. But Julian refused the teacher's offer. "A school band is not what I'm about. The world is screwed up and playing 'The Star Spangled Banner' at a pep rally ain't gone help it," he said to the teacher.

It was now June eighth. Shelly and Myra were again standing at their lockers as Julian passed the girls on his way to biology class. He didn't say a word to either of them, but kept straight into the classroom. Myra blurted out, "Oh yeah, a few weeks ago, how did it go with your tutoring session with Mr. Weirdo Rock and Roll?"

Shelly cleared her throat and rolled her eyes, then said, "Who cares about him? He's a conceited creep." She again rolled her eyes, but this time she smiled wickedly, saying, "Besides, Lance is better in bed anyway." She giggled but then cut it off suddenly, saying, "Yeah, forget him. He's probably gay anyway."

Myra looked at Shelly and for the first time in a long time felt a source of joy. Shelly's face looked perturbed as she talked about Julian Parr. Somebody had finally gotten to little Ms. "I'm better than everyone else." She smiled and said, "Sure, Shell, whatever you say." Yes! Yes! Somebody finally got to the ice princess...Yes! thought Myra ecstatically.

At the end of the school day, Myra told Shelly to walk home without her. She had to talk to one of her counselors. Shelly left the school. Myra then waited until she spotted Julian. He was taking a make-up test in French class and was a few minutes late going home. "Hi Julian," said an excited and nosy Myra. Julian didn't comment. He just put his books in his locker and put on his Clarkston High School jacket. It was June 10, 1987, but still cool outside. Myra then went over to Julian's locker and said, "So, you had to stay at school late today...so did I. I, uh...had to see my counselor about my...."

Julian interrupted her, saying, "You don't have to lie. You were waiting for me." He smiled. His greenish gray eyes sparkled, sending a hole straight through Myra's soul. He then asked, "Why?"

Myra, caught off guard, replied, "What? Why what?" sounding a little dazed.

Julian chuckled. "Why...did you wait for me?" He had an amused look on his face.

Myra cheerfully said, "Like I said, I had to see my...." Julian closed up the locker, then breathed deeply and walked to the school's front door, preparing to leave. All right!...All right!" she yelled, following him down the school's outside steps. "Well, Shelly told me you were gonna help her with her math the other week, and I...I."

Julian didn't listen to her last comment. He walked down the sidewalk, saying, "Oh, I guess you want me to help you with your math, too."

Myra said excitely, "No! No! Of course not. It's just that...well...Shelly...." She ran her fingers through her hair nervously.

Julian interrupted her again, saying, "You know, you're kinda fine. You wanna go somewhere and...."

Myra said quickly, before he finished his sentence, "No! Shelly said you were conceited! I should have listened to...." She then stopped talking and leaned back on the school's fence in disgust. "I don't know why I waited for you," she snapped. "I guess I get sick of hearing about Shelly and her escapades. And...and this time she wasn't happy or bragging so...so I uh...I...."

Julian then said impatiently, as he stood facing her, "Look, I'm tired of hearing about that stuck-up snob friend of yours." He ran his fingers through his hair.

Myra stammered, "Yes, yes...I guess I did, I do want to be with you."

Julian looked at her lovely figure, up and down. It didn't matter that she had on clothes, he had a way of looking at girls that made them feel naked.

Myra then nervously spotted the gold cross hanging around his neck. For lack of words and due to too many nerves, she commented, "I like your cross."

Julian smiled devilishly. His eyes checked out her small but sensuous breasts, the v-neck sweater, and the matching belt she wore around her jeans. He observed, "I like your cross, too."

Myra blushed. He continued, "I don't have a class first hour tomorrow, and I know this great motel." He then looked into Myra's gazing eyes and said, "All I have to do is slip the guy an extra ten bucks and you and I are Mr. and Mrs. Julian Parr for an hour."

Myra frowned, then said, "No, I can't skip class again. If my mom finds out she'll kill me."

Julian shrugged his shoulders, saying, "Suit yourself, you name when." Looking up nonchalantly, she leaned up off of the fence. Her small but curvaceous frame hypnotized Julian, who just stared at her.

Myra then said, "Oh, what the hell...it's only one class. This is a chance of a lifetime. Sure I'll meet you there at eight A.M. Now what motel is it and where is it?"

Julian chuckled, then said, "A chance in a lifetime, huh...? If you say so." He crossed the street, yelling back to her, "Wilmer's Motel on Smith Street!" She smiled. She lived in the opposite direction of his house, so she departed also.

Chapter Twenty
June 11, 1987
Detroit, Michigan

Seventeen-year-old Julian stripped off his black denim jeans and white shirt. He wore no underwear and was now totally nude. His excitement was evident in the hardness of his young masculine body. The sight of his nude body hypnotized Myra. She was seated on the hotel bed feeling a little nervous and a whole lot giddy. "I...I really shouldn't be here," she said. "My mother would kill me if she knew I skipped science to come to a hotel with you, of all people." She folded her arms, feeling a little insecure, as Julian breathed deeply. He rolled his eyes in disgust at her statement.

He walked over to the bed and gently caressed her cheek. He then tilted heir chin slightly so that her face looked up at his. "Baby, you know you want me. I've seen you checking me out for months now," he said. He then shook his head, slinging his long black hair away from his eyes. He pushed her back on the bed. "I don't care about your mama. I want you," he said in a deep, seductive tone. He then caressed her breast and said, "Let's get in bed."

Myra quickly and willingly took off her lime green shell. "Ooh...you know, Julian, I want you so much. I've wanted you since the first time I saw you," she said softly. She licked her lips and stood up from the bed, which Julian had gotten into. A naïve Myra, after stepping out of her flowered flared skirt, followed. He lifted her bra off of her small pouty breast and teasingly caressed and kissed it. She sighed, "You're wonderful Julian." He didn't comment. He just moaned as he continued to kiss her soft body. Myra then said excitely, "I knew you would be. You're so sexy and smart...and so...talented."

Julian, who was still kissing her firm body, moaned in ecstasy. He breathed deeply as he caressed her curvy hips and thighs. "Mmm, baby you feel so good," he murmured.

She chuckled, running her fingers through her black shoulder-length hair wildly as she said, "Well, yes. I'm much better than that blonde tramp, Shelly. She's nothing but a tease. Like I said, you're better off with me."

Julian's thrusts were earth shattering and dynamic. However, the more he made love to Myra, the more she raved on about...everything. "You know what's wrong with our high school?" she asked. Julian didn't comment. He was still enjoying the pleasures of her body. Agitatedly, she snapped, "Julian! are you listen...."

"Will you shut the hell up? he yelled angrily. "Do you want to do it or not?" he asked, his eyes wide with passion and anger.

"Of course, you're sensational, Julian. I'm just glad you haven't been with that Shelly Nohl, slut. She's such a...." He rolled his eyes disgustedly at her constant talking. He again made love to her fervently, wickedly as only he could. He spasmed physically, letting out a horrifying "Uhm!" then rolled over and sat up on the side of the bed. He got up and gathered his clothes.

Myra, looking slightly angry, said, "Wait, what about me? We're not done yet."

Julian looked at her nonchalantly and said, "I'm done," then headed toward the bathroom as he said coldly, "I have to get back to school." He frowned and said, "You need a shrink, baby. You obviously get off on talking and you need to sex someone who gets off on listening to that bull." He went into the bathroom and closed the door.

As he washed up, Myra swore angrily and loudly. But Julian had the water running and didn't hear a bit of Myra's furor. "Fag! No wonder they say you're a weirdo! You creep! You...you jerk!" she shouted. He opened the bathroom door, was now fully dressed. As he stepped out of the bathroom, Myra started silently putting on her clothes. She sat on the bed and said nothing to him. He smiled at her as he opened the motel room door and said to her, "It's been fun. You've got a great ass." He left the room as a stunned Myra just sat there and watched him leave.

Julian went about his day normally. After leaving Myra, he went to school and resumed his classes as usual. When he passed either Myra or Shelly that day, they just looked away as if they didn't see him. He then would smile wickedly, exclaiming lowly, "Horny toads."

After school, Brandie caught up with him as he was walking home. She limped up to him and asked, "Are you done with all your final edams, Jewel? Friday's our last day." She shook her long reddish-brown hair and said, "I finished my last one today. They told me I didn't have to come back until we practiced for graduation." She sighed. He remained silent. She then said, "So...I guess this is goodbye until graduation practice."

Julian quietly said, "This is my last day, too. I hate that school, but at least it took me away from that madhouse I live in." He then frowned.

Brandie, excited like she always was said, "Well, Jewel..." She paused, then continued, "There's always college. Aren't you going to college?"

Julian again frowned. He replied, "Nah, college isn't my thing." He rubbed his guitar case and said casually, "I'm a musician, Red." He swung the guitar case out in front of him, still holding it, then said, "I'm gonna send a few demo's to some record companies and...." He shrugged his shoulders and blurted, "Who knows, Red. The sky's the limit, you know. I got plans, Red, big plans." He then shook his hair away from his face.

Brandie said, "Well, I'm going to Wayne University...I was hoping, you would be going, too."

"Get real, Brandie. College is your thing not mine," he said. He then ran home, leaving her spellbound.

"Goodbye, Julian," she whispered sympathetically to herself.

Julian entered his house enthusiastically. Tracy was sitting on the couch drinking vodka. He said, "Hello," and headed for his bedroom. Tracy came into his room.

"Hi there!" she said.

Julian was playing his guitar said agitatedly, "What is it, sis?"

Tracy slammed his bedroom door and locked it. He frowned, looking curious. She took off her satin shirt and stared at herself in the mirror on the back of his bedroom door. "Tracy, you're drunk. Would you get out of here, please," said Julian. "And put your clothes on," he added.

Tracy turned toward him and unhooked her bra. It dropped to the floor. She then walked over to his bed. He sat there wide-eyed and astonished by his sister's actions. "Come on, Tracy. I'm your brother, stop all this." He stood up. She slid down her skirt, then was totally nude. He shouted, "Hell! Tracy, put your clothes on will you!" She put her arms around his neck and tried to kiss him. He turned his head quickly, avoiding her kiss.

Tracy then got down on her knees and started unfastening his jeans. "Come on, bro," she said in a sleepy voice. "No one will have to know."

Julian whispered, "Tracy, please, get up, sis."

Tracy giggled and said, "Aw, come on, little bro. I'll have fun and you will have a real blast!" She giggled again and pulled down the zipper on his pants. She then said, "You ever had a real blow...."

Before Tracy could finish the question, Julian kicked her to the floor. As he headed for the door, she yelled, "Come on, Julian!" He looked back at her, still seated on the floor. She then said sarcastically, "The family jewel...oh wow! Isn't it more like the family gigolo?" She paused, frowning, then continued, "Mom would love to hear about all those young girls you've been with, I bet. Her little precious jewel wouldn't be looked at as so precious, now would he?"

Julian looked at Tracy with a hate in his eyes that was unnerving. She slyly commented, "Not to mention our neighbor who you screwed that night." He was looking and wondering how she knew about Jolelle when she added, "The next time you two decide to do it, make sure the window on the side of her house is closed. I could hear her screams and moans from here." He agitatedly ran out of the room. "Damn you! Damn you!" he yelled as he ran out of the back door. "I'll never come back to this damn crazy house.... Never!"

Tracy still sat on the floor, half-nude, in his bedroom. She was laughing profusely. Rachel had gone to work early that day to rehearse some new songs. She and Julian had argued that morning before he went to school over her excessive drinking. Nothing was solved, and Julian stormed out of the house. He then went to school.

He headed for the shed to get his ten-speed bike which he had received on his sixteenth birthday the year before. He took the key from under the mat and unlocked the shed door. He stepped over the lawnmower and the numerous basketballs and croquet games until he reached his purple bike at the back of the crowded shed. "I hate that house...I hate that house," he kept murmuring. He thought about Tracy and his anger intensified. He harshly hit the shelf that was against the back wall of the shed, then dropped the key on the floor of the dark shed. "Great! Just great!" he yelled, disgusted and fed up.

He dropped to his knees, feeling and looking for the key to the large shed. After a few minutes, anger got the best of him and he hit the bottom shelf with his fist. He heard a hollow sound and frowned. He lifted the thick cloth that covered the shelf and there he saw it, a lavender guitar. It was broken and dusty, with just two strings attached, and the tuning knobs were gone. Julian thought about his father telling him, when he was younger, of a guitar he had once had. Steven had told him it had been struck by lightning. Julian looked puzzled as he reminisced on his father's words. "Oh shit, this is it," he whispered excitedly. As he was getting ready to stand, he spotted the key to the shed.

Julian picked the key up and put it in his jeans pocket. He then lifted the dusty guitar to his mouth and blew the dust and dirt particles off of it. "It's mine now, Dad. You did leave me something," he murmured.

He walked out of the shed holding the ragged old guitar and pushing out his bike. He closed and locked the shed and then replaced the key back under the mat, where the family had started keeping it. He looked up at the house, thinking of his other guitar he had left sitting in the case on the floor by his bed. He got on his bike and said, "Forget it.... That guitar and that damn crazy house." He then rode off without looking back.

Chapter Twenty-one

Julian rode around the city of Detroit, passing a few of his buddies who were standing on the street corner talking. But with the old guitar in his hand, he just kept riding.

At last, he ended up on Reynolds Street in front of Brandie Charles's house. He rolled his eyes and said, "Where else can I go?" He thought of Jolelle Wilks.... Naw, too close to home, he thought. He then thought about his so-called girl-friends, like Shelly and Myra, among others. They don't give a damn about me, he thought. I've given them all they wanted from me and they've given me all the hell I've really wanted from them. His thoughts then traveled to Brandie. Optimistic flower child, he mused. "Oh well." he sighed. "She probably is the only one who really cares about me. Hell, she cares about everybody," he said out loud.

He got off of the bike and headed up to the brick ranch-style house. He knocked and Brandie opened the door immediately. "Julian, what are you doing here?" she said, inquisitive yet excited.

Julian jokingly said, "Well, Ms. Charles, I could leave if you don't want to see me."

Brandie opened the door wide. She exclaimed, "Of course I want to see you.... Come in. Have a seat." He followed her demands. She closed the door and went and sat on the brown leather chair across from the gold leather couch where he was seated. She noticed the troubled look on his face and asked, "So...what's up, Julian? What did I do to deserve this unexpected pleasure?" She smiled.

Julian ran his fingers through his hair and frowned, then said uneasily, "Uh...I...Brandie, I left home." He shook his hair away from his face and stared down at his lap.

Brandie, astonished by his news, said nervously, "Uh, Julian...just what exactly do you mean, you left home?" She looked at him curiously and frowned.

Julian jumped up from the couch. He walked over to the window and looked out. He replied, "I...I don't know, Red." She still looked concerned. He continued, "My family is screwed.... My dad left when I was seven years old...because I...because I was sick."

"Oh my God, Julian," said an exasperated Brandie. "How could he leave you, just because you're sick?" She frowned again, saying, "What kind of monster would do...."

Julian interrupted her. "Well, as you know I had epilepsy. A real bad case, when I was younger. I used to have these horrific seizures."

Before he could continue Brandie said, "But still...."

Agitatedly, Julian interrupted her. "But still, my father wanted a healthy boy. A basketball player, I guess. Or maybe he wanted a musician...."

Brandie declared, "Well, see there, that's what you're gonna be, right? So...he left you too soon." She licked her lips.

Julian turned away from the window, raised his eyebrows, and said, "Well, Red, that was a long time ago, anyway. My mom started drinking a lot after that and then my sister started drinking just as much."

Brandie exclaimed, "Oh, Julian, how horrible for you." He turned, facing the window again. He glared out of the window, looking, but not seeing anything at all except his own pain.

Julian added, "If that wasn't bad enough...." He chuckled, then continued, "My sister, Tracy, just tried to seduce me." Angrily, he hit the window and snapped, "Damn!"

Brandie ran her hands over her face distractedly. She got up from the couch, walked over to Julian, patted him on the back, then said, "Oh my God, Jewel. What are you gonna do?"

Julian breathed deeply as he looked up at Brandie, who was standing beside him. He replied, "I don't know, Red. But this is the last straw. I can't go back there. Between the arguments with my mom, and now my sister's going freakin crazy, I just can't. Brandie, I just can't go back there," he said, heartbroken.

Brandie hugged Julian, then stepped back away from him. She cleared her throat, trying to forget the feelings she had just holding his muscular body. She hesitantly said, "Well Jewel...what are you gonna do? I would say that you could stay here until you get on your feet, but as cool as my mom is, she's not cool enough to let one of my guy friends stay here."

Brandie went back over to the couch and sat down. She remarked to Julian, who was watching her, "My mom has always liked you and the way you seem to dance to your own drummer, but she also knows that I li...." She changed the subject, saying, "Well, we've got to find you a place to live."

Julian's green eyes sparkled as he smiled and joined her on the couch. She anxiously asked, "Do you have any money?"

Julian laughed and retorted, "Get real, Red." Her big brown eyes widened as he continued, "I'm a high school student, just like you. I have a drunken mom and sister, and my dad split just because I wasn't his idea of the model son." He sighed frustratedly. "I doubt that he left me anything. And my mother...well, I'm sure if I had any savings in the bank, she drank it up. I need to find a job and a cheap place to live. Right now, I'm a homeless, broke, wanna-be musician." He stood up. "Brandie, I got to go," he said, heading for the door.

Brandie got up from the couch and yelled, "No!" He looked back at the reddish-brown-haired beauty with the light brown skin. She had a lovely figure, and the affliction that had caused her to occasionally limp didn't seem to bother Julian. He saw it as a kind of common bond the two of them shared. His epilepsy, which altered his lifestyle in the beginning and his physical actions; and her mild polio condition, which constantly kept her working out in the gym to remain limber.

Julian angrily said, "No what, Red?" He frowned. "You have a nice, peaceful home to live in, and a mom who I am sure isn't a lush. So...what do you want with me?" He again shook his hair, which was more of a habit then a necessity.

Brandie responded, "I...I, uh...I have an uncle who might have a place for you." She grabbed his hand and guided him back to the couch.

Julian asked, "Your uncle, huh?"

Brandie sat down beside him and exclaimed excitedly, "Yes...my favorite uncle. He loves me and would do just about anything for me." She paused, then added, "He's my father's brother. He owns a record store on Lafayic Street and there's a vacant, already furnished apartment just above it."

Julian said pessimistically, "Well, I don't have a job. I can't pay the rent even if he does let me get it."

Brandie took a deep breath, then exhaustedly said, "Look Jewel, I'll talk to him. Maybe he'll cut you some slack until you get a job. You'll be doing him a big favor, anyway. Lafayic isn't the best street to run a business on. So maybe you could look after the place when he closes at night."

Julian suddenly asked, "Where's your mom, anyway? Maybe I'll ask her what she thinks about it."

Brandie bit down on her lip and replied, "My mom's at work until midnight. She's working overtime." He looked over at Brandie, who had a frown on her face. She resumed, "You see, Julian, yours isn't the only screwed-up family around here. My dad left my mom for his business partner." Julian remained silent as she continued, "Oh yeah, she and my mom were good friends, too. She had worked in my dad's private office as long as I can remember. I never really knew what business Dad was in. I was young when he and Mom were together. But my mom just used to say he's just like a movie star himself...damn him." Getting angry, she declared, "'Aunt' Barb was so close to the family. She wasn't really my aunt, but she insisted that I call her Aunt Barb."

Julian said, "That's messed up. She was messing around with your dad."

Brandie chuckled and remarked, "Yeah, tell me about it. My mom has been throwing herself into her job like crazy ever since my dad left her. She's a telephone operator."

Julian commented somewhat sarcastically, "And that leaves little Brandie at home by herself with her peace signs and tattoos, huh!"

Brandie snapped, "You may like being by yourself...you and your dumb instrument. But I get lonely. I miss my mom...and my dad." She looked at Julian's handsome face and said, "You may long for a peaceful home, but I'd give anything to hear my mom argue with me." Tears filled her eyes as she reflected, "To show me that she still really cares about me and not that damn job all the time!" Brandie got her wish and then some.

Julian put his arms around her shoulder, then gently pushed her head slightly to rest on her shoulder. Her eyes again widened. "What are you doing, Jewel?" she asked quietly, raising her head off of his shoulder and looking at him curiously.

Julian replied, "I'm doing what I've wanted to do since I first met you." He then kissed her lightly rouged lips. They kissed for several minutes.

It was Brandie who pulled back, breaking the kiss. She sighed. "Julian, I've always cared about you, you know that don't you?"

Julian breathed deeply and slightly smiled, saying, "Yes, Red, I guess I've known that since we first met."

Brandie continued, "I moved here from Minnesota when I was a kid...and, I...fell in love with the cutest little boy. I've been in love ever since."

Julian embraced her again in his arms and asked huskily, "You think you're in love with me?" Her heartbeat quickened, as did his.

Brandie replied, "Yes, I...I am in love with you, Julian. I have been since the first time we met."

Julian observed, "I think love may be too strong a word, Red."

Brandie looked into his green eyes and frowned, explaining, "I know you couldn't love anyone like me, Jewel. But it doesn't change the fact that I love you." He now had a serious look on his face as she smiled at him and said softly, "I don't want to be alone tonight, Jewel."

Julian kissed Brandie again, stammering, "Uh...Brandie...Where did the "Jewel" thing come from?"

Brandie replied, "I don't know. I've always called you Jewel...every once in a while."

Julian stated harshly, "It's just that...well, my sister was calling me that ...and my dad use to call me Jewel." he said lowly, "And my mom, occasionally."

Brandie caressed his chest and said, "You're my Jewel...my precious Jewel. Just like my jewelry, you're priceless...and I want you."

Julian led Brandie down the hall, asking her, "Where's your bedroom, sweetheart? Down the hall?"

Brandie answered, "Yes, the end of the hall."

Inside Brandie's bedroom, she found out what loving someone really meant. She and Julian made love continuously. A happy Brandie told him afterwards, "It's just like I always imagined it would be. How was it for you, my Precious Jewel?"

Julian had a brand-new light about his face as Mayfield's ballad, "The Makings of You," played on the stereo. He pulled her naked body close to him and replied, "I think I finally know what it feels like to really...you know...?" He didn't finish his statement, even with her insistence. He just ran his hands through her long wavy hair and said, "Come on, sweetie, we're not quite done yet."

Brandie giggled, then got out the bed and went over to her dresser. She looked at Julian, who was still in bed, and said, "I have something for you." He just stared at her without commenting as she opened up her brass jewelry box. She took out a shiny object, smiled, and turned back toward him. She softly said, "So you'll always have my heart. I give this to you." She handed him a golden chain with an engraved heart attached. The engraving was of the same words she had just spoken to him: SO YOU'LL ALWAYS HAVE MY HEART.

Chapter Twenty-two

Julian got up out of bed and slipped back into his black bikini briefs. At the same time, Brandie grabbed her short satin turquoise robe and put it on. She was now sitting on the bed with her back against the plush pillows. He looked back at her as she tied the string on her robe, then chuckled wickedly and said, "That won't be necessary." He opened the bedroom door then walked over to the bed. Her eyes were again wide as she watched his almost nude body approaching her.

Brandie asked, "What?" sounding puzzled. "What are you doing?"

Julian grabbed her hands and gently said, "Come on, I said we're not done yet." He pulled her out of bed.

Brandie, hand-in-hand with Julian, followed his lead. She giggled, saying, "Julian...Jewel, where are you taking me?" Her voice sounded playful. He led her across her large room to the adjoining bathroom. Looking at him with a slight smile on her face, she asked, "Julian...what's going on?" She still sounded inquisitive and playful.

He stopped in front of the sink and said to her, "Wait here." He went to the tub and turned on the shower, then held out his hand to her. His green eyes were gleaming as she put her hand in his and said, "Whatever you want, baby." She chuckled.

Julian assisted her in taking off her robe and said, sounding very enticing, "You said that you wanted to make love to the man you fell in love with in the rain."

Brandie's joy was apparent as she took a deep breath, realizing that he had remembered her comment. She looked into his eyes and smiled, then stepped into the tub. He let go of her hand and slid down his briefs and joined her under the shower's falling sprinkles of water. Their naked bodies embraced as he kissed her neck, her earlobe, her cheek, and then her lips. She moaned in ecstasy, and they then kissed each other's bodies wildly under the shower. He caressed her buttocks and thighs, his hand parading in and out. "Oh Julian," she murmured softly. She tenderly ran her hands over his broad muscular back and shoulders, at last ending at his muscular buttocks. He kissed and softly squeezed her medium-sized breast. Lowering the kisses, he worked his way down her stomach and her entire body above her knees. Feeling an excitement she had never felt before, she gasped hoarsely, "Oh...I love you so much!"

Julian by now was kissing and caressing her shapely legs. He was massaging the back of her legs when he noticed the small tattoo above her ankle. It was a red rose, beautifully crafted. It captured his attention for a few moments, then he looked up at Brandie, who was taken by his touches and the warm shower. She groaned and grabbed the bar of soap from the side of the tub and lathered her upper body. He cleared his throat again, looking at her now soapy tits and stomach, saying, "You really are a genuine flower child aren't you? Tattoos and all." He took his hand and gently traced her ankle tattoo, then rose from the stooped position he was in and looked into her wide brown eyes.

She countered, "I'm a product of God and Mother Nature.... Who knows, they may be one. But I am their's and so are you." She hugged him tightly and kissed his neck and shoulders. She took the bar of soap and lathered his back sensuously.

Julian moaned. "Oh baby.... Where have you been all my lonely life?" his voice was deep and seductive. She shyly looked into his green eyes as he again felt her wet breasts.

Brandie sighed uncontrollably and said, while lathering his hairy chest, "I've been right here, sweetheart." She stopped caressing Julian's body with soap and pointed to the gold chain that hung down on his chest, saying, "I guess it took your misfortune at home and a guiding light to lead you to me."

Julian frowned. He shook his head in confusion, thinking it was a strange way to put his being there with her, "led by a guiding light." He looked seriously into her eyes as he asked curiously, "What guiding light are you talking about, Red?"

Brandie, again excited, said, "God's light...the light of love. We all have it." She jumped into his arms, wrapping her legs around his waist and buttocks.

Julian moaned, "Oh, Brandie...yours is the only light I need. The light that's making my whole body weak, right now. Anyway, I don't know if I believe in that God stuff or not." She was licking and kissing his neck and ignored his comment, giggling in pure passion.

Julian continued, "You're the light that knocks me to my knees." He then pulled her close to him, their bodies becoming one as they moved harmoniously, making love endlessly as the showering water poured.

"Uhhh! Jewel!" she yelled excitedly. "Oh baby, you really are my Precious Jewel." They enjoyed each other's passion once again.

Julian noted, "I'm gonna break your back, Red...or you mine. Why don't we go back to your bed?"

Brandie replied, "Uhn-uhn. No, this is my dream come true. You said it yourself, except...." She paused, looking puzzled.

Julian prompted, 'Except what?"

Brandie finished calmly, "Well...I didn't say I wanted to make love to the man I was in love with. I said," she looked at Julian point blank and continued, "that I want the man who fell in love with me, to make love to me each time it rains."

Julian frowned again, feeling confused by her words. He asked, "Well, what's the difference?"

Brandie replied, agitated, "Do you love me, Jewel? I've told you over and over again that I'm in love with you." She paused, then said, "I haven't heard you say that you love me at all. I don't want to be used, Julian. I know your...." She was looking strangely at Julian. The shower had stopped and both of their heads of hair hung limp.

Julian interrupted her before she could continue saying, "track record with girls," snapping, "Look, Brandie, I never really loved anybody." He paused and angrily said, "What the hell is love anyway?"

Brandie breathed deeply and looked sympathetically at him. She whispered, "My mom will be here soon. We should get dressed." Her joyous expression was now blank.

She started to step out of the tub when he grabbed her arm saying, "No!" She looked up at him. He gently released her arm and said sorrowfully, "Red...The only people who I think I've ever loved are my family." He again frowned. "And look how screwed up they are.

Brandie was now feeling sorry for him. "That...that doesn't have anything to do with m...."

Julian interrupted her. "No...it doesn't have a thing to do with you but...." He paused and continued, "I've used the other girls, women...well, girls and women," he corrected himself. "Because nobody really gives a damn about me, anyway." Anger building inside, he said, "Certainly my mom hasn't cared about anything since dad left, but her booze." He said lowly, "And any poor fool she could sucker into her bed." She caressed his cheek nervously and frowned, staring at him without commenting. Julian declared, still sounding and looking angry, "And my sister's selfish whore ass...she hasn't been the same since she got rid of her kid, which I'm sure she blames Mom for making her do it." Sorrowfully he looked down and said, "Well...Red...that's my dumb dysfunctional family."

Brandie breathed in deeply, not knowing what to say to him. He lifted his head and looked into her brown eyes. "Oh, my sweet and innocent Brandie. You are the first pure and truly innocent person and virgin I know." He caressed her cheek. "I feel like I've been truly honored to be the first guy to make love to you. You've always been there for me...even when," he chuckled, "I treated you like crap. You still cared."

Brandie swallowed hard and uttered weakly, "That's because I love...."

Julian again interrupted her. "I know baby...I know." He hugged her again, kissing her neck softly and caressing her back. He murmured, talking directly into her ear as his hand cascaded through her reddish-brown hair, "The reason I was able to get with all those other girls is because I didn't give a damn about them." He paused as she kissed his shoulder and ran her fingers through his hair.

Julian gasped slightly and continued, "If the meaning of love is always wanting to protect a person and never wanting to see them hurt...baby...maybe I do love you.... Yeah!" He pulled away and looked into her eyes, continuing, "Yeah, I love you...and every crazy, happy, carefree single thing about you." Brandie blushed. "Let's make love huh?" he said quickly. He embraced a now misty Brandie and whispered "I love you, baby, even your flower power ankle tattoo."

Julian and Brandie once again wet and wildly kissed each other. His lips gently caressed every facet of her face as she sighed and moaned in passion. She again turned the shower back on, and they bumped and ground their way into orgasmic ecstasy. "I love you Julian," sighed a naively trusting Brandie.

Julian said, "Me too, baby."

Corina Charles, Brandie's mother, walked into the house at 11:30 P.M. Brandie and Julian were seated on the couch playing a video game. "Hello, Brandie," said a loud and suspicious voiced Corina. She then looked at Julian and said, "Hello, there...Julian, isn't it?" She frowned slightly and cut her eyes over to Brandie.

Julian stood. "Uh...hello, Mrs. Charles. Good seeing you again."

Corina lifted her eyebrows, still looking strangely. "Why...yes, Julian, good to see you too," she responded in a puzzled tone.

Brandie jumped up from the couch. She could only imagine what her mother must have thought was going on. And yes, she was right.... And then some, she thought. "Uh...Mom," exclaimed Brandie. She rubbed her hands nervously on the side of her faded jeans and said, "Julian...had a little problem at home today...and he left home."

Brandie walked over to her mother and put her arm around her shoulder and pleaded, "He can't go back there, Mom. It was awful. Can he stay here? Just for a few days until he can find a job?" her big bright eyes sparkled and she quickly blew him a kiss before her mother could see her.

Corina responded, "Well, it's late. We'll talk about it in the morning. The boy can stay here tonight, and tomorrow I'll talk to my brother-in-law about putting you up at his place. He also has a job for you, if you don't have one." Brandie smiled. She looked at him, knowing that she had told him the exact same thing earlier.

Julian smiled and said happily, "This is too real. You two are the best."

Corina walked over to Brandie. Habitually, she smoothed down her hair and said, "You better be turning in, missy, it's getting late." She flopped down on the couch. Brandie again blew him a quick kiss without her mother knowing. Corina said, "Brandie, your hair is damp. What have you been doing?"

Brandie didn't answer and headed for bed, saying, "I love you. Good night Mother."

Corina went to her closet and got her purse. She gave Julian thirty dollars and said, "Keep this...." He looked at her in amazement. She explained, "It's nothing. I'll talk to my brother-in-law about letting you have the place free of charge until you find a job. He might want to hire you on a job he has available." She covered the top of his hand with her own, and whispered, "Thanks for being friends with my baby. She doesn't have that many, you know." She then winked at him, but he didn't know what she meant.

He hoped that Mrs. Charles didn't suspect he had made love to Brandie that night. He doubted that she knew, because she wouldn't have been giving him cash. Instead she would have been giving him the boot...right out on his ass. Julian stammered, "Uh...you don't have to pay me for being friends with Brandie, Mrs. Charles. I, uh...I care a lot about her." More than I even intended to, he thought to himself.

Mrs. Charles said snidely, "Well, of course I'm not paying you for being friends with Brandie. She's a lovely young woman. Any guy would be blessed to be her friend." She then noticed the scar on the side of his forehead. Corina put her hand to the scar and asked, "What happened to you?"

Julian replied, "I had epilepsy when I was a kid. This is a souvenir left over from one of my seizures."

Corina observed, "Boy, oh boy, you and my Brandie are quite a pair. God's electric lights." She then noted, "Your hair is damp, too. Hmm, it must have been raining while I was at work."

Julian didn't comment. Corina breathed deep and leaned back on the couch as he fluffed his pillow and laid back on the couch also.

"Good morning....Good Morning," said Brandie, always chipper in the morning. As she entered the living room, her mother was seated on the couch. The blanket she had brought out for Julian the night before was folded neatly and placed on the arm of the couch. Brandie looked around the living room with a puzzled look on her face. She shook her hair wildly into place and asked, "Where's Julian, Mom? We've got to call Uncle Everett today." Happiness poured from her.

Corina replied, "He's gone, dear. I gave him some money last night and when I woke at 6:30 this morning, he was gone." She smacked her lips and looked at the folded blanket, jokingly saying, "Neat little bastard though." She chuckled. "He folds better than I do."

A barefoot Brandie pranced over to the open door, saying, "No...no! He can't be gone." She opened the screen door and looked both ways down the street.

Her mother said, "Hey, I'm thinking of getting another tattoo today. Do you want one?"

Disturbed, Brandie stomped over to the couch and flopped down on the cushion. She then looked at her mother, who was polishing her toenails and frowned irritatedly at how calm Corina was. She retorted, "Of course not, Mom. Julian's out there somewhere. He doesn't have a home, a place to eat or...or sleep." She smoothed the side of her face nervously.

Corina countered nonchalantly, "Loosen up, Dee. He's got my thirty dollars." She caressed her daughter's wild, curly, shoulder-length hair and said, "Who knows, he may have went home." Brandie looked at her mom oddly as she continued, "Oh worry wart, he's lived with his drunk mother and sister for all these years. He can take it a little while longer. Besides, isn't he starting college in September?"

"No, Mom," said a still agitated Brandie. "He's not going to college. He's a musician. First he wants to live...you know, without all the discipline of college."

Corina replied, "Oh, well I can respect that."

Brandie resumed, "So can I. He's pretty cool, huh?"

Corina said, "Oh Brandie, you've had it bad for that young man ever since we moved here when you were in the kindergarten."

Brandie blushed and retorted, "Oh Mom, you don't even know him. How could you know I had a crush on him?"

Corina said, "Young lady...I'm not blind." She put the top back on her red nail polish and continued speaking. "I've seen the way you look at him when he passes down the street...damn near breaking your neck getting to the door just to say..." her tone went higher, "hi, Julian."

Brandie stood up and said, "Oh Mom, I was a kid then, and besides, you weren't even here half the time." Brandie went back over to the door, still searching for Julian.

Corina looked back at her and said, "Sure...you were just a kid...then." Brandie paid her mother no attention as she scanned the street for Julian. Corina offered, "Honey, why don't you just call his house. I'm sure he's back at home."

Brandie bit down on her bottom lip, frowned, and shook her head. She blurted out, "His sister tried to seduce him yesterday! I just don't think he'll go back there."

Corina gasped and put her hand up to her mouth, saying, "Oh dear God...that poor boy." Corina stopped. "Try anyway. Call his house. After all it's his home."

Brandie thumbed through the phone directory until she found his number. Before dialing, she sarcastically muttered, "Some home." She rolled her eyes.

"Hello, Mrs. Parr, is Julian there?"

With a slurred voice, Julian's mom replied, "N...no. I haven't seen him all ni...night." She started to rave, "He's a carbon copy of his father. He's...he's probably gone to look for his dad, that stupid sex maniac kid."

Brandie said, "Well, thank you, Mrs. Parr. If I hear from him I'll let you know."

Rachel retorted, 'Thank you, dear," and hung up the phone.

Brandie put down the receiver and said, "Where could he be, Mom" He hasn't been home all night."

Corina got up from the couch, went over, and touched Brandie's tense shoulders, saying, "Go sit down, dear. He'll be back."

Brandie again sat on the couch, looking very upset. Her mother returned from the closet with the beat up lavender guitar of Julian's, telling Brandie, "He left this on the couch, next to the blanket." Brandie took the guitar and caressed it gently. Corina explained, "If he doesn't come back, at least you'll have a little piece of his heart." She frowned and sat down next to Brandie. "That crazy boy carries this guitar with him every time I see him."

Brandie looked down at the worn-out guitar and said, "This isn't it."

Corina asked, puzzled, "What?"

Brandie said, "Yes, he carries a guitar around with him, but not this one."

Corina still held a frown on her face.

Brandie explained, "Oh, I guess this is his. But it's not the one he usually carries with him in school. That one is brown and looks sort of wooden." She paused, then said, "This one is so old and worn. I wonder why he was carrying this one...and where is his other guitar?"

Corina sniffed, "Child, you're going to drive yourself crazy over that strange kid. Let it go." Brandie remained silent. Corina commented, "I think I'll get a tattoo of a dove on my arm." Brandie, in disbelief at her mom's aloofness about Julian shook her head as she asked, "Are you sure you don't want one?"

A few days later, on June 15, 1987, Julian woke up on a park bench. He was now one of the homeless. After waking up in the middle of the night and leaving Brandie's home with a strange feeling of a quest, he now slept in bus terminals and on park benches, wherever he could get a rest. During the day, he looked for a job, however he was unsuccessful. He applied at carwashes and fast food joints. But without having a permanent residence and identification, he usually was turned down. He mastered the streets, just like he mastered everything else. He never ventured back to the vicinity of Station Street or anywhere near his home. He had plans to make a better life for himself somewhere, and he was determined to succeed.

It was now June 18, 1987, and lightning again struck. Julian pedaled his ten-speed down Jefferson Avenue, passing the Mink Nightclub. It had a sign in the window that read, AUDITIONS FOR SINGERS AND BAND MEMBERS, TODAY AT 2:00

PM. Now guitarless as well as homeless and hungry, he said, "What the hell." He got off his bike slowly and walked into the Mink.

He was as prepared as possible. He had been using public bathrooms to wash up, over and over again, both his clothes and himself. With the money Corina Charles had given him, he had bought a toothbrush and paste, along with deodorant. He kept the items with him as he made his travels, in the same small plastic drugstore bag the cashier had placed them in. The rest of the money he frugally lived off of, buying oranges, potato chips, or anything cheap he could eat.

He often just stooped down by an abandoned building and cried for hours and hours. He thought about going home, but in comparison, the street life was better; no drunken whore mother or sister, he thought. He thought of his two school buddies, but the life they led wasn't the life for him. He thought of Brandie, and her uncle's place, which he was supposed to check out.

He frowned, thinking of the blinding light that had once again shone in his eyes early that morning when he left Brandie's house. The light was part of the reason he had left. Many times in the park he had yelled, as he thought of Brandie's lifestyle, "It's not for me! That life isn't for me! I've got to find my own life. I've got to find out who and what I am!" He would then frown once again, tears streaming down his face. He has also yelled many times in the park, "I don't know how to love, I don't love me!" He would then stand, get on his bike, and ride around the city. The park had now become his bedroom.

At 2:05 P.M. Julian joined the others seated at the table in front of the stage inside the Mink Nightclub. The band, loud and very funky, played tunes by Sly and the Family Stone, The Commodores, and many other old but happening jams. He took a deep breath and observed the scenario. He thought, Oh well, I'll either make a fool of myself or maybe they'll love me and...BABY I'M A STAR...the words my dad said to me when I was five years old. He smiled slightly.

A thin, brown-skinned guy named Reggie stood up from the piano. He lazily spoke looking at the cast of characters seated in the club. And, oh what characters, thought Julian. Guys wearing no shirts...cool, thought Julian. Guys with no hair, guys and girls, or were all of them girls? Maybe all of them were guys...cool, thought Julian. He cleared his throat, thinking, If only I had my guitar, I would turn out all of these freaks...so cool! Reggie, the piano player, continued speaking. Clearing his throat, he said, "Okay, we're gonna start with the table on the right. When you're ready, come up to the piano." Reggie breathed deep and rubbed his short cut hair. "Tell me what you gonna do, give me your sheet music if you have it, or if you want to play the piano yourself, it's yours." He then pointed to an unoccupied piano on the opposite side of the stage and added, "Singers, just tell me what number you're doing."

Julian, feeling uneasy and sure that without his guitar he couldn't audition accurately, slid his chair back. He was getting ready to exit the premises when the white guy with long blond hair who had been sitting on the edge of the stage said, "And, uh...yeah man...we do prefer you to have your own instrument for the audition, but if you don't..." sounding dazed, he looked around at the band on stage and continued, "we can set you up." He then shook his straggly hair away from his face, took out a pack of cigarettes from his shirt pocket, and smoked the tobacco filled stick. This was an action he had been doing ever since Julian had sat down in the club.

Julian stayed seated and again said, "What the hell." He slid his chair back under the table. He enjoyed several hours of watching promising and not so promising musicians perform. At around three o'clock, he walked up on the stage and told the guy seated on the stage, "I play the guitar and sing." The band looked at young Julian curiously. Smirks were on some of their faces as the blond guy handed him a guitar. He looked exclusively at the females seated at the front table, and hormones along with adrenaline made him let out a ferocious scream. He shouted, "Excuse me, while I kiss the sky."

Julian then broke into Hendrix's "Purple Haze," capturing his spectator's and the band member's attention. His wild and exceptional way of playing the guitar and his multi-octave voice intrigued the band. They backed him up with satisfied smiles starting to spread on their faces. Julian was amazed how his style of playing and vocals fit with the band. After the audition ended, the band dismissed themselves to their dressing rooms with a, "We'll be back out with our decision."

After a half-hour, the band returned to the stage. The white guy with the long blond hair walked up to the mike and said, dropping his cigarette and stepping on it, "Thanks for coming out. We could have used most of you. But our band, Wild, needed a singer who fit the description of our name." The blonde guy again cleared his throat.

Julian then said lowly, "I know it's not me." He again slid his chair out and was preparing to leave. All the people were a few years older than Julian, and he didn't have a prayer, he thought. As he stood to leave, the white guy with blond hair called out, "Hey, fella, you got the job. You want it or not?"

Julian lowered his eyelids, then looked up at the guy excitedly and said, "Yeah...Yeah, I want it!"

The guy loudly said, "We practice tomorrow at three P.M. Can you make it?"

Julian shook his hair back away from his face and said, "I'll be here, no problem."

The guy then yelled, "Hey! What's your name?" Julian looked toward the guys on the stage.

The other applicants were passing him, heading out the door with frowns on their faces. Some of them commented, "Faggot." Others said, "Young punk."

Julian then said, answering the band member's question, "Julia..." He stopped speaking and thought for a moment, then continued, "Jewel. My name is Jewel."

The guy said, "Well, Jewel, we'll tell you about the job tomorrow. Congratulations." The other band members congratulated him as well.

Julian yelled, "Thanks a lot. I'll be here tomorrow!" He then left, saying, "So cool...so freakin cool!"

Chapter Twenty-three

At home Rachel was going somewhat crazy. Julian had left and she didn't know where he was or what had happened to him. Tracy hadn't told her mother what had transpired between her and Julian that had prompted him to leave. She just told Rachel nonchalantly, "He's probably somewhere with some hot chick playing house." On this day, June 18, 1987, he was supposed to be graduating from high school. But he hadn't showed up at any of the rehearsals or at his home. Rachel's drinking increased due to her worry over his disappearance.

The teachers had contacted Rachel concerning his whereabouts. Her comment was, "Sorry, I have no idea where my son is. Just mail his diploma home." Brandie had been going just as hysterical as Julian's mom about his disappearance and was going through a seriously depressed state. Her mom, Corina, sat her down the day before graduation and said sternly, "Look, Dee, what's going on with you?"

Brandie sat silently and rolled her eyes. Corina then said, "You haven't been the same since that young man...." She ran her fingers through her hair and continued, "left here! What is it? Did you think you were in love with him or that he honestly loved you?"

Brandie retorted, "I do love him, Mom!" Corina looked at her and raised her eyebrows, looking puzzled. Brandie went on, "...and he said he loved me, too, in so many words."

Corina laughed and declared, "My poor, dear, darling daughter. Boys like Julian don't want innocents like you, babe. They want hot, fast, make-up wearing girls who put out."

Disgustedly, Brandie looked at her and objected, "Mom!" She then rolled her eyes.

Corina said, "Really, honey, I'm not trying to be cruel...but peace and love preachin' virgins like you don't turn on guys like that Julian boy."

Fed up with her mom treating her like a kid, Brandie angrily said, "Mother, I hate to burst your bubble, but...." Corina just stood there in front of the red couch with black fluffed pillows with a blank look on her face. Brandie continued, "I'm not a virgin anymore."

Corina Charles looked stunned, as though she had seen a ghost. She flopped down on the couch with her mouth was open in surprise. She looked, and was, flabbergasted. She stuttered, "You...you're not a...a what anymore?" She heard Brandie's last statement, but somehow hoped she had heard wrong.

Brandie replied, "Mom, I said I'm not a virgin anymore. Julian and I made love."

Stunned, Corina said, "Oh my God! Dee Dee. When did all this happen?" Before Brandie could answer, she demanded, "Why didn't you tell me?"

Brandie angrily stood up and walked to the open front door. She again scanned the street with her eyes, but this time was looking for, or at, nothing. She snapped, "I was stupid all right! I've always had a crush on Julian, since kindergarten. And the other day, when he came over here and needed help...." Brandie paused, "...needed my help...well, one thing led to another and I told him I loved him." Corina stared at Brandie, listening carefully. "He said he loved me, too, in so...."

Her mom angrily interrupted her, "I know...I know Brandie! In so many words!" She repeated Brandie's earlier statement. She then angrily said, "So what, Dee? What were you thinking? You couldn't have...." She stopped her angry comment and thought for a moment, then shouted, "Oh God! You might be pregnant!"

Brandie turned from the open door and closed it behind her, saying "Oh Mom...we did use protection. Would you give me a little credit for having common sense?"

Corina stood up from the couch and said to Brandie, who was leaning against the door, "Common sense! Common sense! Dee, God! I used to think you were the smartest kid I knew." Brandie's big eyes were now even wider as she looked at her mother. Corina continued, "But...having sex with that teenage Romeo! Oh Dee Dee, how could you?"

Brandie then ran down the hall to her room, shouting, "I love him! And I thought he loved me, too! I'm sorry I even met him! I hate him!" She slammed her bedroom door, threw herself on her bed, and cried. Every once in a while she peered up at her graduation gown, which hung on a hanger on the back of her door. It made her sadder, and she cried longer.

On Station Street, Rachel taught her class as normal. Life went on, but instead of being a joyous day in her son's life, graduation day, it was just like any other ordinary day in the Parr household, except no Julian. At the nightclub, she thought of him, then went and poured herself a drink. She thought of Steven occasionally and would turn up the whole bottle.

Brandie Charles, on that day at five o'clock, had graduated along with the rest of her class, minus Julian. The ceremony was beautiful and so was Brandie, who had made up her mind as she was getting dressed that all boys were creeps and she couldn't depend on anyone but herself for happiness. At the graduation, Brandie found out she had a four-year scholarship to UCLA. This thrilled her and excited Corina even more. She would finally be able to forget about Julian Parr, thought Corina.

Tracy was now twenty-one years old and beautiful. She and Rachel lived in the same house, but after Julian left, they were now like strangers. Tracy would still get angry at her mom's host of male friends, and Rachel equally felt the same about Tracy's flamboyant lifestyle. On a many of the tension-filled nights and days at the Parr house, World War III would almost break out, it seemed. The fighting would get that bad.

The band was already on stage and playing a wild and funky rock tune. Ricky, the lead singer, a medium-height, skinny white dude with long hair and a soulful voice, belted out, "This Is It." As Julian approached the stage, the loud blaring music seemed to lower. Ricky stopped singing and said, "Take five, guys." The music totally stopped as Julian reached the stage. He said loudly, due to the acoustics in the hall, "Hey guys! You were sounding good." Ricky called out, "Jewel, come on up and join us. Your guitar is over there." Julian walked up on the high stage and grabbed the guitar leaning against the wall.

The band members were greeting Julian from their standing positions, saying things like, "Hey man, welcome aboard. What's up!"

Julian replied calmly, "Hey guys," and revved up the guitar and the small amplifier beside him. He played "This Is It," the same song he had heard the band playing when he walked in. Julian, however, played the tune wilder and funkier. The band joined in, sounding dynamic. Ricky's singing, however, was overthrown by Julian's raw, raunchy voice along with his guitar. After a while, he just stopped singing, and was staring at Julian with a look of fascination—or was it fear?

Julian kept on singing and playing, even though Ricky's eyes held a look of utter annoyance as he stared at him. When the band finally stopped playing, the other members were praising Jewel on his singing and exceptional guitar playing. "Man!" said an astonished-sounding Jeff. He was the white blond guy playing drums. "That's the best we ever sounded playing that song." Jeff hit his cymbal and said, "Freakin' damn good, man." Julian shook his head, slinging his long black hair back away from his face.

Reggie then said, "Yeah man, what are you anyway?"

Julian looked at Reggie directly and in his normal, slightly deep tone said, "What am I?" He had a slight frown on his face as Reggie said joyously, "Yeah man. You sorta sound like a white dude, but then you sound like a brother." Pausing, Reggie continued, "What the hell are you, with all that hair? You just never know...you know?" Reggie had a sincere look in his eyes as he tried to find out the makings of Jewel.

Julian said solemnly, "It doesn't matter what I am. We all freakin' shit, don't we?" His look was as solemn as his tone. The other band members stared at him as he continued, "I listen to a lot of rock. I listen to a lot of soul. If you want a black soul singer, I'm your man." He again paused as all the band members stared at him, without a word. "If you want a white rock singer, that's me too." He ran his fingers through his hair and said, "If you want a mixture of the two, here I am." He looked at the band members and remarked, "Now, what songs are we rehearsing next?"

The band members chuckled. They were saying things like, "Weird man. He's a fruitcake. I don't think he knows what he is."

They all burst out laughing, except for Ricky, who was staring at Julian strangely. Ricky smirked, saying disgustedly, "Look at him, man. He's a black-and-white, male-female freak."

Julian looked at him and retorted, "I think you got me mixed up with your girlfriend."

The band laughed. "Ooh's" and "He told you," were said loudly.

Ricky fanned his hand at Julian and said, "Forget that faggot creep!" He then said, "Our manager's coming in a minute, and this bum," he paused, pointing to Julian, "will be history."

Reggie, the African-American piano player slyly said, "Aw Rick, you're just jealous."

Ricky returned lowly, "Fucking asshole." The door of the club opened immediately and a medium height and build, light-complected black man walked up the aisleway. A happy Ricky said, "Here he is now. Sayonara, weirdo creep."

As the man approached the stage, Julian looked as if he was in a state of shock. Tears filled his eyes as the man proudly said, "Hey, fellas...so, where is the new member?" The manager was looking around the slightly dim room and stage and had overlooked a tearful, choked-up Jewel. Before the other members commented, the man aught a glance of the light-skinned, long-haired young man with the guitar strapped around his shoulder. That voice, those eyes, thought Julian.

The man stood in front of the stage with a frown on his face as he stared up at Jewel. That face, that body, that...demeanor, thought the manager. Julian then croaked out, "Dad?...is it...really?"

Before he could say another word, Steven Parr was up on the stage with his arms around an emotional Julian. Tears rolled down Steven's cheeks as he and his son hugged each other. They hadn't seen each other in ten years, but they knew each other right from the first look. Love knew. "Oh my God! Julian...son," exclaimed an equally tearful and emotional Steven. He and Julian hugged each other for thirty seconds. The band was silent, observing the strange but joyous reunion of father and son.

Jeff, the drummer, then said, "Well...you know what color he is now." The band was still silent.

Julian and Steven finally let each other go. Steven then said excitedly, looking at Julian, "Look at you, son. You're all grown up."

Still hurt, Julian said snidely, "Yeah,...you grow up rather fast when you don't have a father." He then looked directly into Steven's grayish eyes.

Steven responded, "You've always had a father, Julian." Julian rolled his green eyes in disgust. Steven looked at the stage and said, "Maybe a not-too-bright-one...maybe a chickenhearted, cowardly one, but you've always had one." Julian sniffed and wiped away a fallen tear. With the same hand, he then pushed his long, straight, black hair away from his face. Steven noticed the scar and reached up, caressing Julian's forehead. He frowned, worried, and said, "What happened to you there?"

Julian grimaced then chuckled slightly, saying, "Oh...I call it my birthmark."

Steven, looking puzzled, said, "What?" He remembered his son's birthmark was on his thigh.

Julian retaliated sarcastically, "Oh...that's right. You left our home that night, didn't you?" Steven didn't comment. Julian continued, "Remember, Dad? I had a seizure and almost burst open my head on the kitchen table leg...and you had had enough. You couldn't take it." His words were spoken coldly and cruelly, full of hurt and anger. He looked at Steven and smiled, saying snidely, "Ain't that what you said, Dad?"

Steven cleared his throat and looked at the other band members, then looked at Julian and said quickly, "We'll talk about it later, all right?"

Julian chuckled and said, "Don't worry. My band, I'm sure, is used to your...bowing-out antics." He looked over at the members. They all had smirks on their faces, but they all seemed to adore Steven. Julian said, "Well, maybe not. You walked out on a wife and two kids, but you seem to have adopted a rainbow family."

Steven commented, "So...This is the one you all told me about last night when I came to the club, huh?" He was now looking at the spellbound, quiet band. None of the members answered. Thinking for a moment, he then said, "Jewel, huh? So you're Jewel?" He observed Julian.

Julian cleared his throat, slung his hair back, and said, "Yes, Dad.... Yeah, I'm Jewel."

Steven smiled slightly and said happily, "Well, at least you took something I gave you." Julian frowned in confusion as to what he was getting at. Steven resumed, "I nicknamed you Jewel when you were a little kid, remember?" He touched his son on the shoulder fatherly like.

Julian pulled away quickly and said, "I got the name Jewel from...." He rolled his green eyes. "From the only person who really loved and cared about me."

Steven, feeling the chill from his reaction and remarks, cleared his throat. He asked, "Well, Jewel...how are your mom and your sister?"

Julian replied coldly, "You know the address. Why don't you go find out for yourself?" He held a stern look on his face.

Steven chuckled. He patted Julian on the back and said, "I'm gonna do that...I'm gonna go and see my family." Julian stood there nonplused at his father's words. The band members still observed the younger and older Parr men. Steven turned, looking at the band, and said, "Fella's...you didn't tell me the new member was my son, here."

Jeff, the drummer, retorted, "We didn't know, Steve. We didn't tell him our manager's name."

Julian played a few cords on the guitar and said to Steven, "Naw...I sure as hell didn't know you were their manager."

Steven, looking at the band, declared, "Let's break for a half an hour guys. I have to talk to my son here." Steven smiled with fatherly pride.

The band scattered, murmuring amongst themselves as they left the stage. Some of the band members went outside. Jeff and the other members remained in the building, going to their dressing room or sitting at the small tables inside the nightclub. Jeff sat at one of the tables drinking a soda.

Steven went to a table in the back of the club and invited Julian to join him. When Julian sat down, Steven slipped him a fifty dollar bill. "To keep the monsters away," he said jokingly. He used to tell Julian that when he was a kid and Steven would slip him money. Jeff saw the transaction between father and son, but acted as if he paid no attention.

Julian and Steven talked for half an hour with heated words being yelled out by both. "We're your family dammit! My mother needed you! I needed you," yelled an angry Julian. "Mom started drinking because you left us!"

Steven countered, "Correction—your mom didn't start drinking; you mean she started drinking again!" Julian was quiet as Steven began telling him something he never knew. He continued looking nonplused as Steven lowered his voice. The band members who were seated at the other tables had began to look at them, obviously hearing their conversation. Steven took a deep breath and said, "Your mom was a heavy drinker before I even knew her. The way she misused her body with alcohol might be the reason for your epilepsy, son. We don't know. We never really talked about it." Julian just shook his head slowly in disbelief that his mom had a reckless and abusively sad life before she ever met his father. Steven continued, "Your mom told me that she was a heavy drinker even in high school. She stopped when she met me, because I don't drink."

Julian angrily remarked, "Oh, now you're blaming mom for your leaving...what I guess you're gonna tell me next is that...the reason you left us is because she started drinking again!" He stood up angrily and yelled, "Well you know what? You can go to hell! I know why you left, and I'm the reason." He sighed as tears filled his eyes, then he yelled, "Be it me having epilepsy or Mom's drinking, you should have stuck by us. You're my and Tracy's father and Mom's husband...your wife dammit!"

Steven's conscience was quickly becoming guilty. He pleaded, "Sit down! Don't leave yet, please." Julian hesitantly sat back down. Steven said, "Son, I'm dirt. I deserve every bit of hate that you feel for me. I left you when you needed me. I just walked out, like a punk, a real sissy. I didn't think about Rachel or my daughter. I just didn't want to see you helpless anymore and...." Tears filled his eyes as he thought about the former days, then he said, remorsefully, "I ain't saying that your mom wasn't drinking back then. Your illness put a halt to that and that's not why I left. I was just a coward. A feeling sorry for myself coward." Julian didn't comment. Steven asked, "So...how are you doing now?"

Julian chuckled and said, "I'm fine and I'm cured. I have been...ever since I was fourteen."

Steven was overwhelmed by his son's good news. 'God Almighty!" he shouted. "Thank you! Forgive me for not being there for him...but thank you!" He was looking toward the ceiling as he spoke, then he reached across the table quickly and hugged Julian.

However Julian was not ready to receive his father's apology or love. He just tensed up as his father hugged him, and his eyes stared straight ahead, emotionless. He stood up. "I've got to go," he said.

Steven chuckled slightly, feeling his son's rejection. He acknowledged, "Sure son. We'll call it a day." He yelled, "Rehearsals tomorrow! You're dismissed!" talking to the rest of the band. Julian was headed out of the club behind the others as Steven called, "Tell the others who are outside, will you, Julian?"

Julian looked back and said, "Sure, Dad." He smiled. For the first time that evening, Steven felt as if his son had forgiven him, and Julian felt a lift once again. He had a dad.

Most of the band was now outside of the nightclub. The musicians were in their cars, pulling off. Julian was standing outside of the Mink unlocking his bike. He was preparing to leave when Jeff ran out of the club. "Jewel! Jewel, wait!" shouted Jeff.

Julian looked around at the Caucasian drummer and said, "Yeah...What is it?"

"I...uh...do you know anyone who needs a place to stay?"

Julian climbed on his bike and said, "Wh...why do you ask, man?" He slung his hair to his back.

Jeff replied, "It's just that I have a flat above my house I'm renting. If you know anyone who needs a place, it's available."

Julian frowned. He looked at Jeff and said, "Oh yeah, I...I'm kinda looking for a crib myself."

Jeff chuckled and said joyously, "All right, man. Our last guitar player used to live there, but...." Jeff looked down at the sidewalk, then said casually, "Well...he quit the band."

Excitedly, Julian asked, "Cool, when can I see it? Where is it?"

Jeff, seeing Julian's enthusiasm about the flat, told him the address and to come by in about an hour to check it out. "If you like it, it's yours," Jeff then said.

Steven left the club while the boys were talking. He patted Julian on the back as he passed by. Julian explained to Jeff, "I won't be able to pay until we get paid Friday. I'll move in then and bring the cash."

Jeff asked, remembering seeing Steven pass Julian some money, "How about tonight? You just pay what you can and pay the rest on Friday."

Julian replied, looking at Jeff with a frown, "Nope, Friday's fine. I'll have the cash then." Jeff looked at Julian curiously. He frowned and said, "Hey, you're that homeless kid who sleeps on the park bench." Julian didn't respond. "Yeah, it is you. But...why are you homeless with Steven Big Bucks being your dad and all?" He had a smirk on his face that made Julian's skin crawl.

Julian shook his head and said, "Naw man, that wasn't me. I...I have a home." He looked down at his bike seat and then back up at Jeff and said, "I just don't get along with my mom and sister. That's why I need a place to live for awhile, that's all."

Jeff rolled his eyes and said nonchalantly, "Whatever you say, kid. The rent is one hundred twenty dollars a month." Julian was about to comment when Jeff continued, "I'll give you a break for a couple of months, since you look like you're just barely making it.

Julian frowned, wanting to deck the guy, but he knew Jeff was right, so he just said, "Thanks, man."

Jeff then said, "Well, Jewel, gotta get to work." He gave Julian the keys. "Here...you can just go check the place out yourself. I trust you. If you like it...it's yours. I'll stop by there in about a half hour to see how you like it."

Julian was suddenly in agony. He yelled in pain, "Oh shit! Oh no, make it stop! No!" He grabbed his eyes. Bending down, he yelled, "Agh! Agh! No! Dammit no!"

Jeff was in total confusion, alarmed by Julian's reaction as he was once again hit by the horrifying, blinding light. As he stood back up straight, the light had diminished. Breathing deeply, he looked at Jeff and said, "Sorry about that, man, it's...."

Jeff, still looking confused said, "You doing drugs, bub? Bitchin! I can take care of you! I know a guy who'll...."

Julian interrupted Jeff's excited conversation, agitatedly saying, "Look, uh...uh...Jeff, man...Jeff."

"Nagy...Jeff Nagy," said the blond guy soon to be Jewel's landlord.

Julian continued, "Whatever man.... Look, I don't do drugs. I, uh...I have these headaches, that's all," Trying to explain the incident that had just occurred. "These damn headaches are back." He tried to sound believable to Jeff. He wouldn't dare tell him about the light. He didn't understand it himself and thought, He would probably think I was psycho if I told him the truth.

Chapter Twenty-four

Two months had passed. It was now August 24, 1987. Tracy, who had gotten a better job in a women's boutique, was attending AA meetings weekly, trying to get herself back on the right track. This was due to the encouragement that her new boss had gave her. She had a new boyfriend who was also a designer and attended AA meetings as well.

It was a sunny warm day. The grass and leaves were green and exceptionally beautiful on Station Street. They seemed to yell, "Oh, what serenity!" But in the Parr household, there was anything but serenity going on. "Uhn...uhn.... Make love to me! Oh yes," screamed Rachel from her bedroom.

Tracy came in from work at around four o'clock that evening. Rachel's clothing and underwear, alone with a man's shorts and tie, made a path up the stairs to where her mother was. Tracy picked up an empty vodka bottle from the floor and was furious. She said, "Dammit! Does she ever stop? She doesn't even care about my brother being gone...or my father." Her greenish gray eyes flickered in the bright sunlight shining in the window. She then angrily threw the bottle against the wall. Glass shattered everywhere. She dropped to the floor exhaustedly and cried, "No more...I can't take it anymore."

As she was on her knees, she thought of Julian and the incident that caused him to leave. She laid out on the brown carpet and began beating on the floor, saying, "My God! What have I done? It can't go on like this. I've got to...." She didn't finish talking. Instead she got up off the floor and laid on the couch.

She cried as she thought of the clothes she had designed for the boutique she worked for, Laboutique. She was an exquisite clothes designer despite her drinking habits and had made clothes for many of her friends, receiving top dollar for her work. She had made clothes and submitted them to her boss, Mrs. Dean, who then submitted them to her supervisor, who in turn told her, "They're very good, but since the maker has no experience or training, we will sell them under the label...LaBoutique Fashions."

This devastated Tracy, but she couldn't complain. She had always planned on going to school for clothes design, but just never got around to it. After Mrs. Dean told Tracy she wouldn't get name credit for her fashions and she would only get a small percentage on what was sold, Tracy missed three days of work because she went home and drowned her sorrows in booze. For two days she had a hangover, but she went back to work on this day, Tuesday, August 24. She was now determined to stay sober this time, no matter what happened.

When she was leaving her job, she passed by a handsome, clean-cut gentleman who stopped her as she was leaving. The man with the pleasant look and voice to match grabbed a hold of her hand, saying, "I've heard so much about you. You must be Tracy." She stood there speechless with her eyes wide and her mind wondering as the gentleman continued, "You are beautiful. Hi, my name is Allen Dean. I'm a clothes designer and I'm an alcoholic."

Tracy quickly was jarred out of her daze. She said, sounding puzzled, "Dean?"

The medium-height man replied, "Yes, my mom, Dorothy Dean, is your boss. She told me all about you, Tracy Parr."

They made plans to meet up at their AA meeting the following night and then go to dinner. Tracy left the boutique and Allen went in to talk to his mother. As she passed by the boutique's glass window, her boss smiled and threw her an okay sign. She smiled and walked on to her car.

As she continued to cry and reminisce about her day's events, she fell asleep. Her mother's moans of passion were still going on.

At eight o'clock that night, Rachel shook her arm, saying, "Wake up, wake up sleepy head. Are you gonna stay there all night?" Rachel had been drinking, but she wasn't drunk.

Tracy's long black hair hung down in front of her face as she sat up on the couch. She said, "Mom?"

Rachel replied, "Yes dear," and sat down beside her. Tracy, rubbing her tired and a bit swollen eyes, said, "Mom...I've got to find Julian."

Rachel frowned slightly and said, "Wh...where would you look dear?"

Shaking her head, Tracy said, "I...I don't know. All I know is that I've got to find him, Mom." She stood up and ran her fingers through her black hair, lightly frizzing it out of its long, hanging curls style. She frowned at her mother and said, "Oh...Mother, I'm an alcoholic...." She then said angrily, "Hell Mom, you're an alcoholic too."

Rachel, still seated on the couch, said, "Wait a minute, now." She was getting slightly ticked off by Tracy's statement. "Just because I like to drink and have a good time every now and then," she looked at Tracy. "Ms. High and Mighty, don't you call me an alcoholic. You're no better than I am, daughter dearest...don't you forget that."

Tracy rolled her puffy red eyes and sat back down on the couch next to her mom. She held her mom's hand and said solemnly, "Mom, I know I'm no better than you are. If it weren't for Mrs. Dean, my boss, or AA and the members there, I wouldn't have known I was an alcoholic either. I wouldn't even be attending Alcoholics Anonymous meetings, let alone admitting that...." She looked into her mother's eyes deeply. "Yes, Mom...I am an alcoholic." She then lowly said, "It's not really anybody's fault but mine, and that booze. It's a wonder Julian didn't get caught up in the booze thing; it's an illness. I've got to try to control it."

Rachel took her hand away from Tracy's and said, looking wildly upset, "Well...well that doesn't mean that I'm a drunk. You're just a...hot thing, always have been." She looked at Tracy angrily. "And you probably always will be." Tracy took a deep breath and closed her eyes, trying to control the building anger that wanted to explode. Rachel suddenly snapped, feeling as if she had shut Tracy up about her drinking and all, "So...what did your mean, evil behind say to Julian this time to make him leave home." Rachel paused. "You know, he's almost been gone for three months.

Tracy again stood. She paced the large living room for several seconds. Rachel just sat there on the leather couch watching her. Finally Tracy looked at her mom and said, "Well, I didn't exactly say anything to him." Tracy paused. "I, uh...." Spit it out, Tracy. Just tell your mother that you tried to have sex with her pride and joy, her precious jewel. She tried again, saying, "I, uh...well, I'm an alcoholic and...uh...our...I...uh...."

Rachel stood up, exclaiming angrily, "Dammit Tracy! What is it? Where is Julian?" All sorts of things entered Rachel's mind. Maybe Tracy had been drinking and driving drunk and...oh God, no! thought Rachel. She went over to the small built-in bar and poured herself a drink.

Tracy saw her mother and anger again started to build as she yelled, "I tried to seduce him, dammit!"

Getting ready to drink some of the scotch from her glass, Rachel suddenly lost the urge. She set the glass on top of the bar with her mouth and eyes wide open as she slowly sat on one of the bar stools. Her back was to the bar as she frowned at Tracy.

Tracy continued, saying angrily, "I was drunk, Mom, and I tried to fuck my own brother!"

Rachel said, astonished, "My dear God. You didn't...." She stopped. Looking puzzled and confused she stammered, "You didn't actually...."

Tracy interrupted her mother's question and snapped, "No! No, Mother, no he knocked me down and ran out of the house." Rachel breathed a sigh of relief. Now crying and shaking, Tracy walked up to the bar, looked at Rachel, and yelled angrily, "You! You're the reason I got rid of my kid! You're the reason this place isn't a home! It's a whorehouse for you and your johns!"

Tears filled Rachel's eyes. She raised her hand and slapped a hysterical Tracy.

"Great Mom! Just great. But you know I'm right," said Tracy. Rachel again reached for her glass of scotch. She didn't comment. Tracy said, "That's our answer." Rachel took a drink, still not commenting, but listening to her intensely as she continued, still crying, "My dad walked out on my epileptic brother and on us. You turned into a fucking drunken whore and I'm your fucking drunk whore daughter, screwing every man we can get our hands on! And how does it end? With me trying to do it with my own brother!"

Rachel grimaced and kept sipping her booze. Her mind was now opening, not from the booze, but from Tracy's comments. She knew they were true.

Tracy suddenly picked up the booze bottle and threw it against the other bottles lined up on the bar wall. "Enough is enough, Mother!" she shouted. She then took the small glass her mother had been drinking scotch from and threw it as well. Rachel and Tracy looked at each other. Tracy said tearfully, all choked up, "Oh, Mother!" She grabbed her mouth disgustedly and ran down the hall to her room. Rachel looked at all the broken bottles behind the bar, then stared at the broken vodka bottle on the living room floor by the wall. Tears filled her eyes.

After months of self-denial, fussing, and Tracy's fussing, Rachel finally decided to go to Alcoholics Anonymous. She and Tracy came together in their search for Julian and their quest for sobriety. For months they went around the neighborhood asking his friends and enemies if they had seen him. Before Brandie left for college, Tracy went to her house and asked a cold and distant acting Brandie if she had seen him. She told Tracy, "You and your brother have a lot of problems, and I don't particularly care for either one of you."

She was about to slam the door in Tracy's face as she stood on her porch. "Look, I know you like Julian a lot." She folded her arms in frustration. "I remember you from high school. I was a senior when you and my brother were in junior high school."

Letting down her defenses Brandie said lowly, "I...I saw Julian on the day you tried to...." She didn't finish her statement. Instead, she looked down at the floor. Feeling embarrassed, Tracy looked down, too. "I...I...I was sick. I didn't know what I was doing. I was drunk." She bit down on her bottom lip in nervousness.

Brandie frowned and said, "I'm sorry.... He came here and I thought he was going to stay the night, but when my mom woke up the next morning, he wasn't on the couch." Sadly, she added, "He left before the next morning." Tracy rolled her eyes and soon left. Brandie sighed sorrowfully and...let it go.

Chapter Twenty-five

At the Mink, Wild's practices were amazing. Their nightly shows were dynamic due to Julian's exceptional and raunchy style and sexual flair. He played the guitar like a demon stirring up sin, playing all the tunes Wild had been playing for years like he was a veteran band member. He felt he was right where he belonged. The five-piece band fit his lifestyle like a charm. He got along with all the members and the fact that the band was paid was phenomenal for his first job.

His father was rarely at their shows. When Steven would show up, however, he spent an inordinate amount of time with Julian. He was fascinated by his son's style of playing. At most of the practices, Steven showed up with a white, middle-aged man who stared at Julian intensely. He had become annoyed by the man's constant stares at him and asked Steven who the man was and what his deal was. Steven had replied, "He's just a friend of mine."

Reggie Casey, the black keyboard player, said to Julian in the middle of one of their practices, "Look, man, you're showing all of us up."

Julian just chuckled and turned away from him. What he didn't see was the hate-filled look Reggie gave him after his comment. Julian replied, as he tuned his guitar, "Aw...give me a break. You guys are a dynamo." He shook his hair away from his eyes and said, "You guys play like monsters. I'm just a guitar player. I hope one day I could be half as good as you guys are." All the band members chuckled and gave high fives to each other. Julian smiled, feeling satisfied, but he knew he was probably better than each of the band members. They ranged from age seventeen to twenty-four years old, and belted out a few classic Brown tunes, along with some classic Stones.

Months passed, with Wild becoming well known in Detroit. Julian was becoming well-known as "Wild" by himself. The other band members were quickly becoming nonexistent because of Jewel—"Wild Jewel," as the regulars coming into the club would call him. The rest of the band was becoming steamed. But still the band played on. Wild played at the Mink Nightclub three nights a week to a packed audience, but the jealousy toward Jewel was becoming intense.

It was Friday, December 17, 1987, a cold, snowy day. Flurries had been falling off and on all day. There was a fresh smell of winter snow in the air. Julian hadn't yet arrived at practice, and it was five P.M. exactly. His father had gotten him a job at WKBK-TV station, where he was assistant to Steven while he operated audio equipment. The job wasn't hard, but the work was tiresome. Julian would go home to his apartment and sleep for hours, resulting in his being late for band rehearsals often. He still, however, played the guitar fiercely.

Ricky was standing on stage. He said, speaking into the microphone, "Man...the guy is crazy. I don't know why we just don't get rid of him." He rolled his brown eyes. "We got rid of that other chump. Why can't we get rid of this one?"

Reggie replied, sitting at his piano. "He's the manager's son, Rick, remember?"

Keylon, the bass guitar player, who never had too much to say, chimed in, "Yeah, since that kid got in the band, Steven acts like...that dumb kid is the whole band."

Jeff added from behind his drum set, "He's always late for practice, anyway." Julian had only been late for three rehearsals. He continued, "He's a show-off, punk, and I'm tired of the freak living with me."

Ricky frowned at him and said, "What do you mean, you're his..." he chuckled and said sarcastically, "you're his landlord."

Jeff took a drag from his cigarette and said, "That fool has women coming to the apartment practically every night. They practically throw themselves at him."

Reggie laughed and said, "So...what's wrong with that?"

Jeff ran his fingers through his blond, stringy hair and said, "Fifty thousand women throwing themselves at that...that fag, and I've only seen him date two of them."

Ricky jumped in. "Forget that. What are we gonna do about the party on Saturday?"

Jeff replied, "He doesn't work on Saturdays, so he'll be there." He hit his drum harshly. "Damn...I want to get rid of that show-hog faggot.

Keylon said softly, "What can we do? His dad is running the show."

Jeff suggested, "Uh...you know, we can always set him up. He'll have to quit then."

Reggie objected, "You guys set up that other lead guitarist the same way."

Keylon agreed, "Yeah, he was a good guitarist, too." He then looked down at the floor shyly. There was a silent, tense moment.

Ricky frowned and asked, "Are you sure somebody isn't gonna get suspicious? He looked at Reggie and Keylon, then continued, "All of our new band members suddenly having to leave the band."

Jeff cleared his throat and responded, "Hey, man, it's our band. These fools get in and try to take over."

Reggie acknowledged, "He's right, you know. We can't have amateurs coming in and taking over." Reggie sounded frustrated. "I'm the one who started the damn band. We were first named 'Black and White,' remember?"

The band members all said, "Yeah."

Jeff stated, "The party's Saturday. I'll get the stuff and Jewel's history, agreed?" The band members again high fived in agreement.

Just then, Julian walked into the club. He took off his coat and his hat and stamped his feet, releasing the snow that he had tracked from outside onto the mat. He walked onto the stage and said, "Hey guys, sorry I'm late. Did I miss anything?" He picked up his guitar and looked at the band. They were whispering to each other and acting strange. He noticed this, but ignored it. Many of the band members had smirks on their faces.

Keylon finally answered his question, saying, "Naw...Naw, Jewel, man. We're just ready to rehearse, that's all." The others chuckled.

Jeff commented, "Yeah, we were also planning our annual after New Year's party. We have it up in the flat that I rented to you." He looked at Julian and said, "Is that all right?"

Julian nonchalantly said, "Cool, man. Whatever." He then revved up the amplifier and played his guitar wildly. The others just watched him. He then said, "Let's run through the songs for tonight's show." The band practiced the set of songs. Julian had written all of the songs the band now played at their shows. They went through the set perfectly. Julian sang half of the songs, and Ricky the other half. After a few hours, the band went home and got ready for the night's show.

At ten P.M. Wild went on stage at the Mink. "Jewel! Jewel! We want Jewel!" were the chants coming from the crowd, male and female. The curtain went up at 10:05 P.M., and the noise from the crowd was deafening. The spotlight on the dark stage shone on Jewel. He experienced, as always when the stage light shone on him, a certain sense of deja vu. Jewel solemnly said, speaking into the microphone, "It's the light that takes me on. It's the light that makes me strong. It's the light that rules the night, and it's the light that lights up my life!" His long hair fell in front of his face dramatically. He took his hand and pushed it back away from his face. The audience's claps and screams were out of control. The stage then lit up. The whole band was in clear view and playing Jewel's opening song and anthem. "The Light." They smiled and played vigorously. However the looks of jealousy flowed, unnoticed by Julian or the audience. He just jammed. He was clad in gold silk shorts. He didn't have on a shirt and he wore his traditional suspenders and gold chain Brandie had given him.

Jewel put on a next-to striptease show. He had the women fainting from excitement. His sexy falsetto singing voice had them throwing their bras and panties on the stage at him.

Chapter Twenty-six

It was now Saturday, January 18, 1988. New Year's had come and gone. Wild was still planning on getting rid of Jewel by any means necessary.

The band played loudly inside Julian's apartment, which was full of partying people. It was open to the public and there was a mixed crowd of blacks and whites, men and women. "Hey! Par—tay! Par-tay!" yelled one guy. He then turned up a bottle of beer, guzzling it.

"Oh, yeah, all right!" said a Caucasian black-haired girl of around twenty-two years of age. The crowd was dancing and partying to the band's music. There were a few couples making out on couches and in chairs. Julian's falsetto then alto soprano voice crooned as the women screamed in ecstasy.

Ricky was standing in the background like a backup singer. He had started singing lead vocals on "Dizzy Dame," however, the song took on a new meaning and beat as Julian sang to the cheering and screaming women at the party. Ricky was miffed at being upstaged by Julian once again.

"Jewel! Jewel!" the women changed. Ricky sang low in the background. He looked at Jewel with all hell's hatred as he sang the words, "I won't complain, but that's how I started living with this dizzy dame!"

The partying crowd cheered, danced, and shouted, "Jewel!" Ricky's face was red with anger. He gritted his teeth in frustration at Jewel's once again upstaging him. This occurrence happened often that night, and since Julian joined the band.

The party went on till late. At around four A.M., the crowd started leaving Jewel's apartment. "The party was jamming, man!" said Reggie happily to Jewel.

A little later, the band packed up and prepared to leave. Jewel noticed how slowly and strangely the guys were looking as they packed away the instruments.

Keylon then said, as planned, "Hey guys, let's go get some beer and come back here to relax and rap about the party." He looked at Jewel and Jeff. "If that's all right with you guys?"

The other band members were saying, "Yeah, cool, sounds good to me."

Jeff replied happily, "Cool, I'll go with you. The store down the street is open."

Julian flopped down on the couch and said frustratedly, "Uh...you...uh, I'm kinda tired, you guys. I'll sit this one out."

Jeff grabbed his coat, along with the other guys, and said, "Thank God it's Saturday, Jewel. Stop being a grandma." He playfully punched Jewel in the stomach. "We'll be back, Jewel...wake up!"

The guys left the apartment. Julian stretched out on the tweed couch and closed his eyes. He was tired after working eight hours and performing almost eight more.

Down at the corner store, his band members stood outside the phone booth while Jeff made the call. "Hello, I want to report drug possession at this party I was at tonight. It was given by Jewel Parr on 6th Street in the upstairs flat." Jeff paused. "The guy is in a band. He just had a wild party. I'm a neighbor across the street and I'm calling because I'm a concerned citizen." Jeff hung up the phone. He ands the other guys laughed and gave each other high fives. Jeff then said, "It's done.

Keylon agreed. "He's history."

Ricky said excitedly, "All right!"

At five in the morning, Julian was still sleep on the couch when he was abruptly awakened by several loud knocks at his door. He sat up quickly and looked around the apartment, dazed. He was quickly reminded of the party that had just take place there. Beer bottles, cigarette butts, and pretzels were all over the floor and table. He stumbled exhaustedly over to the door, running his fingers through his hair. Thinking it was his band members, he yelled, "Keep your pants on guys! Keep your damn pants on!" He then opened the door.

The taller officer said in a deep voice, "Mr. Jewel Parr, we've been ordered to search your place. We've had a report of drugs being on the premises."

Julian shook his hair away from his face and said breathlessly and tiredly, "Man...ain't no drugs here. I don't do drugs. I'm...."

The other officer interrupted, "May we come in and look around, sir?"

Julian sighed and said casually, "Why not? I told you, I'm not into drugs." He opened the door wider.

The two officers stepped inside his apartment. Immediately they began opening drawers and closets and looking under the seat cushions on the couch. They also frisked Jewel. He was clean. The stout officer opened the drawer of the end table by the couch, searching through piles of Julian's written song lyrics and phone books.

Jewel said, "Look...my band will vouch for me! They...," he looked over at the clock on the wall, "will be back in a minute." He frowned, seeing 5:00 on the clock.

The officer searching through the drawers suddenly said, "Ah ha!" Julian looked at the officer, who held up a plastic see-through bag. Inside it was a white powder-like substance.

Julian shook his head saying, "Naw...it's not mine. My friends will be...." Julian was suddenly hit. He fell to his knees screaming, "No! Oh No! Stop it, I can't see! I can't see!"

One of the officers stood beside him shaking his head. He told the other officer, "He's stoned now. Just look at him."

Julian was on his knees, holding his eyes in pain. The light had returned, striking his eyes with a blinding force.

The officer held onto Julian's arms tightly and said, "You just hold on there, fella." The taller officer, after sampling a taste of the substance, said, "Coke, just like I thought."

Julian was now regaining his composure after again being blinded by the light. He then said to the officers, "I...I had a party tonight. Some other guest must have left that here."

The officer beside him replied, "Whatever you say, liar. You're under arrest." The officer then read Julian his rights.

The shorter officer mused, "I think we had another arrest here a year ago."

Julian was silent, his green eyes glistening in the confusion. The taller officer said, "Huh. In this damn neighborhood, what would you expect?"

Julian just shook his head sorrowfully. "You racist, stupid jerks. I didn't live here a year ago. Let me go."

The taller officer retorted, "Dopehead sissy." The officers then took him out to the car.

All during the ride, Julian mumbled, "I'm going crazy...I must be crazy.... Lights, the police." He frowned. "What the hell else can it be?" He thought about Brandie's speaking of a higher power and then thought about his screwed-up childhood. He breathed deeply and sarcastically mumbled, "Higher power, huh." He rolled his eyes. "Yeah right."

On Sunday morning at six A.M., Julian was put in jail. When the officer informed him of his right to a phone call, he called his father. "Julian...son, I'll be right there."

A panicked Julian stammered, "Dad, I...I think the guys may have set me up."

Don't worry, son. I'll be right there," exclaimed Steven. He immediately came down to the county jail with his attorney.

Jewel was going a little ballistic being behind bars. 'You can't trust any-body!" yelled Julian. "Not even your own damn band! I don't understand! They're trying to make me look bad...why? Why? Why would they do this to me? Why? I don't do drugs! I don't do drugs!" Steven came to the cell with his attorney.

Julian ran over to the bars of his jail cell saying, "Dad, when do I get out of here? It isn't fair! I was set up!"

Steven replied, "Don't worry, son. I believe you. You'll be out in no time." The lawyer gave Julian a pep talk also.

Julian told the lawyer and his father, "The guys in the band have sort of been acting weird for the last few days. I think they wanted to get rid of me."

Steven responded, thinking back to another incident, "That may be true, Julian. I got rid of our former lead guitarist because he kept getting into trouble with drugs. He denied it, but I let him go. He and Jeff were good friends. Jeff rented him an apartment and everything, just like you." Steven frowned. "The guys may have framed you, too, thinking I would get rid of you, or that you'll go to jail."

Julian rolled his eyes and flopped down on the chair inside the cell. He said disgustedly, "Aw man!"

Julian was in jail for two weeks. After the judge heard his side of the story, the charges were dropped with a warning: "Watch your friends." He was sent home with his father.

A few nights later Steven caught up with the band members of Wild at the Mink Nightclub. "Hey boss, where's Jewel!" asked Jeff, as if he didn't know that anything had taken place.

Steven looked seriously at the happy and nonchalant-looking band and gri-maced. They were all snickering snidely. He replied, "Break time, fellas."

Keylon, Reggie, Ricky, and the rest of the band had strange and guilty looks on their faces. Reggie then asked Steven, "What's up? What's going on? We're in the middle of a set."

Steven retorted, "Someone set Julian up. He was arrested for cocaine possession a few weeks ago...after you guys had your so-called party."

Jeff shook his long stringy hair in amazement and said, "Aw man...I knew he was heavy into drugs."

The other members mumbled, "Yeah, yeah, yeah, all that energy—what else could it be."

Steven's rage was building up as he looked around the room at each of the guys. He calmly walked over and grabbed Jeff by the collar, looking as if he could kill the drummer right there and then. A panicked Jeff said nervously, "Steve...hell! You know I gave the kid a place to live when he was living on the park bench." Jeff paused. Steven's hold on him increased. In a strained voice from Steven's tight hold, Jeff squeaked, "Let...let me go, Steven. It...it wasn't me."

Steven through gritted teeth said angrily, "Look punk!...I know my son."

Reggie chuckled in the background and cracked, "That's not what we heard."

Steven ignored the piano player's snide comment and continued, "My son didn't have those drugs." His hold on Jeff's neck tightened further. "They must have been yours or your punk friends." He looked at Jeff with hate in his eyes, then looked around at the other band members. "You all planted those drugs in my son's apartment for him to take the blame! And I'm telling you now, I won't have you screw me.... I'll kill each and every one of you!" Now at the boiling point, he took Jeff and threw him against one of the tables in the club, breaking the table in two. He yelled angrily, "I haven't seen my son or any of my family members for more than ten years! But I'll fuck up anybody who tries to hurt him."

Jeff was now on the floor, still looking dazed and in pain. His heart was pounding as he listened to Steven go off on the band profusely. Steven went over to Ricky and grabbed him by the collar also, saying, "I know you're into drugs, punk. All of you. But trying to set up my son is the last straw, do you hear me? The last straw." Ricky was sweating buckets after the outburst. Steven turned to the rest of the band and said, "Ricky, you're fired!"

Ricky laughed and rolled his eyes. He looked at Steven and said, "You can't fire me, I don't work for you. I work for the Mink."

Steven pulled out his knife and yelled at Ricky, "And who do you think is in charge of getting entertainment for the Mink?"

Ricky's eyes widened, along with the rest of the band. This bit of info they weren't aware of. In a quivering, unsure voice, Ricky said, "But I've been in the band for three years now." He frowned, looking at Steven. "It wasn't me who set Jewel up, it was...." He felt the tension building in the small room. He also saw the hateful, alarming stares at him coming from the band. Changing his words around boldly, he said, 'If you fire me...we all go. Isn't that right, fellas?" He looked at his fellow band members and knew that his last statement was a lie.

He heard the other members mumble, "Hey, Rick, I got a daughter to support...Hey, you know, Rick, I started the band," said a slow-voiced Reggie.

That was all he had to hear. He picked up his coat and other personal belongings and left.

Steven then looked at the band and said, smiling, "Now...Let's put all this behind us. We have our lead singer. You all are his backup band. Case closed."

The band was looking a little on edge. Steven continued, "Oh yeah, take the rest of the night off. Practice is at five P.M. tomorrow. Julian will be here as lead vocalist, and all is right with the world." Steven put on his hat and smiled at the band. "I pay your salary." He then walked out of the door, leaving behind a spellbound band of Reggie, Jeff, and Keylon.

That night, a distraught Ricky went to Flames Go-Go Bar on the west side of Detroit. He was drinking heavily while he watched the strippers perform. "Yeah! Yeah baby! Bring some of that over here!" he yelled to the strippers. The blonde stripper sighted him and kept on performing. After her performance, the girl dressed and joined him at the bar.

"Hi there," exclaimed Shelly, the stripper he had been ogling at all night.

A drunken Ricky then said, "Hey sweet stuff.... Life stinks, you know that?"

She ordered a drink and shook her long blonde hair away from her face. She then said, "What do you mean, cutie? What's wrong?" She could tell by the guy's demeanor that he wasn't totally a drunk or a louse—she hoped.

He blurted out, 'Nothing babe. My band just dumped me, that's all." he took another drink of the alcoholic beverage he had been nursing all night. "They threw me out for a punk. A punk named Julian. Julian Parr...Jewel—what a freakin' joke. The kid can't be no older than sixteen years old."

Shelly's eyes lit up. She cleared her throat and excitedly said, "Julian Parr! The Julian Parr?" She felt like she had struck gold.

Ricky said roughly, "Yeah...you probably threw your panties at him, too."

She said, "Huh! I'd like to throw a brick at his using ass." After graduation, Shelly had tried to get her former boyfriend, Lance, to find Julian Parr and beat him senseless, something to show that he couldn't take advantage of Shelly Nohl.

But Lance just said nervously, "Leave the freak alone."

She had then angrily shouted, "Lance, you coward! If I didn't know any better, I'd say you were scared of him." Lance had just looked away. The truth was, Lance was scared. This was one of the factors that led to he and Shelly's breakup the year they graduated high school.

Chapter Twenty-seven

Twenty-one-year-old Ricky and seventeen-year-old Shelly sat in the bar drinking and becoming acquainted. The two of them exchanged numbers that night. For the next several months, they quickly became a couple. They dated only each other, resulting in their falling in love and gradually became the equivalent of Bonnie and Clyde. Shelly and Ricky schemed, plotted, and planned their way to much money, inevitably using Shelly's sexy and gorgeous looks to con rich bankers, businessmen, and fools out of credit cards, money, and jewelry. Ricky was an expert thief, however, murder never was a part of their schemes and maneuvers. They just laughed, loved, and lavished themselves with their ill-gotten wealth. Conscience was a minus.

"Uhm, Julian, you're great. More...more...yes, baby, don't stop, more!"

Julian caressed her lips and said huskily, "You're great too, baby." His thrusts were hard.

The woman sighed and screamed, "Oh yes! Yes, yes!"

At the same time, a deep-voiced Julian yelled, "Oh baby, uhn! I'll never leave you...again, I love you, Brandie!" He then spasmed uncontrollably.

Lanora, the woman he was with, sat up from the kitchen floor and said, "Who the hell is Brandie?

Returning from the Mink, Steven suddenly entered the kitchen and snapped, "That's more like, 'what the hell is going on here'!"

Lanora Jenkins, Steven's live-in girlfriend, said, "My God! Steven!" She then grabbed her dress from the floor and put it on, covering her totally nude body. Julian grabbed his clothes from the floor and quickly left the kitchen. Steven exploded as soon as Julian was gone. He yelled, "Dammit, Lanora! This is the last straw! You slept with a lot of my friends and I forgave you, but my own son! I won't have it! One of you has got to leave!" He sat in the kitchen chair, his head dizzy with confusion.

Lanora looked at him and went over and sat on his lap. She ran her fingers through his black hair teasingly saying lowly, "Look Steve, I need you so much. I love you."

Steven replied tartly, "If that's the way you show me that you love me, I guess I would have a real big problem if you hated me." He then stood. "Get out of here, Lanora. It's over!"

Angrily Lanora said, "Dammit, Steve, you're never around here, so what if I screwed a few of your friends...and your son!" She shrugged her shoulder. "I needed someone."

Lanora was a thin and beautiful woman. She had a fabulous light-brown complexion and short curly hair. Her big brown eyes attracted both Steven and Julian. She was a beauty, and frankly, a free-for-all. Steven knew this all too well, but what the hell, he thought.

Lanora left the kitchen. She passed Julian, who was on his way back into the kitchen to speak with his dad. She then said to him, "You're good kid," she chuckled. "A damn good lay." Julian sighed disgustedly. He rolled his eyes, ran his fingers through his long hanging hair, and proceeded toward the kitchen doorway. Lanora called, "Hey Jewel, you know almost everytime we did it, you called me Brandie." He was now standing still, looking back at her questioningly. She continued, "To have someone like you who loves her so much, she must be pretty important." Julian was silent. Leaving the living room, she suggested, "I think you'd better find this girl, or you'll never be happy...trust me. I wish I had someone who cared about me as much." He looked around at Lanora. She continued with tears in her eyes, "I guess if I had someone who loved me that way, I wouldn't be so screwed up."

He replied solemnly, "You aren't screwed up, Lanora. My dad belongs with his wife, that's all. And somewhere there's a guy for you as well, you'll see."

She chuckled. "You're sweet, you know that?" She caressed Julian's cheek. "But you've got a lot to learn about life, kid." He didn't comment. He walked away, venturing into the kitchen with his father. Lanora whispered, "Dumb jerk, just like his father. I'm getting thrown out just for a crazy kid, hmm!"

When Julian entered the kitchen, Steven forgave him. He told Julian about the new band arrangements, then sighed, rolling his eyes nonchalantly. 'Chicks...just treat 'em like clothes. You can always get more." Julian didn't comment. Steven solemnly sighed again. "Shh...damn tramp." He rolled his eyes. "She's a good lay, isn't she?"

Julian, angry and disgusted, said firmly, "I'm the one's who's good, dammit!" He declared, with hate in his eyes, "And your wife is good! She gave you two kids, didn't she?"

Steven chuckled lightly and replied, "Yeah...yeah, your mom is the best. I still love her, you know?"

Julian rolled his eyes and said, "Yeah right.... You wouldn't know it by the way you just left her."

Steven patted his son on the back and smiled. "My son. You're my son all right."

It was now Sunday, March 2, 1988. At practice the next day, things started out strained, with Julian being uncomfortable and the other guys as equally ill at ease. However, music being a bridge that can mentally bring you through troubled waters, in no time the band was playing spectacularly and Jewel was singing dynamically as ever. The absence of a jealous co-lead singer made the atmosphere a lot calmer. Julian told the guys, "Look, I might be a stage hog...but hey, I come alive up here. And from now on, each of you will have solos so all of our talents can be displayed."

Reggie nodded. "Cool, that's cool with me." The other players agreed as well.

That night, Wild was back on stage at the Mink. At nine P.M., the band went on and played the first song, titled "Red." It was a wild rock tune. Jewel looked at the screaming women. He then pulled open his shirt, exposing his bare, hairy chest. "Oh Jewel! Jewel!" exclaimed the women. He was suddenly hit in the chest by a woman's bra, a pair of panties, and other articles of female clothing. He caught some of the articles and kept singing. "She is an awesome girl, with pretty red hair. Every time I see her, I imagine her bare." The music continued to play. "Totally red hot, all red, I want you, no maybes. I need you to have my baby." There were more cheers and applause, along with more articles of clothing thrown on the stage. The crowd went wild and rushed the stage, attacking Jewel, tearing and ripping at his clothes in a fanatical frenzy. He was escorted off stage by the club's bodyguards.

As the crowd still went wild in the club, Jewel, sitting alone in his dressing room, laughed. "Sex...all they want is sex." His mind wandering, he continued, "Sex in my music...I'll be a star." He again laughed. The band was still onstage playing, without him of course.

Steven was not at the show. He had sent his friend, Leonard Higgins, to check Julian out without a father's prejudiced point of view. This was Steven's way of getting Julian away from the loser band and onto bigger and better things. The middle-aged Caucasian watched the show and Jewel's magical performance like a hawk.

Julian remained seated in his dressing room thinking on his future. All of a sudden, there was a knock at the door. Thinking that some of the customers had somehow gotten back stage, he yelled, "Yeah...who is it?"

The man said, "I'm Leonard Higgins, your father's friend. May I talk to you please?" Julian rolled his eyes and opened the door for him. "Jewel, I've heard you play guitar. I think you're really talented and...." Mr. Higgins paused. "You could have a great future in the music business."

Cocky and a little rebellious, Julian asked, "Yeah, yeah...so what? Where's my father anyway?"

Mr. Higgins scratched his head, then said, getting a little restless, 'Look! Kid, I don't know where your dad is. I'm from Bazaar Records and I'd like to sign you up with our company."

Julian's eyes widened. He ran his fingers through his hair and disbelievingly shouted, "Bazaar Records! You want us to sign with Bazaar Records!" He excitedly spun around, then jumped up and down and shouted, "All right! All right!" Settling down, he said, "Have a seat, Mr. Higgins."

The middle-aged, slightly gray-haired man went over to the long, hard, blue couch and sat down. He then told Julian, "Babe, your band is great. But Bazaar Records is just interested in just you. I see real potential in you, your raunchy style...real potential. You could be big someday, kid." Mr. Higgins boosted Julian's confidence and then stood up from the couch.

Julian wasn't too disappointed in Mr. Higgins's comments. Since his arrest, he had an uneasy feeling about being in the band. He felt now that while he was performing he should have a bodyguard to watch his back. He never knew when he would be stabbed in it by his fellow band members. He happily shook his hair away from his face and asked, "Who, how?"

Mr. Higgins informed Julian that his dad was well aware of Bazaar Records' intentions and in fact, Steven Parr had arranged for him to come see the band in the first place. Mr. Higgins observed, "The band is average, but you...you Jewel, are extraordinary."

Julian slung his hair away from his shoulders and said, "Ain't that the truth. Thank you, Mr. Higgins." The two sides of Jewel struck again.

For the next couple of months, Jewel and Steven, along with Mr. Higgins, held contract meetings and signed contracts.

It was now April 11, 1988, and Julian was rehearsing with the band. Approaching the stage, Steven informed them of Jewel's record contract. He also told them he was quitting as manager as well as music organizer for the Mink.

"Ever since your damn kid got in the band, you haven't given us the time of day anyway," shouted Jeff.

Reggie then said, "I knew something was going on. Ever since Steven and that suit-wearing guy have been coming to our shows, I knew something was up."

"We're getting Ricky back in the band," shouted Jeff.

There were more shouts of hatred and even threats toward Julian. Finally, Jewel and Steven departed the Mink Nightclub. Steven just sighed and said, "I'm glad I wasn't under any contract with those bums." He and Julian got into Jewel's black Firebird and pulled off.

Chapter Twenty-eight

JEWEL SPARKLES! read Morningstar's magazine. JEWEL BUYS NEW HOME, read Starstruck magazine. PREACHING SILENCE IN SEXUALITY...JEWEL, read Blackstar's magazine.

It was seven P.M. on April 14, 1992. Twenty-two-year-old Jewel had become major force in the music industry and among music fans everywhere. He had been selling out concerts everywhere, and was now going back and forth from Detroit to California. He was promoting his solid gold album, Jewel.

Meanwhile, parents had began picketing Bazaar Records. They were protesting Jewel's "dirty music" and sexy performances, as they had been ever since he hit the professional music scene. He didn't care, though. He kept writing raunchy lyrics and performing to still sellout crowds. In fact, his songs were raunchier and his performance...well...almost nude.

Through his stardom he had purchased a beautiful home in Belleville, Michigan, and a summer house in California.

On the west side of Detroit: "Did you read this, Ricky?" shouted an excited Shelly. He was sitting on the couch with Shelly next to him reading the fan magazines. They were now living together in an apartment on the west side.

Ricky, who was clad only in jeans, said, "You've had that stupid magazine all day, Shell."

She ignored his comment and said, "That damn rock star Jewel's album has gone solid gold, and he's been voted one of the richest singers around."

He yawned and disinterestedly said, "Oh yeah? That's nice."

She then shouted, "He's worth almost fifteen million dollars!"

His eyes widened. His mouth went dry. He swallowed hard. "Fifteen million...my God!" he shouted.

"Yeah," she said gaily. "And to think...I slept with the boy when we were in high school."

Ricky, now very interested, said, "Oh yeah? Really?" He folded his arms as his mind was racing a mile a minute. He opened his mouth, beginning to speak, but Shelly beat him to it.

She jumped up from the couch excitedly, shook her head full of blonde locks and yelled, "I could have been rich! If only that...." She paused, and after thinking for a moment, looked at Ricky. He had a devilish grin on his face, as if thinking the same as Shelly. She then yelled, "We're gonna be rich, Ricky!"

He agreed excitedly. "Yeah, all you have to do is make him fall in love with you, Shell." Shelly nodded her head in agreement with Ricky. He added, "Luscious hips, now I know you can do that." He smirked. "Every guy you meet wants to get you under the sheets." He and Shelly both laughed.

Her look of joy suddenly ended as she then remembered how cold, cruel, and heartless Julian was in high school. She thought about how he had screwed her and then left her house. After that, he acted as if she didn't exist. Anger and thoughts of revenge once again started building up inside her.

At the same time, anger and hatred was building inside Ricky as he thought of how the long-haired freak had taken his job as head singer of Wild. Both Shelly and Ricky then grunted and evilly smiled. He asserted, running his fingers through his blond semi-short hair, "I'm gonna kill that effeminate bastard." He looked at Shelly. "All you have to do, my love, is...get engaged to the creep."

Shelly, looking puzzled, said, "Huh?"

He stood and hugged her, patting her rump gently. "Do whatever it takes, love. Just get engaged to the bum if you have to. All we need is access to his money...and you're the key to that." He explained, "Shelly, just get engaged to him and tell him that you want a joint bank account with the idiot."

She excitedly chuckled and commented, "Before the wedding day comes, we'll be gone!" They exclaimed together, "And we'll be rich!" They kissed each other and laughed. Shelly, then looking as if she was far away, said, "I'll get that using loser."

Ricky agreed, "I'll get that show off job stealing son of a...." However it wasn't until two months later that they contacted Jewel. Shelly caught a plane to Los Angeles, California. She and Ricky had started their plan of action.

On Friday, June 6, a day before Jewel's birthday, he performed in California at the LA Forum. Julian sang. "I'll brand your name to me, if ever again it's you I don't see," a song he had written about Brandie Charles on one of his many lonely nights. He continued to sing, "...You thought I was too good for you...I'm saying that's not likely true! You were the one who made me doubt me, I started to question who I am and what I'm about, that's why I had to go and find out...about the me I didn't know!"

The packed arena cheered and roared as he ended his song titled, "The Me I Didn't Know." The lighted stage turned colors as he performed. It went from yellow to blue, from blue to green, and then to black. The concert was then over. The crowd was disappointed because the show ended, and they sighed in dismay. Jewel's voice finally echoed, "If you ever need a rule...always count on your Precious Jewel! I love you all. Stay precious.... I'm Jewel! Good night!"

The crowd cheered again and headed for the exit. Surprisingly, in the crowd exiting Jewel's concert was UCLA graduate and now a raving beauty striving for her master's degree, Brandie Charles. She was now known as "Bread" around the campus because she had gone on a bread and water fast in college. She who was never really fat, but had always been slightly plump. The bread and water fast gained her a new name, and at last, her girl-next-door image had died. She now had a sexy, feline look.

She was uncertain about going backstage to see Julian after the show. After all, he had used her in high school, Just like all those other stupid girls, thought Brandie. He would probably just laugh in my face. She sighed and said, "Screw him." She had heard the last song he sang, but with all the commotion from the crowd, she didn't hear the words clearly, only the beat of the music. She had no idea that he was singing a song about her. With her mind made up, she walked out of the stadium.

Julian was now in his dressing room. He had a strange feeling that someone was there, but it was just a feeling. As Brandie made her way out of the stadium, following the large crowd, she thought about their lovemaking when they were younger. She then thought of his departure from her home and life, without even a goodbye. She remembered her mother's rage and words after learning that she was no longer a virgin and that Julian was the reason. The words still echoed: "Boys like Julian don't want innocents like you. They want girls who put out, fast girls who put out...fast girls who put out...." She shook her head vigorously, trying to clear her mind of her mother's comments. She thought of all the women she had read of Jewel being linked to. "Oh, forget him," she then whispered to herself. She then left the arena and got into her Ford Escort. Forgetting Julian was easier said then done.

Julian was exhausted from his two-hour performance. He was seated in his dressing room in front of his dresser, wiping off his stage makeup and listening to the crowd's departure. However just like after many other concerts, some fans always found his dressing room, and this concert was no exception. Artie Toggle, his personal body guard, held back the group of females who crowded outside Julian's dressing room door. Julian, shaking his head in disbelief, just chuckled. Suddenly the door was pushed open. He quickly looked around instinctively when he heard the cheers become louder. Artie was easing open the door. A blonde and very shapely female pushed her way into the dressing room. Julian jumped up from his chair and shouted, "Artie, what the hell are you...."

Artie closed the dressing room door and interrupted, "She said you invited her, Jewel. She said...." Julian grunted angrily. Artie continued, "Yes...she said she knows you."

Jewel angrily shouted, "Don't you know a groupie when you see one, Art!" Artie replied, "Yeah boss, but...."

Jewel, devastated by how easy someone could con Artie, interrupted him, "Man! You've been doing this for eight years. Don't you know when a groupie is handing you a line?"

Shelly, straightening her mini dress and hair, snapped, "Julian! I'm not a groupie, babe. It's me...Shelly, Shelly Nohl. We went to school together, remember?" She grinned as she brushed her hand over her silk mini dress. Julian, still standing, just stared at her movements. She then said wickedly, "Well, we did a lot more than just go to school together, now. Didn't we Jewel?" She chuckled again and so did Artie. Julian's face remained stern.

He looked at Artie, who was leaning back against the closed dressing room door, and said, "You can go now, Art...and no more being a pushover for a sexy body."

Artie once again laughed, saying hoarsely, "All right, boss." he then went back out to the mob of fans standing around Julian's dressing room door.

Julian ran his fingers through his slightly limp black hair and said to Shelly, "Have a seat, please.... It's been a long time." Shelly smiled, looking at him. She then sat on the brown cloth couch. He sat back down in his swivel chair and continued removing his make-up as he looked at her through the mirror. "So...how did you like the concert?"

Shelly shook her head, swinging her long blonde hair away from her face. She answered, "You're good. I've loved all your albums."

Still viewing her through his mirror, he said, "Thanks. I'm glad you liked it."

"Of course I like it," she said. She then stood and walked up behind him.

She wrapped her arms around his shoulders sensuously, then whispered in his ear. "Do you want to play around? I'm very horny right now." He still viewed her in the mirror. His expression was blank. She breathlessly added, "You've always gotten me so hot." He swung around in his chair, getting ready to comment, when she went down on her knees. She let her long blonde hair swing down, cascading over his satin short-covered loins. She then said, "I bet I could get you hot and horny, too.... I remember how much fun we had in high school."

He rolled his eyes disgustedly. Voiced angrily, "Would you get up off the floor? You're acting like a damn slut."

Her blue eyes widened as she stood up, looking flabbergasted. "Wha...well."

He looked at her with a serious expression on his face. He cracked, "I've been horny ever since I was twelve years old." He looked at her again. She laughed wickedly, then walked over to the other vanity mirror in his dressing room.

She again pushed her hair back in place and said angrily, "Oh...I get it now, you don't like white chicks anymore, huh?" He remained silent. "You prejudiced mother...." she said. His eyes held a look of anger as he looked at her. She added, "You've got your fame and fortune...and now you think you're too good to get with me, huh?" She slung her hair to her back and folded her arms. He frowned. She then took out her lipstick and started applying it to her already rouge-colored lips, then suddenly stopped and said nastily, "Mr. High and Mighty rock star, you think you're too good to screw." He chuckled slightly. She continued, "Or is it that you only screw around with famous chicks?" She then rolled her eyes. "What is it? You only get hard from those famous and rich bimbos?" She finished applying her lipstick, put the top back on the lipstick tube, and dropped it into her purse.

His face took on a stern expression. He breathed in deeply and snapped angrily, "My guitar gets me hard. And when I want an orgasm, it'll do that for me, too!" She remained silent, looking at him inquisitively. He swirled back around in his chair. He again looked in the mirror and said to her, "Where are you staying, baby? My guitar has retired for the night."

She giggled and replied, "I'm at the Best Southern Hotel." She reached into her purse and pulled out a small vial of coke. She smiled at Julian and said enticingly, "Yeah baby, tonight you're gonna feel more pleasure than your guitar will ever give to you."

He stood up, looking at her, and said, "Would you get rid of that shit? I'm not into it, baby."

She took a snort and demanded, sounding agitated, "What kind of musician doesn't do a little coke now and then?"

He grabbed ahold of her hand and headed for the door, guiding her along as he answered, "A live one, honey...a live one."

They went to dinner in his stretch limo. After that, they went straight to her hotel room in California's Best Southern Hotel.

Chapter Twenty-Nine

It was now 2:00 A.M. on Saturday, June 7, 1992. Julian undressed Shelly as they made love ecstatically. He caressed her breasts and nibbled on her nipples endlessly. "Oh Julian...yes!" she shouted. He then threw all the bed sheets and blankets off the bed wildly. Delirious, she dazedly said, "Wha...what are you doing?" looking at Julian.

He huskily said, "I don't like distractions, and all those sheets were distracting me." He then kissed Shelly wildly, then pulled away and breathlessly said, "Totally raw, that's the way I like it...you and the bed."

She ecstatically shouted, "Yes, yes! Oh yes!"

He then pressed his body wildly against her. His thrusts were rough and gentle at the same time as she met with his jolts. He caressed her tiny but voluptuous buttocks as she caressed his. They made endless love for endless hours, and came simultaneously.

A happy Shelly then got up and went into the bathroom, yelling to Julian, who was still laying in bed, "You're still a super lover, Julian! This night's gonna be incredible."

Julian yawned and murmured, "Yeah, I'm a super lover. But I'm not in love with you." He got up from the bed, put on his clothes, and yelled to her, "I'm out of here, Shelly." He closed the door as she quickly ran out of the bathroom. Her make-up was now on impeccably.

She was calling ecstatically, "Julian! Julian! Don't...go!" But he was already pulling off in his limousine. A now distraught Shelly flopped down on the bed. "It isn't over Jewel...it isn't over. It's just beginning, punk." She went over to the closet and pulled out her suitcase, opened it, and pulled out several newspapers and magazines. She also pulled out a pair of scissors, some glue, and a pack of white typing paper. She began cutting letters and gluing them to the typing paper.

By 9:30 A.M., June 7, Julian was back his house on Sunset Boulevard. He was sitting on his dark green leather couch listening to soft music on the radio. It was his birthday and he was now twenty-three years old. He was about to doze off to sleep when the phone rang. He was still exhausted from his concert the night before and Shelly earlier that morning, and clumsily reached over for the phone.

"Julian, I have bad news!" said a firey voice, Mr. Higgins.

Julian was suddenly wide awake. He heard the urgency in his manager's voice and suddenly became alarmed. He frowned and asked, uneasily, "What is it Leonard?"

Mr. Higgins, sounding angry, replied, "Just get your butt back to Detroit. I'll tell you when you get to my office. Make it pronto!" Mr. Higgins then hung up. A dazed and confused Julian went and took a quick shower, his mind all the while wondering what his manager wanted with him. After showering, he dressed and called the airlines to find out when the next flight out to Detroit would be.

Back at the Best Southern Hotel, Shelly was now dressed in a yellow silk dress and standing outside of the hotel. She dropped a letter in the mailbox, smiled, went back inside to her hotel room. She sat down on the bed and phoned her boyfriend, Ricky. "It's happening, Rick, honey. The only part I hate is that I had to sleep with that conceited creep," said Shelly.

Ricky frowned slightly, thinking, I know you Shelly, and the sound of your voice is not a sound of an unhappy woman. He swallowed his pride, thinking about Shelly being in bed with Jewel, then said, "Don't worry about it, honey. It's all for the money, remember?"

She then said a giddy, "Uhn-huh."

He continued, "Just like that rich banker you slept with a few weeks ago, remember?" She didn't comment. "That rich fool guy wanted you and we wanted his money...and that all panned out when you poisoned the sucker."

She chuckled and said happily, "You're right baby. We wiped out his bank account and his credit cards before his wife even found out he was dead.

He declared, "Of course I'm right. We're the new Bonnie and Clyde." He then took a snort of cocaine as she did the same in her hotel room. He went on, "Oh baby, yeah...and I mailed that fag, Jewel, a letter the day you left for Cali, so he's in for a real thrill." They laughed hysterically.

Taking another snort, she then said, "When he gets my letter, the punk is going to freaking crap in his pants." She then burst out laughing along with Ricky. After the laughter stopped, a still excited Shelly exclaimed, "We're gonna be rich, baby! We're gonna be rich as hell, baby!"

He excitedly agreed with her. "Come on home now, honey. We can think of our next plan then."

She replied, "I'm on my way!" They both hung up the phone.

At 10:00 A.M. Saturday, Julian boarded the first class flight to Detroit. He sat in the rear seat with his sunglasses on and a cap pulled down so as to not be recognized by the passengers. However he wasn't successful. After the semi-crowded plane took off, the blond stewardess who had been catering and greeting all the other passengers, finally walked to the back seats. Julian's eyes were closed and his head was resting on the back of the velvety cushioned chair. The stewardess, named Meg, approached Julian's chair. "Hi sir, is everything all right? Do you need anything?" she asked cheerfully.

He impulsively slid his sunglasses down on his nose and looked at her, observing the curvaceous brunette from head to toe. He replied sounding seductive, "No, I'm fine, thank you."

The stewardess, who seemed not older than twenty years old, swallowed hard. Her eyes widened and her voice went up an octave higher. "You're...you're Jewel!" she exclaimed excitedly.

He put his finger to his mouth and said, "Shh, shh. I don't want the whole plane to know. I thought the other stewardess informed...." He paused, then said quietly, pushing his shades back up on his nose, "You knew that I was on board."

She whispered, "Who? Sandy? No, she didn't tell me. That Sandy! I'm gonna kill her." She asked, "Can I have your autograph? I'm a big fan of yours." She took an ink pen and a small pad from her uniform pocket and gave them to Julian.

Jewel again smiled and said, looking up at her name tag, "Meg...please don't make me beg." He had a sensuous look on his face as he spoke. As usual, the stewardess chuckled. He then scribbled, "With love...Jewel," on the scratch pad. She walked back to her workstation, where Sandy, the other stewardess, was standing. The girls started happily talking about the famous star on the plane. They weren't the only ones glad that Jewel was aboard the plane.

He again closed his eyes, trying to rest. Someone came and sat in the seat right beside him. "Hey baby. You don't just walk out on your Shell like that," the sexy voice said.

Knowing who the voice belonged to, he opened his eyes. Shelly was smiling at him. "Shelly...what the hell are you doing here?" He was surprised to see her again...so soon.

She replied nonchalantly, "You're not the only one who flies first class, Julian." He didn't comment. "Get yourself a private plane—you're a rich guy now."

He laughed. "How do you know about my finances, Ms. Nohl?"

She rolled her eyes and said, "Aw, come on...Jewel, you're a big star now. Of course, you can afford a private plane." She avoided answering his questions about his finances.

He retorted, "Well, I'm not one for all the extravagancies, but you know...you're right.

She chuckled. Plan in action, she thought to herself. Aloud she said, "Of course I'm right, silly." She caressed his cheek. "You see, you need someone like me."

He said, "I do, huh?" again sounding extremely seductive.

"Yes you do, or you're gonna die a very old and lonely musician. You need someone to show you how to have fun. Life isn't just gold records and concerts, you know?"

He raised his eyebrows, not taking her words seriously. "And what is life, according to you, Shelly Nohl?"

She slung her hair away from her face and replied, "Well, Jewel, life is having someone you love to share it with...to act crazy with, to wake up with every morning...and if you have money, to buy lots of clothes and jewelry with, to have a mansion and servants with...and to...."

He laughed, interrupting her last words. "Hold up, hold up," he said.

She agitatedly said, "What?"

He replied, "I was with you in the beginning, when you were talking about life being about loving someone and sharing with that someone."

She interrupted him, tartly saying, "Well, that's in fairy tales. So what?"

He went on, "When you go to talking about being rich and having lots of clothes and servants and all that shit...I had to draw the line."

A little confused by his comment she asked, "What's wrong with servants and all of the clothes you want, houses, mansions...everything!" She had a far away look in her eyes as she loudly spoke.

He hushed her up by putting his finger to her lips, then said, "That's a fairy tale life...all the houses, cars, clothes." He frowned and said sadly, 'Life...life is love." She looked at him strangely. He continued, "I love my music, my concerts,

Shelly...and that's my life. And it would be a happy one if I had someone who loved me to share it with, like you said in the beginning." He sorrowfully shook his head. "Screw it." He turned his head and looked out of the window.

She raised her eyebrows again, looking nonchalant, bit down on her lip, took a deep breath, and said, "I love you Julian. I always have and I'll share the rest of your life with you."

He once again frowned, looking at her in disbelief at her comments. He chuckled slightly. "Aw Shelly, you don't love me. You just love the quote, unquote good life...the stars, the money, the...whoopla."

Looking sincere, she replied, "No...really, I do love you. Let me come live with you?"

Surprised by her words, he stammered, "What? Live with me?"

She replied, "Yes...I'll show you that you can enjoy the fringe benefits of fame...and that's life." She looked at him. "You know we're good together in bed, Jewel. How about it? Let me live with you?"

He sighed. "You don't really love me, Shelly." She slowly slid down in her seat as he looked back out of the window. I only want to live with and make love with the red-haired girl I left in Detroit back when I was seventeen. Not you dammit! Never you, he thought.

A few hours later, the plane landed at Detroit's airport.

Chapter Thirty

Julian got into his waiting limousine, telling Shelly, "I'll drop you off at home, Shell."

She put down the outside pay phone receiver and joined him. "Honestly, Julian, it will work. I'll cook for you sometimes and we can make love for days if we want to. It'll be perfect." They rode to her apartment in his super-stretch limo. Ricky was inside waiting for her call so he could pick her up from the airport but Julian wasn't aware of this and Shelly didn't let him know.

At 3:00 P.M. they pulled up in front of her beautiful apartment building. "I would walk you up, Shelly, but I've got an appointment in an hour," said Julian.

She kissed him on the cheek and said, "You're gonna be mine, Jewel. You'll see." He didn't comment. She chuckled and got out of the limo, looked at him, and said a casual sounding, "See ya." She then ran up to her apartment.

The limousine driver closed the car door. He walked around to the drivers side, got in, and said to Julian, "Your place, Jewel?"

Julian replied, "yeah." The driver then pulled off.

Ricky and Shelly made love as soon as she walked into the apartment. While laying in the king-size bed, she said, looking at Ricky, "You know, Rick, if I started living with Julian, I would eventually gain all of his trust. That would make our plan go even smoother."

Ricky sat up and said, looking at her, "Well, the idea is for you to get engaged to the creep, and then you can take out an insurance policy or get a joint bank account with the nasty bum." He angrily frowned, then said disgustedly, "I didn't want you to live with the bastard for God's sake!"

She irritatedly sat up next to him and snapped, "But...."

He interrupted her. "What! Did that creep ask you to damn well live with him already!"

"No, of course not," she exclaimed. She got out of bed and put on her pink bathrobe, then sat on the edge of the bed looking dazed and saying frustratedly, "Julian is still the same arrogant tease he was in high school. He's gonna need a little nudging before I can get my hands on any of his money." Ricky then got up and sat beside her. He quickly reached down on the floor and grabbed his jeans. Shaking her hair fiercely, she continued, "I know I can persuade him to let me move in with him, honey."

Stepping into his jeans, Ricky asked in a rough tone, "Oh yeah, how?"

She bit down on her bottom lip and said, "Regardless of all his money, he's...he's lonely, Rick. I can tell." She paused and looked at him. "I'll get him to let me move into his house...and then I'll get him to trust me with his money, and voila!" She smiled at him. "The money is ours!"

He raised his eyebrows. Feeling uneasy about Shelly's plan, he said, "I don't now about this, Shell."

She then said gleefully, "Look, he'll be out of town doing concerts half of the time. You and I can have his house all to ourselves, honey." She hugged him, kissing him on the neck.

He shrugged his shoulders and said, "I don't know Shell, you'll still be living with that creep." She continued to kiss him passionately. He smiled excitedly and said, "All right, all right baby, I give up. Besides, it might be fun to make love to a woman Julian thinks is his...and in his own house, too."

"Oh yeah baby, yeah!" she moaned. He grabbed her and kissed her, pinning her to the bed. She giggled wickedly and passionately, and they again made love.

It was now the month of June, and Julian walked into Bazaar Records at 4:30 P.M. His white stretch limousine was parked outside. Mr. Higgins said calmly, "Have a seat, Julian. I have to talk to you about a couple of things." Julian shook his hair wildly, then sat down in one of the two director's chairs in front of Mr. Higgins's desk. Mr. Higgins opened his desk drawer and pulled out an open envelope, frowned, and said, "One of the things I have to tell you, Jewel, is..."

Julian frowned, interrupting him. 'What's up Leonard? What's going on?"

"You've received death threats, Jewel," he replied. "You got one letter yesterday and one today." However Mr. Higgins's expression was blank. He took the two letters out of his desk drawer and gave them to Jewel.

Julian's eyes widened. He asked, sounding surprised, "A death threat?" He pushed his long hair away from his face and read the two letters Mr. Higgins had handed him. Jewel's green eyes widened further and he chuckled a little. But the laughter ceased as he read the brutal letter he'd taken out of the envelope. Your days are numbered, pretty boy. When you least expect, I'm going to cut your throat, faggot. I'm then going to use your head as a showpiece for my mantel. So when you least expect, sl——ice.
Goodbye forever.
Ha ha ha!
The letters were cut out from magazines and newspapers and pasted to a white sheet of typing paper.

He read the second letter. So you think you're sexy, huh? You know what is sexy to me? Seeing them lower you in your grave. Pow! Pow! You're dead.

He folded the letters and put them back on Mr. Higgins's desk. Seeing the worried look on his face, Mr. Higgins said, "I wouldn't worry about them too much. It's common in the music business, Jewel."

Jewell sighed. "Man, oh man."

Mr. Higgins scratched his head. "Especially with you...Jewel, being so...." He paused. "Uh...so different...so controversial."

Julian cleared his throat and said in a deep voice, "So...if it's common, why did you want to see me so urgently?"

Mr. Higgins's look turned from blank to serious. "Well, Jewel, those letters came this week and I know from past experience that there will be more."

Julian shrugged his shoulders and looked at Leonard, then said, nonchalantly, "Some obsessed nut case. I'll just have to hire more bodyguards, right?" He started to stand, saying, "If that's all, Leonard, man, I've got to be going."

Mr. Higgins quickly replied, "Sit down, Jewel."

He sat back down looking puzzled. "What is it, Leonard?"

Mr. Higgins stood up and said, "Look, there's no easy way to say this, Jewel. I'm afraid Bazaar Records has cancelled your contract."

Julian jumped up wildly, then yelled, "You can't do this! I...I have a contract for three years.... I'll sue this company!" He again slung his hair back, exposing his scar that had now become his famous trademark. The mark was a part of what made rock star Jewel genuine.

Mr. Higgins sat back down and took Julian's contract out of his desk drawer. He looked at a now furious Julian and said, "See here, son. The contract says if you become a danger to the company's reputation...you're out!"

Julian grabbed the paper contract from him, balled it up ferociously, and threw it across the room into the garbage. Still a super shooter, the balled up contract landed in the trash can. He shook his hair away from his eyes and said, "You can shove this whole damn company up your a...."

Mr. Higgins interrupted him sternly. "Julian, you brought it on yourself! You're too vulgar...your music and your performances are bad for the business! The parents are complaining and picketing us."

Julian, who had flopped down in the chair after making the basket with the contract, yelled, rolling his eyes, "So, you just say the hell with me, huh? Just because some small-minded uppity parents don't want to hear my music!"

Mr. Higgins replied solemnly, "We...me and my staff, have to do what's right for Bazaar Records, Jewel. And you're not it."

Now furious, Julian got up and headed for the door. He grabbed the knob, looked back at Mr. Higgins, and said, "They're only complaining about me being a bad influence on their kids. Well, half of what I sing about their kids are already doing. Because when I was a kid I was doing it, too." Mr. Higgins just stared at him without comment. Julian opened the door and said, "It's a tough world. If parents only would talk with their kids, they wouldn't be picketing me!" He left Bazaar Records.

Chapter Thirty-one

Julian went home and for several days and nights locked himself in his house. He didn't hire any more bodyguards like he had planned. He just stuck with his original guards: Artie, Stan, and Eric. Artie lived in the left downstairs wing of Julian's house as his personal security. Julian locked himself away from the world, so Artie would go out to buy groceries and things like that. Julian had become a hermit.

On July 30, 1992, he called his agent, Phillip Emery, and told him he was going on vacation for a few months. "You sound awful, Jewel. You doing all right?" asked Phillip. He was a bright-complected black guy who could have easily passed for Julian's brother, although his hair was shorter and he was a little stocky, unlike Jewel's thin but muscular body.

A depressed-sounding Jewel whispered, "Yeah...yeah, man, I'm just a little tired, you know?"

Phillip didn't comment. He did know tiredness, and he also knew the sound of a burnt out rock star. He had been an agent for several years. Raising his eyebrows, he just said to Jewel, "Well, I hate to tell you this, but...you have been receiving numerous death threats."

Julian lazily asked, "Yeah?"

Phillip replied sternly, "Yes, Julian! Whoever it is sent them to Bazaar Records and they sent them to my office."

Julian, who was laid out in his bedroom said roughly, "Don't worry about it. It's probably just some jealous dude who can't get it up, and his girl has to get it on by listening to me." Julian then laughed, but Phillip didn't find anything funny.

A stern-sounding Phillip said, "Julian, I haven't seen you in a while. I'm sorry about Bazaar Records letting you go. They sent me a letter informing me of the cancellation. Man, you still have a few more concerts to do under their contract. Why don't you come down to my office, we can talk. It's better than being locked away in your house all the time."

Julian frowned and snapped, "I told you man...I'm going on vacation for a few months! I'll get back with you when I get back!" He hung up the phone, then reached for it again. He sighed, "Might as well get it over with, before Phil tells him." His father, Steven Parr, had chosen Phil to be Jewel's agent. Julian dialed him at the television station where he still worked.

"Yeah, Steven Parr, here," said Julian's dad when he answered the phone.

Julian said, "Dad...what's up?"

"Hey, Jewel!" said Steven joyously. "How's it going, son? You still fighting off the ladies?"

Julian cleared his throat. Scratching his head, he said, "Uh...Dad, I...uh, I guess I sort of got canned from Bazaar Records a few weeks ago."

Steven heard the tone in his son's voice and knew he wasn't joking. Getting angry, he snapped, "You screwed up, huh?"

Julian replied, "Naw, Dad. It's just...." He started to say, "all the small-minded managers and shit and the protests against me," but Steven interrupted him. "You shook your ass right out of there, didn't you?"

Before Julian could comment Steven, still angry, said, "I went out of my damn way to get freakin' Leonard Higgins to take you on, and you couldn't even handle it! You're not star material, Julian. Face it!"

Julian's hurt now turned to anger. He yelled, "Listen, Dad! You're the one who can't handle it. And you're the one who's not star material, so...."

Steven interrupted Julian saying nastily, "Ahh...tell it to Bazaar Records! You're just gonna be a has-been, a wash-up, an oversexed wash-up! All you're good for is sexing older women!"

Julian retorted, "Oh yeah, Dad...just like you, huh?"

Steven was now even angrier. "Don't try to insult me just because you're an insult! All that screaming and shaking your ass didn't do anything but shake your ass right out of a record company. The damn smallest company around at that."

Julian's green eyes saw red. He didn't want to mention to his two-timing father how he hadn't even been man enough to stick around when he was a sickly kid. He wasn't going to mention how Steven was off getting it on with some tart instead of his wife when Julian ended up, by fate, back together with him. He just swallowed hard against the lump of rage in his throat, and said angrily, "You'll see, dammit! You'll see...me!" He frowned, wondering how Steven had heard the record company fired him because of his vulgarity. "How the hell did you know why they fired me anyway?"

Steven replied, "Phillip Emery informed me of it."

Julian said disgustedly, "Of course...leave it to good old Phillip to spread the 'good news' about his loser client." He hung up on Steven. However he had no idea what he was going to do. Most record companies wouldn't let him be himself, so he wouldn't dare try to get signed with one of them. Laying in his bed, he heard his father's cruel words echoing in his ears: You can't handle it! You're a has-been! Has-been...a has-been." He took the beer he had been laying in bed drinking and angrily threw it toward his blaring stereo system.

For months, he went through hell to find heaven. He still had concert dates to fulfill and he did, somehow. Phillip constantly told him he was working on trying to get him another record company, but Julian had started drinking a little too much instead of coping.

Saturday, March 19, 1993, he flew to California for a concert. He was scheduled to perform at a posh club called "The Mirror." The concert went off without a hitch, and Jewel performed perfectly, as he always did. After the concert he flew back to Detroit.

The next day, twenty-three-year-old Julian was invited to a party by Rocker Eli. He wasn't going to attend, but after being coaxed by his bodyguard, decided to go. He dressed in an aqua blue suit and shoes and, accompanied by his bodyguard, Artie Toggle, arrived at the party at twelve A.M. in his white stretch limousine. He had drunk a few bottles of beer, so he was ready to party.

Rocker Eli had an elegant home in Southfield, Michigan. Jewel ate a little, drank a lot, and partied non-stop for hours. He danced the entire time with four young women in particular, exchanging one with the other during each song.

The women, all in their twenties or late teens, weren't or didn't seem to be in show business. They all giggled and danced with him like star-struck groupies, so he figured they weren't entertainers. Two of the women were white and two were black. At six in the morning, when the party ended, he was still a little tipsy and a whole lot sexy and said to the women, "Come on...you're going with me."

The four young women giggled and looked at each other, saying, "All right! Sure, why not? Let's go."

Julian, followed by his bodyguard and the four young women, headed out to his limousine. The driver took them back to his house in Belleville, Michigan. When they got there, the girls were busy oohing and aahing about how beautiful his home and the view was. Julian told Artie, "You can leave, Art. I'll be fine." He then looked over his shoulder at the giddy girls who were bunched around the window, looking out.

Artie smiled wickedly, also looking at the women, and said jokingly, "You lucky dog, you."

Julian shook his head exhaustedly and said, "Get out of here."

Artie chucked. "I'm going down to the bar. If you need me, you know the number." He opened the door, and looking back at Julian, said, "I doubt..." he chuckled "that you will," and left.

Julian locked the door, then went over to girls and said, standing behind them, "How about breakfast?"

The Caucasian girl with the long curly blond hair, named Shannon, turned from the window and, looking at Julian, said, 'Sure, what are we having?"

Julian pulled off his blue shirt and replied, "I thought you already knew the answer to that." He smiled at Shannon sensuously. All four girls chuckled. Julian walked over to his leather pull-out couch, laying it out into a bed, then reached into the drawer on his side table and pulled out red satin sheets and blankets, covering the bed with them. He took off his blue dress pants, socks, and shoes, then got under the satin sheets. He looked over at the four women and said, "I think I want you all." The girls once again looked at each other unsurely and slightly giggled. Sitting up in the bed, the fluffy pillows behind his back, he cracked, "Did you all come up here to look out of my window...or do you want to do it?" He looked somewhat amused by the situation, but still sounded very sexy.

Shannon exclaimed giddily, "Yeah! Come on you guys." She took off her dress and stepped out of her camisole. She ran over to the bed totally nude and got in next to him. They began kissing passionately, seeming to forget about the others watching. He caressed her breast. She was running her fingers through his hair and moaning. Damn, I'm in bed making out like crazy with rock star Jewel!

Ashley, one of the African-American women, had watched his moves with her friend and was getting hotter by the minute. She remarked, "Uh...she doesn't even know how to kiss you," as she looked at him.

He said, "And I guess you do." Before she could answer, he added, "Why don't you do it, then?"

She was taken aback by his sexy voice...by his sexiness. She breathed deeply and smiled as she pushed her long hair away from her face, then uneasily said, "Uh...well, sure.... I'll try anything once." She smiled at him. Shannon was dizzily caressing his hairy chest with a satisfied smile on her face as his hand moved all over her naked body.

Ashley swiftly removed her black leather mini dress and placed it on the chair. Her big brown eyes sparkled as she gazed at him while she was undressing her shapely body. She was soon nude, except for her stockings and pumps. She kicked off her pumps and stepped out of her stockings. He was watching her sensuously as he nibbled on Shannon's breasts and nipples. His eyes were wide from the arousal of both watching her disrobe her lovely, tan-colored, shapely body, and from sucking and nibbling on Shannon's tits.

Ashley, not the least bit embarrassed at disrobing in front of him, looked over at Pamela, the other African-American woman, and Lindsay, the other Caucasian woman, and said, "Come on, you guys.... Don't be such stuffed shirts." Julian and Shannon were now under the sheets kissing and caressing like crazy. When he glanced up at Ashley, he quickly said, "Shannon don't be greedy, huh." He looked at her coldly.

Shannon frowned in surprise as she started getting out of bed, asking, "What?"

He reached for Ashley, telling Shannon, "Go take a shower or something, okay?" Ashley was now snuggled beside Julian in the full-sized bed.

Shannon angrily replied, "You creep! I'm getting the hell out of here!" But he was busy making love to Ashley. Shannon dressed and left the house. His hands held firmly onto Ashley's hips as they kissed and caressed each other's bodies in ecstasy. She disappeared under the covers and all that could be seen was her body's form on top of Julian, moaning and making out like crazy. His face held a look of pure pleasure as she breathlessly said, looking at her other two friends while kissing his hairy chest, "So...wha...what are you two waiting for?"

Pamela ran her fingers through her short cut but full-bodied hair and said angrily, "We're not pieces of meat! I...I did want you...but now, I wouldn't touch you with a ten-foot pole, you lousy son-of-a...." Her brown eyes seem to turn reddish as she angrily spoke.

Lindsay interrupted Pamela's furor. "He's not even worth it." She rolled her blue eyes and looked at Julian, who was in pure ecstasy from Ashley's caresses. She and Julian were still under the covers.

"Oh yes, Jewel, baby." She kissed him erotically. "Mmm, you taste so good...I just want to eat you alive."

As she continued to kiss his neck, he motioned to the other two women, "Hey! Show's over, so get the hell out."

"Yeah baby, mmm," she moaned in ecstasy. The other two girls were making their was out of his house. He let out a loud yell as he spasmed uncontrollably. She soon climaxed as well. She hugged him and kissed him provocatively again. "You're good baby," he said breathlessly.

She was now getting out of bed saying proudly, "Of course I am." She got dressed.

Just then, her other three friends came back into the house. Ashley, who was now fully dressed, was putting on her shoes. He was still lying in bed looking satisfied. Lindsey began, "You know what girls," speaking to and looking at her other three friends, "you all might love this guy or think you love this guy."

She looked over at Shannon and Ashley. "But you know, love comes from above." She looked up toward the ceiling and smiled. "From Him, the Almighty. We don't have to take off our clothes and get naked for His love." All three girls were silent as Lindsay spoke.

Julian, who was still laying in bed looking self-satisfied, said nastily, "Would you all get out of here? I've got things to do."

Lindsay said sternly, "You see that? He doesn't give a damn about us. I read the Good Book and even though I want to fall in love just like every other woman, I'll wait, until the Man upstairs sends him to me." She paused. "I'll then know that he's Mr. Right." Julian had gotten out of bed and put on his pants. He was now sitting on the bed fiddling with some papers he had taken out of the table drawer next to his bed.

Julian was looking through the papers blindly, but his ears and mind were in tune to what Lindsay was saying. Ashley was neatening up her hair. Lindsay continued, "We don't have to demean ourselves, doing unspeakable acts that should only be for your lover or husband...for this creep." She looked at him spitefully. She glanced over at Ashley, who was finished doing her hair and looking at her as well. Ashley rolled her eyes. He stood up and looked at the girls. Ashley was getting her purse from on the chair.

Julian said, clearing his throat, "I, uh...hate to interrupt your lesson in life day." He smiled his gorgeous smile and said, "First you got laid, then...you heard a sermon."

The girls had blank looks on their face. "What is it Jewel?" said Shannon. "We've got to go. Now that you've gotten your jollies."

Julian chuckled and said, "Hey...back to the real world." He paused. "I'm a famous musician, you know? So I need you all to sign this. It's...uh, it kinda says that if you ever told the tabloid about...you know?...You guys hanging out with me, my agent can sue your asses off."

All four girls again looked at each other. Shannon rolled her eyes and said disgustedly, "What the hell. I just want to get out of here." She snatched the paper from him and signed it, then passed it to her friends, who signed it also. Pamela handed the paper to him.

He said, "Thanks. My driver will take you back to where he picked you up at." He opened the door for the four young women and said snidely, "Thanks for the company."

Julian may have seemed calm and cool as the young women left his house, but as soon as he closed the door, he broke down and cried. "I've screwed two women today, and if I wanted to I could have had all four!" He was on the floor on his knees in front of his front door. Tears streamed down his face and fell onto his bare chest. "It's not enough!" he screamed loudly. "I can fuck fifty women and it's still isn't enough! I'm not happy. Something is wrong! Something is wrong! Please help me! Please help me! It isn't enough. It isn't enough!" he cried out, looking up toward the heavens. He curled up on the floor and continued, "It's not...it's not enough. I need something more. If you're up there listening...please help me, I need something more."

Artie came into the house as he was on the floor in a fetal position. He frantically said, thinking some fan may have attacked him, "What the hell happened in here? Jewel, are you all right? What's going on?" Artie then helped him up off the floor. He had a wild look on his face and his eyes were bloodshot.

He quickly went over to the door and locked it. Looking around wildly, he said frantically, "My home...they want my home...they want my body...they want my life!...They want my life! But they're not gonna get it. They'll never get it!" Artie looked at him with a concerned frown on his face. He continued to rave incoherently. "It's the record company, Bazaar Records...they did this to me, and they're after me. No!...It's my dad. He thinks I want that bimbo girlfriend of his. He wants to get me, he wants to kill me!"

Julian looked around madly as he heard his mom's voice say, "He's famous now, that son of mine. If only I knew where he was."

"Mom?" yelled a disturbed feeling and looking him. "I'm here, Mom!"

Artie took a deep breath, shook his head sorrowfully, and said sympathetically, "Come on, Jewel, let's go sit down. I think you're tired. All the concerts, all the parties, you're just tired." Artie had a puzzled look on his face. He then told him, "You've been hitting the booze bottle a little bit too much also."

Julian, seeming to calm down a little, licked his lips. He took a deep breath as he sat down on the leather couch. He covered his eyes with his hands and said, "What's happening to me? My God, I'm going crazy! I can't take this anymore. It's too much, it's all too much!"

Artie sat beside him and in a comforting tone said, "I think it's time for you to take a vacation, Jewel. Let's face it, you're a relatively young man to have all this fame happening to you."

Julian chuckled. "Maybe you're right, Art." he sighed. "I'm going back to my house in California, man. I need to get away from all of this." Artie didn't comment. He continued, "Away from the groupies, the music scene, the everything. I've got to get away." His voice was sounding exhausted. Artie patted him on the back and went to his room. As he sat there, slightly frazzled, his slight nervous breakdown was followed by a blinding flash of light. "Oh hell! Stop! Not again!" he yelled. He grabbed his eyes trying to protect them from the blinding light that only he could see. Again he pleaded, "Please help me! If you're up there...please help me!" The blinding light seemed to diminish. He got up from the couch and called the airport, making reservations to leave Detroit for California.

Chapter Thirty-two

At 8:00 that night, Julian arrived at LA's airport. He stopped at a small gift shop by the airport and purchased a few books and a strawberry soda pop. The small shop was free of shoppers, though a sunglasses-clad Julian proceeded cautiously. Artie stayed in the limousine at Julian's request. He shopped quickly, picking out books—The Quaran and the Bible—and a Song Lyrics magazine, on the front of which was his picture, under the title, FIRED FROM BAZAAR RECORDS...JEWEL...WHAT WILL HE DO NOW.

He thumbed through the magazine and read the article about himself. A woman walked inside the store, but he was totally engrossed in the article, which he noticed was filled with all sorts of misleading accounts. He was disturbed by the lies in the magazine he didn't notice the shapely, thin, beauty with reddish-colored hair. However Brandie, who was standing at the dairy freezer choosing a low-calorie ice cream, noticed him.

Brandie frowned, gazing at his disgruntled disposition. His hair hung long in length, and he looked unshaven and somewhat agitated. She whispered to herself, "Oh my God, Julian," then quickly took the ice cream from the freezer. She took a fifty dollar bill from her purse and quickly went to the cashier and gave her the money, saying, "Keep the change."

She quickly headed out of the store.

The older cashier, surprised by the customer's actions, said, "But, this is too much! Miss!" Brandie had left before the cashier could give her change back or ask if she wanted a bag. Artie, who was sitting in the stretch limo outside of the gift shop, noticed the woman's quick departure but thought nothing of it. Brandie got into her Escort and drove off. She could not stand the thought of getting involved with Julian and being made a fool of again.

A few minutes later, he came out of the shop and got into his limousine. Artie asked, "All set, sir?"

Julian responded, "Yeah take me to my house, please."

Artie then slyly asked, "Did you get her number?"

Julian frowned, puzzled by the question. He then asked, "Whose number?" he shook his hair away from his face.

Artie replied, "The red-haired fox who went into the store after you did."

Julian, puzzled, said, "I didn't see any red-haired fox. I was in there alone."

Artie asked incredulously, "You mean you missed her, Jewel?"

Julian nonchalantly retorted, "I didn't see her."

Artie shook his head, smacked his lips, and said, "Pity. She was a real looker, too. Who knows, she could have been your wife!"

Julian rolled his eyes disgustedly and said sarcastically, "My wife! Yeah, Artie, right."

Looking out at the California sun and scenery, Brandie thought back to the gift shop and to her early days in California. She had joined California's Gala Spa. A friend had told her of their fabulous reputation and wonderful workout equipment. Brandie's doctor had assured her he would have her dancing and agile in no time. He also told her to join a spa, to "keep it limber." She trusted the elderly doctor and signed up for several spa sessions, thinking, What do I have to lose? California is full of beautiful, active women, and I'm going to become one of them. And become one of them she did, with a vengeance. She was now thinking of how she had seen Julian at the gift shop. She thought about how unruly and sad he looked, nothing like the Julian she remembered and had once known.

She was still a student at UCLA. She had received her bachelor's degree and was now going for her master's. Twenty-three-year-old Brandie hadn't changed that much during her years in college. Despite her businesswoman-like manner, she was still a faded jeans, tattoos, and peace sign wearing Detroit love child.

She continued looking out at the beautiful, sunny California as she thought about her mom, Corina Charles. She thought of the words her mother had told her before she left for college. "Dee Dee, you must always think ahead of time before you allow yourself to love a man. They'll disappoint you if you don't know what to expect."

A then wide-eyed Brandie had said, "Mom...whatever happened to Dad, anyway? Why did he leave?"

Corina had told her daughter, "Your father is a businessman. He's an investor and he owns many businesses."

Brandie asked solemnly, "Where is he?"

Corina responded, "I don't know, sweetie. The last time I heard from your father, he was investing in some businesses. I don't know what he's been up to lately, though."

Brandie frowned, then quickly asked, "Business? I wonder what kind of business?"

Corina sighed. "Oh honey, when I met your father, he and your uncle Everett were trying to start some sort of business back when we lived in Minnesota." She caressed Brandie's hair and said, "We were teenagers then, Brandie. Your father and uncle has always had big ideas of making it to the top, one way or the other."

Brandie looked stunned. She told her mother, "I never knew that, Mom."

Corina said, "Yeah, that's the Charles family. They all want to be Big-Time Bob's." Sorrowfully, Corina continued, "I guess that's why he left me. I wasn't trying to get rich quick like he was." Tears then rolled down Corina's face.

Brandie, who was sitting on the couch with her mother, hugged her and said, "Oh Mom, I...I'm sorry. I didn't think mentioning Dad would make you so unhappy."

Corina had patted her daughter on the back and said, "Don't worry about me, Dee Dee. Just learn as much as you can and rule the world."

Brandie replied solemnly, "Yes, Mom." She then raised her eyebrows as she thought of her dad and uncle, then hugged her mom as her mind raced and she stared into the distance. She was again seated, staring out of the window of her dormitory as she reminisced on her past conversation with her mother.

She had one more year to go at UCLA, and she would then have her master's degree. Twenty-three-year-old Brandie was an avid fan of rock star Jewel, even though he had walked out of her life almost six years ago. The pain of his cruel departure from her life hadn't left her. However she did go on with her life, pushing him out of her life and mind.

Brandie had started several clubs while attending college. She was also asked to pledge with several sororities, but she turned them down in pursuit of her own clubs, "Women of Wonder," and "Peace with Life." She had also started a support club titled, "Love and Peace in the 80s." The club was a huge success, helping out women with problems such as relationships, dating, and other personal topics. Along with her college studies, it took her mind off of Julian. But when he became famous, became number one on the record charts, she had to see him again! Julian Parr, alias Jewel!

She had seen his dynamic and very explicit show and drove home with a feeling of joy and sadness inside. She also had a smile on her face. "My precious Jewel," she had whispered. A tear fell from her eye.

Nine months later, back at his house in Belleville, Michigan, a recuperated Julian was laying on his bed. He opened up the Bible he had purchased, read a few pages, and closed it. He frustratedly said, "God, huh? Yeah right. Look at my screwed-up life." He then dozed off to sleep.

This kind of action went on for a few of months. He didn't leave his house. He didn't call anyone or receive calls. Artie would tell callers he was out of town, however he was usually on his couch reading the Bible or the Holy Quaran.

All this changed, however, one night in March, 1994. Artie had gone to the store to get Julian's favorites—spaghetti, orange juice, and Oreo® cookies and had been gone for about an hour. Julian, who hadn't eaten all day, had just finished meditating and got up from the floor and sat on his red leather couch. There was suddenly a knock at the door. Julian, thinking it was Artie, got up from the couch, walked over, and opened the door.

"Jewel, sweetheart...where have you been hiding?" said Shelly giddily.

Stunned, he replied, "Shelly! What? How did you get through the gates?"

Shelly joyously said, "Your bodyguard let me in." She then pushed her way past him. She was busy looking at his lavishly decorated living room. She went over and stared at his gold album inside the tall, see-through, glass trophy case.

Julian, still holding the door open, said sounding puzzled, "Where is Artie, anyway?" He then frowned at a smiling and cheerful Shelly as she sat on his red leather couch and sighed from the comfort.

"Artie," Shelly paused and sounded nonchalant, "I guess that's his name, said to tell you that he forgot a few items at the store and he'll be back momentarily."

Julian closed the door. He then rolled his eyes disgustedly. Walking toward the couch and Shelly, he asked angrily, "So...what are you doing here, and what's with the suitcase?"

Shelly giggled. He sat down next to her. "I think you need a woman around here, Julian," she said.

Julian cleared his throat, and looking at her said, "How would you know what I need?" He raised his eyebrows. "How the hell did you know where I live anyway?"

Shelly folded her arms and sighed. "Well, Jewel...for one thing, when we were together in California, you struck me as an unhappy, lonely man, with nobody to keep him company but his guitar." She added, "And anyway, I adore the fan magazines, and I am a fan of yours. And everyone who's a fan of yours knows where you live. I'm sure you know that, though. That's why you have all the security gates outside, right?"

Julian sternly said, "Wrong! And I'm not unhappy or lonely." He added, "And I don't have a guitar anymore." He stood up from the couch and said, looking angrily at her, "Look, I don't need any live-in guests! So, it's been nice seeing you again but I'm afraid you'll have to be going."

Shelly ignored his temper and said, "You may not need any live-in guests, but what about a live-in lover?" She stood up and put her arms around his neck.

Suddenly, Artie walked in the front door. Julian sighed. He said, sounding rough, "Good!"

Shell, ignoring his comment, ran over to him happily and exclaimed, "Hi...Artie, isn't it?"

Artie looked past Shelly at Julian. He sensed something intense was going on. Julian just rolled his eyes. Artie laughed and said, "Ye...Yeah, I'm Artie, Julian's bodyguard and personal assistant. How are you? I remember you from the concert in California. That's why I let you in the gate."

Shelly then said, "I'm Shelly Nohl." She took the bag from Artie. "I'm fine, Artie. You're Julian's personal assistant, huh?" she took the bags to the clearly visible kitchen.

Artie, looking at Julian, shrugged his shoulders. Julian again rolled his eyes and disgustedly flopped down on the couch as Artie chuckled. He walked over to the kitchen, where Shelly was busy putting milk into the refrigerator, and answered Shelly's earlier question. "Yeah, I'm Jewel's assistant, Ms. Nohl. What are you doing here?" He started putting away the groceries also.

Julian walked into the kitchen. Shelly looked back at him. As she put bread inside the bread box, she said, "I'm trying to get Julian to let me stay here with him, Artie. The house is beautiful, but it needs a woman's touch." She giggled. "This house is just like Julian...all male." Julian stood silently in the doorway. He observed and listened to Artie and Shelly. She continued, "It's obvious he doesn't have a cook or a maid, so...I could do all those duties for him. That way, Artie, it'll take a load off of you."

Julian's deep voice then filled the kitchen as he said, "I used to have a maid, a cook...all those extravagancies." He sat down at the kitchen table. "I like my freedom, my privacy." He slung his hair away from his face. "Artie and I keep the house up better than any maid."

Artie agreed, "That's right. I give him his space and he gives me mine. I live here with Jewel, Shelly."

Shelly was now placing canned goods in the cabinet, saying sarcastically, "The real odd couple, huh?"

Julian agitatedly then said, "Naw, it's more like the real lifestyles of the rich and famous. Artie has his quarters downstairs, and I have mine."

Shelly's pale face seemed to turn red as she said meanly, "Well, aren't you just the lone...I mean, the only one."

Julian stood and said, "Weren't you on your way out, Shelly?" She again looked back at him. "I have a song to finish writing. I'll be in my studio."

Shelly sat down and said, "Artie...I used to go to school with Julian." Artie just listened to her as he started preparing dinner. "I fell in love with him back then, but he wouldn't give me the time of day."

Artie was shredding lettuce. He said, "Funny, Jewel never mentioned you."

Shelly rolled her eyes, swung her hair back, and said, "Talk to him for me, Artie." She thought for a moment. "I...I mean, don't mention our high school days, but tell him to let me move in here with you guys." Artie began boiling the spaghetti as she continued, "Tell him I can help him."

Artie thought for a moment. He then said, going toward the guest room, "I'll talk to him for you. I've been telling Julian it's time he got married." Shelly laughed. Joyfully she followed Artie upstairs to the guest room.

After the spaghetti was cooked a little later, Artie went down to the end of the hall and opened the door to Julian's studio. He went into the quiet, spacious room. "Dinner's ready, Julian," he said.

Julian, who was writing in his tablet, asked, "Is Shelly gone yet?"

Artie sat on one of the recording stools and said, "Julian, she isn't a bad-looking girl."

Julian agreed, "Yeah, she's all right."

Artie added, "She's also crazy about you. I can tell."

Julian chuckled and said, "She wants a permanent bed partner, that's all."

Artie stood up. "You should get with her, Julian. You need a good woman."

Julian, disgusted, exclaimed, "Yeah, maybe you're right." He then got up and followed Artie into the dining room.

As they were headed down the hall, Artie said, "She's gonna stay with us for dinner, if that's all right with you?"

Julian eyes widened. He shouted, "You mean she still here?"

"Yeah, she's here. Shelly! Dinner's ready!" yelled Artie.

Shelly came downstairs. All three of them then ate a delicious spaghetti dinner together. Artie and Shelly had wine with their meal while Jewel had fresh-squeezed orange juice. "Oh my God, don't tell me you don't drink either," said Shelly as she observed Julian pouring juice from the tall glass pitcher.

Artie had prepared a delicious tossed salad, hot buttered rolls, and a pan of his special spaghetti sauce. He had placed the food, along with a bottle of white wine and a pitcher of orange juice on the square glass dining room table.

Shelly was seated across from Julian. Artie was seated at the other end of the square table. Julian snapped angrily after Shelly's comment, "You know Shelly, every musician's not a drunk or a dopehead!"

Shelly, stunned by his angry mood and tone of voice, swallowed hard. She frowned and then said, "Julian, I...I was...."

Julian interrupted her statement, still angry. "After dinner, you're out of here, all right!"

Tears filled Shelly's eyes. She looked down at her plate of food and then back up at Julian. She glanced over at Artie, who had stopped eating and was looking curiously at Julian. She then looked at Julian and, sounding all choked up, said, "I...I have no place to go, Julian."

Julian looked at her. He then said, surprised, "What?" Artie just sat silent. He was wondering what Julian had against her.

Shelly, now in tears, told the two of them, "Well...my lease is up today, and my landlord has raised my rent. He raised it another five hundred dollars." Julian, used to people trying to get money from him, just sighed. He looked at Artie and then at Shelly. "He told me that he might raise the rent...but I didn't know that it would be this month," she said. Tears were now streaming down her face.

Julian, getting angry, disgustedly asked, "What do you want, Shelly? You want me to give you some money, huh?"

Shelly rolled her eyes. She took a napkin and then dried them. "No...no, of course not, Julian. I'm gonna find myself another, cheaper place to stay. I...I just need a few days to find one." Julian cleared his throat, preparing to speak. Shelly added, "I...I put my furniture in storage today, so that's no problem. As soon as I find a place, I'll get it out of storage and be on my way." She paused and then whined, "Please, Julian...let me stay here? You know, I don't have any real reliable friends...no one but you. I...I love you, like I said on the plane."

Julian took a bite from his roll and a sip of juice. He said, pushing his chair back from the table, "What about your parents?"

Shelly slung her hair back and said, "Naw...I don't really see eye to eye with them."

Julian stated coldly, "Well, I'm sorry, but you can't stay here."

Shelly agitatedly shouted, "You can't put me out on the street!"

Julian replied, "I'm not putting you out on the streets, "I'm just putting you out of here."

Shelly sighed sadly. "Well, I guess I can stay at a motel for a while."

Artie interrupted. "Come on, Julian, man. You can't just put her out of here."

Julian, standing away from his chair looked, at Artie for a moment. Giving in, he said to Shelly, "You can stay here a week. By then, you should have yourself another place." he went into the living room, picked up the Bible from the bookcase, and sat down on the couch, reading some the verses.

A little later, as he was reading, Shelly walked into the living room and sat down next to him. She looked at Julian's masculine physique as he read. She said, swinging her hair away from her face, "You're kinda religious, huh?"

Julian closed the book and said solemnly, "I find the peace and knowledge I yearn for when I read the Word."

Shelly, ignoring Julian's placidity, reached over and put her arms around his neck. She said to Julian, speaking sexily and softly, "I'll tell you all the words you need to know." He looked at her in disbelief. She said seductively, "Now...Why don't we go to your bedroom?" She paused. "I'll give you what you really yearn for."

Julian pulled back. He grabbed her arms and angrily took them from around his neck. She was surprised by his actions and said loudly, "What's with you, Jewel?" The phone rang before she finished saying his whole name. She jumped up from the couch, shook her long, blonde, curly hair, and went over to Jewel's telephone. Angrily, she pouted as she walked. "All this religious stuff...huh! I bet this is one of your women calling now!"

Julian, still used to being in isolation from the world, said suddenly, "Don't! My answering service will get it."

Shelly said angrily, "Huh, it's probably one of your groupie girlfriends!" She picked up the receiver. "Hello, Jewel's secretary speaking. How can I help you?"

He just sat silently, observing the tornado that had swept through his house.

Phillip Emery, Jewel's agent was on the line and said, sounding panicked, "I need to speak to Jewel! It's urgent! This is Phillip Emery."

Shelly looked over at Julian and said, "It's Phil Emery. He says it's urgent." She again slung her golden curls.

Julian sighed. He then got up from the couch slowly, walked over to his telephone stand, and took the phone. "Yeah Phil, what's going on?" Shelly went back over to the couch sat down.

Phillip told Julian, "Jewel! Where the hell have you been? I was worried sick. You've been hiding out for a year. Man, your career is going down the drain!"

Julian exhaustedly replied lowly, "I...I've been writing some tunes, Phil, calm down. I...I'm just a little burnt out. I had to get away from all this...the music, the parties, I...just had to get away."

Phillip then said, giving in to Julian's words of weariness, 'Okay, Jewel, okay. But look here, you've been receiving a lot of threatening letters!"

Julian acknowledged nonchalantly, "Well, I guess when it's my time to die, they'll get me."

Shelly, who was reading a magazine, looked up as she heard his words. The plan is working, thought Shelly. She smiled and looked back down at the magazine page.

Phillip then said, "You better beef up your security. These letters are damn eerie! Thank goodness whoever it is, doesn't know where you live!"

Julian cleared his throat and said calmly, "I'm not afraid to die. It's inevitable."

Phillip now furious at how nonchalant and uncaring Julian's attitude about the matter was, said, "Listen you fool! This nut says he's gonna tear you apart limb by limb! He's psychotic! He's really gonna kill you, Jewel. It's serious!"

Julian raised his eyebrows. Rolling his eyes, he said lowly, "God is my defense and the God of my mercy."

Phillip snapped angrily, "Well, good...Julian. You're gonna need something, cause whoever's writing these letters means to do you real harm!" The two men were silent for a few seconds. Phillip then said, "Well, Jewel, thank God they don't know where you live. Whoever it is is totally ballistic about getting rid of you."

Shelly was listening intensely, even though she pretended to be totally engrossed in the magazine article that she was reading.

A few minutes later, Julian and Phil hung up. Julian went back over to the couch and sat down. Shelly closed up the magazine she was reading and animatedly shouted, 'My God, Julian! You've been getting death threats!"

Julian said snidely, "You were listening to my conversation."

Shelly shouted, "Yeah, so what? I heard your phone call—big deal! You've been getting threats, Jewel! You've got to do something. It's probably some sick, obsessed fan."

Julian just stood up from the couch. "You just worry about finding a place to stay, huh? You've got a week." He then went to his bedroom and closed the door. The guitar sound blasted from his room.

Shelly mumbled to herself, "You'll see, pretty boy, you'll see." She laughed and went up to the guest bedroom.

Shelly ended up staying with Jewel for over a week, always looking but never seeming to find a place to stay. She went out to work each day and came back each evening, complaining to Julian that she couldn't find a place. She had told him she went looking after work and there were no affordable apartments available. She had told him that she was a full-time secretary, but in all actuality, she worked part-time. She went to work each morning and got off work at one o'clock, then would head back home to the apartment she shared with Ricky Hodges. Julian was none the wiser of her whereabouts or activities. He took her at her word.

Shelly had quit her night job as a stripper when she and Ricky found out about Julian's millions. Her main job and goal now was maneuvering the money away from him. She and Ricky were finally going to strike it rich with...Jewel's gold.

Chapter Thirty-three

It was now Friday April 13, 1994. Shelly again went back to the apartment she shared with Ricky. It was one-thirty P.M. Unemployed Ricky was lying on the tweed couch in their medium-sized living room. "Shelly, sweetheart! I was just lying here thinking about you." he stood up.

Shelly ran over to be near him and embraced him passionately. They kissed for several minutes. "Oh baby, I missed you so much," said a giddy Shelly, then lifted her top off.

Ricky sighed, saying, "Oh yeah baby, me too. I hate the idea of you living with that faggot."

Shelly was busy unbuttoning his shirt. She took it off of his shoulders, and it fell to the floor. He then lifted her and took her to their bedroom. "Uhn...Uhn!" he groaned as he made love to her vigorously. She caressed his buttocks and back as she moaned in heated ecstasy. 'Oh baby, I missed you so much," he said breathlessly.

Shelly sighed and moaned, "Oh yeah, me too, baby." In ecstasy, she cried out, "Don't stop! Don't stop, please!" They continued to make love for hours, resulting in an explosive and very passionate end.

Shelly, sitting up on the side of the bed, said, "We have work to do, love, enough play." Her eyes sparkled as she kissed him on the cheek and opened the drawer to the table beside the bed. She pulled out more magazines and typing paper.

Ricky whined, "I need you Shelly. Come on, forget all that stuff and get back into bed." He reached over for her arm.

Shelly reached over to the bottom of the bed and grabbed her robe. Putting it on, she said, "Ricky, baby, we'll never get rich, if every time I come home we spend all day doing it."

Ricky sighed. "Yeah...you're right, babe." Excitedly, he got out of bed and went over to his closet. He took out a pair of jeans from his closet and put them on, then reached back into the bottom of the closet and pulled out a gun. "This is going to sign Julian's death certificate." He held the revolver out so she could examine it.

Shelly was busy cutting and pasting letters, making up another threatening letter to Julian. Ricky cleared his throat, getting her attention, and she looked over at him. He was bare chested and holding out the black revolver. "All right, Ricky! You got it!" she shouted excitedly. She then slung her blond hair away from her blue eyes and smiled, pleased with his purchase.

Ricky laughed. He said, "Of course, I bought it yesterday at the pawn shop."

Shelly giggled, then shouted, "Pow! Julian, you're dead, and we're rich!" They laughed hysterically.

Meanwhile in California, Brandie Charles continued her studies. She had become and continued to be a California beauty. She worked out daily at the Here's to Your Health spa. She had dated many guys who had also attended

UCLA during her years there. However she kept on comparing them to Julian Parr, and nothing compared to Jewel.

It was a month before her college graduation, on a Monday night. She had been dating Cyris Grant for three months. Cyris, who was getting his master's degree in accounting, had fallen head over heels in love with her, and was not about to let her get away from him.

On the other hand, she liked Cyris as a friend, but thought he was a dreadful self-righteous bore. Although she now wore designer jeans instead of faded ones and silk dresses and high-heeled shoes and may have looked conservative, she was still a flower child at heart. Underneath all the makeup, the business-like clothes, the big words, and proper speaking voice, she still had her tattoos. In fact, she had added a tattoo of a dove on her left thigh. She had also added a tattoo of a diamond on her right breast, with the word "Jewel's" above it. She was indeed still a flower child, constantly calling her mom and complaining, "I don't care how many degrees I get...I'll never turn my back on the things that are truly important, like air pollution, the hole in the ozone, and starving people." Corina had agreed with her. Brandie would say, "Peace, love you, Mom, goodbye," and hang up the phone.

Cyris and Brandie dined at the Jaquii Restaurant on that Monday night. They were celebrating their upcoming graduation. Cyris never saw her passionate side and never agreed with any of the views about which she felt so strongly. When she did speak of such matters, such as homelessness, Cyris laughed and said, "Lazy bums! They need to try to get a job and quit relying on the welfare system. I know I'm personally tired of paying their way through life while they just sit around and have baby after baby."

Brandie became outraged at Cyris's comment. She stood up angrily and shouted, "You heartless jerk!" then walked out of the restaurant.

She went home and laid on her couch, furiously thinking about Cyris and his narrow-mindedness. A little later, he came over to her dormitory. She calmly opened her door and invited him in. He sat down on her couch and aid, "You're a bleeding heart, Bread. I'm gonna have to help you get over that nonsense."

After a while, she forgave him for his opposing views, and they affectionately kissed each other for hours as they sat on her small couch. He eventually went over and turned on her stereo. A rock tune played on the radio.

Cyris was a thin, brown-skinned, scholarly looking man. He had on a white shirt covered by a black and red checkered pullover sweater vest and dress pants. He returned to the couch and they continued kissing passionately. He unbuttoned her black silk blouse and slid it down from on her shoulders. Brandie sighed breathlessly, "Cyris." He started to unhook her bra.

"This is Jewel, singing, 'Many Girls, One Woman,'" the radio announcer said as her bra dropped to her lap. She and Cyris still passionately kissed.

"Mmm, baby," murmured Cyris. "I know I told you before that I wasn't going to pressure you, I'm going to make love to you tonight." He again kissed Brandie, who was feeling sort of vulnerable and didn't comment. They had been going together for months, but they had never been intimate, due to Brandie's insistence that they wait. She had gone out with many guys, but had never been intimate with any of them.

The song on the radio played on. "I've had many girls in my world, but I'm gonna be honest, if I can. I only loved one woman...I've only been in love with one woman." Jewel continued to sing on the radio.

Cyris started sliding down Brandie's skirt, his hands grabbing at the waistband. She shouted hysterically, "No! Don't.... Stop!" She jumped up from the couch and said angrily as she put on her blouse, "I told you before, Cyris, I'm not ready!"

He rolled his eyes and disgustedly said, "Aw come on, baby. I'm a man with needs. You don't want me to satisfy them elsewhere, now do you?" He sat back comfortably on the couch.

Jewel's song was ending on the radio. "Many girls...one woman.... Where is she? Many girls, one woman, I need her to set me free."

Brandie was now hysterical and frantic as she heard the words to Jewel's song. She looked at Cyris and shouted, "Get out, Cyris! Get out, now!" She pointed to the door and then went over to open it for his exit.

He slowly got up from the couch, chuckled dryly, and walked over to the open door. He then said, looking at Brandie, "You're a fool. You're gonna be a lonely, old-maid bitch... You know that?" She didn't comment, still thinking of the words to Jewel's song. As he left the dorm, he looked at Brandie and again chuckled wildly. "Waiting for some damn prince charming, huh? Or maybe you're waiting for that damn fool Jewel who was just singing on the radio."

The expression on her face convinced him his last question was right on the money. Her eyes were wide with enthusiasm after hearing Jewel's name mentioned. Shaking his head remorsefully but comically, Cyris then said, "You fool! Will you wake up!" Before she threw him out of her dorm, he left quickly. She went over to the couch and flopped down on it. Thinking of Cyris's words, she cried until she slept.

Back in Detroit, Shelly headed to Jewel's house. She drove down to the corner of the street, then got out of her car, and dropped yet another threatening letter in the mailbox for Jewel. She sighed. "Huh, your days are numbered, Jewel. Your days are numbered." She chuckled and said to herself, "Sorry." She got back into her car and drove off happily.

May 15 had arrived. Shelly was still living with Julian, and lovely Brandie had just graduated. After the ceremony, she searched the California auditorium for her mom. Suddenly, she slowed as she saw her mom seated by and talking with a very attractive African-American male. Brandie being only eight years old when he left, nevertheless, recognized the man right away. She approached the two individuals. "Daddy?" she asked as she walked up to the both of them. They were deep in conversation and didn't even notice the graduate who was approaching them. There was first an awkward silence when Brandie walked up to her mom and dad.

"Dee Dee?" said Jarrod Charles. Tears started to fill both his and Brandie's eyes.

She said calmly, "Yes, Daddy, it's me."

Jarrod grabbed Brandie and hugged her intensely, unleashing the last fifteen years of missed hugs that he hadn't received.

"Oh my God! Daddy!" shouted a now crying Brandie. "I wanted you to come, but we, Mom and I didn't know where you were." Tears dropped from her eyes onto his Armani suit. His tears also drenched the shoulders of her gown.

He then said, choked up and breathless, "My little girl! Whe...where's the limp? I hardly recognized you." She didn't comment. She just kept crying tears of joy. He then said, "Your mom knows where I've been. She's known since last month, when I phoned her."

Brandie let go of her embrace with her father. Looking confused, she stammered, "But how? Mom, you said you didn't know where he...."

Corina interrupted Brandie's puzzlement, putting her arm around her shoulder. "We wanted to surprise you honey. Your father and I are thinking of getting back together."

"Oh, Mom, Dad, that's great!" shouted Brandie. She smiled at her mom and then her dad.

"Come on, puddin', I'm taking you and Corina out to dinner."

Brandie said, "That's wonderful, Dad, let's go!" She took off up the aisleway, then looked back at Jarrod. "Hey, Mom didn't tell you. The doctors out here, along with a lot of physical exercise, helped to improve my physical condition. I no longer limp."

Jarrod joyously said, "Congratulations baby, I'm so happy for you. You came to California and became a real Soul Train dancer." Jarrod and Corina continued to follow Brandie out of the auditorium.

Brandie retorted sarcastically, "Really, Dad, Soul Train dancer? Me? I highly doubt that."

Corina remarked, "Well, Dee Dee, you have changed from that eight-year-old flower child your father remembered." Approaching Jarrod's car, she proudly caressed Brandie's long reddish-brown hair. "You certainly don't look like that hippie seventeen-year-old daughter who left my home six years ago.

Brandie laughed. "Oh, I'm still a hippie at heart, trust me." She opened the car door. "I had to go through a lot of extensive therapy and exercise in California, Mom and Dad and...." She did a little dance. "Voila! Here I am." She held out her arms in a dance-like manner and laughed. They all got in the car laughing and pulled off.

At the restaurant, Jarrod pulled out a chair for his wife and daughter. He then went and sat down at the table himself, smiling and looking at his daughter. "Dee Dee, I have a surprise for you."

Brandie asked, "What is it, Dad? Where is it?" She was excited by her dad's statement.

He took a sip of water from the glass the waiter had just set on the table and said calmly, "Well, Dee Dee...Corina." He looked at both women as he mentioned their names. "For the last couple of years, I've been starting a record company."

Corina disgustedly said, "Another business venture, huh, Jarrod?"

He rolled his eyes, smiled, and said, "It's a graduation present for Dee Dee." he corrected himself. "I mean, for Brandie."

She shouted, "What! Are you serious? For me!" Her eyes were wide with excitement.

Corina gasped, "Oh my God." Her mouth remained opened in total shock.

Jarrod said joyously, "Yeah, the name of it is 'Dee's Records.'" He paused and bit down on his lip. "I already have a few artists on the label. They're not major, but they have potential and with Dee's records, I expect all of my artists to go to the top of the charts within the next couple of years." Brandie, looking very interested, was totally attentive to her father's words. He continued, "I already have The Landers, Tianna, and Crosswinds, a white funk band you'll soon be hearing about."

Brandie excitedly exclaimed, "You've got Tianna on your label? She's great! I've got her album." Her eyes widened again. She then said in amazement, "Oh my God! I did see the Dee's Record label on the album, but...." She paused. "Oh, Daddy! I had no idea it was yours."

Jarrod laughed. "It's not mine, sweetie, it's yours. And with my help, we're going to make Dee's Record Company the biggest around.

Corina observed, "Well, Brandie, it's time to put that master's degree in business and music to work, huh baby?"

Brandie smiled and ran her fingers through her reddish hair. She said to Corina, "Yeah, I guess it is." She took a deep breath and said, "I've always wanted to work for a record company, but I never thought I would own my own company." She laughed. "Oh well...time to get to work."

The waiter returned to their table and took their order. After all three of them had ordered, Brandie frowned in deep thought. She then said, "Jewel! Rock star Jewel. I went to school with him."

Jarrod raised his eyebrows and Corina sighed and said lowly, "Oh no."

Brandie excitedly continued, "I read that he hasn't been signed to a record company." She rolled her eyes. "He got fired or something from his old company."

Corina exclaimed, "That nasty sex fiend, no wonder!"

Brandie touched her mother's hand. "Mom, come on. He's a good guy. He'll make Dee's Records number one, I just know it!"

Jarrod remarked, "He's a bit raunchy, Dee Dee, but...."

Brandie interrupted him. "He'll be perfect!"

Jarrod cleared his throat and said, "I don't know, Dee Dee. I'll call your Uncle Everett when we get back to Detroit."

Corina said, sounding surprised, "Phillip? What on earth does Phillip Everett have to do with this? Where is he anyway? I haven't seen him in years."

Jarrod replied, "He's a big-time record agent these days."

Brandie interjected, surprised, "I can't believe it—Uncle Everett, an agent? Whatever happened to his record store?"

Jarrod answered, "He turned his store into his office. He has clients from all over Detroit. He changed his name for business reasons. He told me that Phillip Everett Emery Charles was too damn long."

Corina laughed and said, "Honestly, Jarrod, where did your mom get that name from for him?"

Jarrod replied, "She named him after all of my uncles, all her brothers. Now, he only goes by Phillip Emery." Brandie laughed. "Yeah, like I was saying, he has clients all over, some from Detroit, some from California, everywhere."

At the same time, Brandie and Corina dropped their elbow on the table, cupped their chins in their hands, and looking stunned said, "Unreal!"

Jarrod laughed. "Aw man, I'm back all right! Back with the hippie twins from the sixties." He again laughed. "Anyway, Phillip has a lot of info on the rock stars. He'll tell us if this...this Jewel is worth our time. He'll tell us if he's just another doped-up punk rock star."

Corina then said, sarcastically, "The latter is probably true."

Brandie again rolled her eyes. "Mother please! You never really got to know him."

Corina sighed in disgust. She thought of the rude young man who broke her daughter's heart and took her virginity. "Yeah right, Brandie. I know him just like I know a lot of other punks."

Brandie sighed. Looking as if her mind were on a million dreams, she said happily, "My own record company! Far out!" The waiter soon returned with their orders.

When the Charles's returned to Detroit, not only did they find out from Phillip Emery Jewel's whereabouts and what he was up to, they also found out that Phillip was his agent.

Chapter Thirty-four

Back in Belleville, Michigan, Shelly arrived at Julian's home at 7:35 P.M. Artie was again leaving the house as she entered the tall iron gate. "Hey, Shelly," he said as he walked to the gate. He unlocked it for her. "Good to see you. Julian's having another one of his depressed days. He's been locked up in his room playing the guitar all day."

She swallowed and said, "What he needs to do is to start performing again. It's not good, his staying in that house all the time."

Artie sighed and agreed with Shelly. "Yeah, all he's been doing is sitting around playing that damn guitar and writing sad love songs."

She asserted, "He's not doing himself or his fans any good just hiding away in that house like that."

Artie sighed again. "You're right, Shelly. But what he really needs is a good woman." Artie paused and walked out of the gate. As he was locking it, he looked back at Shelly, who was still standing on the walkway. "A wife, Shelly.... He needs a wife." He repeated, "Jewel needs a wife."

She bit down on her bottom lip, wondering if Artie was implying what she thought he was.

Artie, looking between the bars of the security gate, said, "He needs a woman who really loves him." He paused. "Oh, sure, he's gone out with a few women, but it's just to pass the time anyway. He isn't serious about any of them." He chuckled. "The guy hasn't been serious about women for as long as I've known him."

Shelly asked seriously, "Why? Is he gay or something?" Artie laughed. "Nah, it's nothing like that. It's just...."

She interrupted, "It's just what?" She was now very interested in what he had to say about Jewel.

He sighed, ran his fingers through his hair, and said uneasily, "I guess...." He frowned and then continued, "Well...Julian has always talked to me about some girl he went to school with. He said she had red hair." She frowned and folded her arms as he reflected, "Julian told me that she was the only girl he really ever loved...been in love with."

Shelly mumbled, "That fool, Brandie, no doubt."

Artie didn't hear her mumbled words. "All you have to do, Shelly, is make him fall in love with you." She stared blankly at him without commenting. "I know you care about him, and I think he cares about you, too." He chuckled. "Why else would he let you live here for so long?" Artie then walked away from the gate and got into his black BMW and pulled out.

Shelly smiled wickedly in deep thought. "Hmm, this is going to be easier than I thought it would be...with the help of that dumb bodyguard." She then walked up the walkway humming gleefully and went inside Jewel's house.

"Julian...Julian, honey! I'm home!" she yelled. She then headed upstairs to his bedroom. She knocked twice, then opened the wooden door. "Hello, Jewel."

She then walked into his room. "Why are you couped up inside this bedroom on such a beautiful day? she asked vivaciously.

Twenty-four-year-old Julian lay on his full-sized bed. The one hundred watt stereo played lowly in his bedroom. He glared at Shelly and frowned. "I don't think I have to explain my every movement to you," he retorted, sounding agitated by her question.

Shelly, ignoring Julian's mood, took off her coat and threw it on the chair in the corner of his room. She then said, "It was a beautiful day...a little cold, but beautiful." She then stripped nude very provocatively. His green eyes widened. She looked at him. He was staring at her nude body. She then walked over to him and said, "Come on, Jewel, make love to me." He remained silent. His eyes were caressing her shapely form. She then danced closer to him and grabbed his hand, saying, "Please, Jewel...dance with me."

Julian grabbed her, sat her on his lap, and kissed her very passionately. They kissed for several seconds. Finally, he pulled back from her kiss. Exhausted, he said, caressing her cheek, "I'd better stop." His voice was sounding deep and a little raspy.

Shelly got off of his lap smiling, and said snidely, "You've always wanted me Julian...." He stared at her blankly, but said nothing. She continued, "And you want me now. So...why don't you stop all of this self-righteous bullshit and get undressed." She caressed his cheek, then walked over toward the bathroom.

Julian stared at her pale body with devilish eyes. However he still didn't say anything. He was imagining her naked breast pointing out in front of her.

Shelly entered the bathroom. Looking in the mirror, she ran her fingers through her shiny gold hair, then called to him, "I'm gonna take a bath, honey. Come on...join me."

Jewel replied, "No thanks, doll. You go right ahead. I'll be out here waiting for you."

Shelly again yelled to him, "Get ready, baby. When I get out of here, we're gonna finish the dope in my purse and you're gonna have the best fucking night that you've ever had." She raised her eyebrows and scratched her head. "How many years has it been since you've had a woman anyway, Jewel?" She giggled and stepped into the bath.

Jewel yelled to her, "I've been celibate for quite awhile now...it doesn't really matter!" She turned on the water. He breathed in deeply, thinking about her statement of him having the best fucking night that he's ever had. He had been celibate and loving it. Drug use wasn't his scene either. Yeah, Shelly looked good. Her lips tasted divine, he thought. But he was tired of affairs that didn't go anywhere. He didn't love her...so what the hell was he about to do, he thought.

He stood up, reached into his pants pockets, and pulled out the gold cards he had made when he first vowed celibacy. He found a verse and left it on top of Shelly's clothing that was in a pile on the floor. He dropped the card on top of her clothing and left the room. The card read, "Blessed is the man that walketh not in the counsel of the ungodly, nor standeth in the way of sinners, nor sitteth in the seat of the scornful. But his delight is in the law of the Lord, and in his law doeth he meditate day and night." On the other side of the card was Julian's name and number. These kind of events had happened several times since his slight nervous breakdown and his declaration to stay celibate.

Shelly came out of the bathroom. She looked around the room. After realizing that he wasn't there, she said, "Damn!" then started picking up her clothes from the floor. She noticed the gold card that was on top of them. She picked it up and read what was on it. After reading the card, she chuckled, then balled up the card and said, "Fool." She smiled and tossed the card in the small wastebasket that was in his room. Even though she found his actions sort of peculiar, they also intrigued her.

It was now July 31, 1994. Shelly found Julian's being enigmatic fascinating. The more she tried to get with him, the stronger his will became. However they had seemingly become best friends. Even though she had the sizzling hots for him, he treated her as only a good friend. She still stuck by him, no matter what. She respected his privacy, his lifestyle, and his glamorous life.

Julian and Artie sat in Jewel's lavish living room. "Jewel, you're not getting any younger," said Artie.

Julian stood up from the couch and said, "So...what does that mean?"

Artie replied, "I know you don't want to hear this, but I think that you should think about getting married to Shelly Nohl."

Julian gasped. "What?"

Artie continued, "She's in love with you, Julian." Jewel frowned as he stared out of the window. "She's been here for months now. She does the cooking and cleaning for you. Man...that's wife material, if you ask me."

Jewel rolled his eyes in disgust. "I don't love her, Artie."

Artie retorted, "She loves you, though. She's been here all this time just trying to prove it to you."

Julian laughed. "She's in love with my lifestyle, Artie. I seriously doubt that she's in love with me.

Artie shouted, "So...you don't love her and you think that she don't love you. Make her love you! Love will happen for the both of you, Jewel...trust me." He then went to his room, and Julian flopped down on the couch tiredly.

The next day, when Shelly came home from her supposed job, Jewel asked her to marry him. She accepted right away. A few days later, he went and bought a diamond ring. Meanwhile, she slowly withdrew money that was in their joint bank account. Julian, sticking to his guns and just being Jewel, continued his vow not to be intimate until marriage. Therefore Shelly continued to sleep in the guest bedroom.

Shelly still wanted to be intimate with Jewel, but nothing more was ever done than heavy kissing in the house of Julian Parr. The money she withdrew from the joint bank account she deposited into her account with Ricky.

It was now August 15, 1994. Artie again left the house. Julian went over to sit on the couch, Shelly excitedly following behind him. "We haven't discussed when or where, Jewel. I have so many things to do. I have to go see about getting a dress."

Julian sighed and said, "Hold up Shell, hold up. We're going to have a long engagement.

Shelly breathed in deeply, disappointed by his statement. "Sure, baby, whatever you say," she said humbly, giving in. She then wrapped her arms around Julian's neck and said, "I am so happy. We're going to have a wonderful life together." She kissed him on the cheek and on the lips.

Julian, looking nonchalant, sighed. He then sat up and grabbed the envelope on the table in front of him. He was ignoring her signs of affection and trying to be intimate. He commented, "I received another death threat today."

Shelly disorientedly mumbled, "Hmm, wha...what, honey?"

Julian angrily stood up and shouted, "Damn it, Shelly! Someone is threatening to kill me and all you want to do is screw around."

Shelly sighed. "All right, all right. Let me see the letter?" All thoughts of being romantic with Julian were now gone.

Julian handed her the letter. It read, "I'll get you, you show off sissy. You're a danger to today's kids and the world! Bang! bang! Faggot, you're dead."

"Oh my God! What are you going to do?" said a stunned Shelly.

Julian sighed and sat down beside Shelly. "I don't know. I'm not even performing or recording and they're after my ass."

"Oh my poor baby. This is horrible," she said. She then laid her head on his shoulder lovingly.

For months after their engagement, all Shelly did was spend his money. She began showing her true colors, and her change of attitude often got on Jewel's nerves as they lounged around the house. All she now seemed interested in was his bank account, stocks, and bonds. Her dope use had ceased, but her "You got money, so let me spend it" attitude drove him crazy. He often became sad and depressed, thinking, My God, this is gonna be my...my wife? He would then sigh and say, "Well, at least I won't be alone."

Chapter Thirty-five

It was now September 10, 1994. Shelly had come home at 7:00 A.M. in the same clothes she had worn the day before. She yelled to Julian, "I had to work over again!" She had just come back from an intense evening with Ricky. They had made love the entire day before, resulting in Shelly falling asleep and not waking up until five o'clock that morning. She headed for her bedroom in the outfit that she had purchased on Julian's credit card the week before. She had bought an entire wardrobe, in fact, with his credit cards. She took off her clothes, threw them on the floor, and got into bed. Julian was lying in his bedroom half-asleep when she entered the house. He found the fact that she worked overtime so often odd, however, he didn't question her about it. Groggily, he just yelled to her, "Okay, sweet dreams."

The sun was shining into Jewel's bedroom window. He covered his head completely with the covers to block out the sun. He was about to drift off again when the phone began to ring. He waited for her to answer the phone in her room, but after the phone rang several times, he angrily threw the covers off of him. He rolled his eyes and picked up the receiver. His agent, Phillip Emery, was on the line. Phillip, happily said, "Good morning, Jewel. Long time, no see."

Julian just moaned, "Uhn-uhn."

Phillip continued, "I got a call from a record company that was interested in you."

Julian yawned and said, "What company is it?"

Phillip said, "Uh...it's a fairly new company, Julian." He was looking through the papers on his desk for the notepad where he had written the record company's name. Finally he found the pad and said, "Dee's...Dee's Records."

Julian was still lounging in bed. He yawned again and said, "Never heard of it."

Phillip retorted, "Well, my boy, they've heard of you and they want you." Pausing, he continued, "Look! You haven't done anything for months now. You've been out of work long enough, Julian. Listen, you don't have any concert dates—in fact, I'm sure that the only dates you are keeping are with a different woman every night."

"Screw you, Phillip," said Julian, now getting angry. "It's none of your damn business anyway. But if you must know, I haven't gotten laid since last March."

Phil disgustedly said, "Yeah, well, Julian. What about the company? Do you think you want to see what they are about?"

Julian sighed. "Yeah man. Give me the dude's name and number. I'll give him a call."

Phillip did exactly that, and both he and Julian hung up the phone.

However Julian didn't call Dee's Records that day. He fell back to sleep, only to be wakened forty minutes later by the phone ringing again. He sat up on the side of the bed, tiredly rubbed his eyes, and exclaimed, "Damn, why the hell doesn't she answer the ph...." He didn't finish his rage. He just picked up the ringing phone's receiver and grunted, "Yeah, who is it?"

"Hi, " said the cheerful-voiced, soft-spoken woman on the other end of the line.

An irritated Julian snapped, "You must be crazy, to be calling at this time of the morning."

The woman laughed. "Good one, Jul...." She cleared her throat and corrected herself. "I mean, Mr. Parr." She spoke in a very proper and professional manner, in a kooky sort of way.

He asked, "Who the hell is this?" sounding more curious than angry.

The young woman replied, "I'm...co-manager of Dee's Records." Julian was silent. "My name is Br...Bread, Bread Stockwood. The manager...Mr. Chuck...Jarrod Chuck, wanted me to set up an appointment with you...for say, uh, tomorrow at 8:00 A.M." Julian shook his hair away from his face and said, "I don't get out of bed until noon. And if you're in bed with me, I won't be getting out until day after tomorrow."

The woman laughed. "Same old Jul...." She corrected herself again and said, "Same old jargon. Same old rock star jargon."

Jewel cleared his throat, thinking, What a freakin' flake. "I'll be there," he said in a deep, clear, and sexy voice.

"That'll be grand," she said excitedly.

She was about to hang up the phone when Julian said quickly, "Hey! Before you go, what are you on? Uppers or something?" He sounded sarcastic but serious. The woman was silent. "Uh...What was your name again?"

She replied, "Bread, Bread Stockwood."

Julian chuckled. "Bread? What the hell kind of name is Bread?" The woman was still silent. Julian then asked jokingly, 'And Stockwood? No, no, sweetheart, I take my question back. You're not the one on drugs, your parents must have been, naming you Bread Stockwood."

The young woman said sternly, "Mr. Parr, my parents were not on drugs and neither am I."

Julian retorted, 'Well, I don't know, something weird was going on." He spoke in a joking manner.

The young woman wanted to burst out laughing herself, but she kept her cool demeanor. "My father's last name is Woodstock and his father's last name is, too. Our family name goes back a long way."

Julian said, laughing, "You mean your last name is actually Woodstock? Yeah, your family name goes back a long way all right...back to New York in 1970, during Woodstock with Hendrix and all the other rockers."

Bread laughed also. "Good one, Mr. Parr. Are you sure you aren't in the wrong profession?"

Julian replied, "Naw, are you sure your parents weren't hungry when they named you Bread?"

The young woman, sounding serious, said, "My name is food for thought, but yours is a materialistic object—Jewel."

"Naw though, you're cool. Don't get all hot under the toaster. My mom and dad use to call me Jewel when I was a kid. That's where my stage name comes from." He ran his fingers through his hair and frowned. "This chick I used to know called me her Precious Jewel...and I think that's going to be the name of my next album. Cool, huh?"

The woman on the other end of the line was all choked up and emotional. She just had to ask, her voice cracking from held back tears, "Whatever happened to the girl who used to call you Precious Jewel?" Julian was once again silent. "Huh? Just like all musicians, you used her and dumped her didn't you?" Bread tried not to sound angry or too close to the question.

Julian, however, did sound angry. "I'm not all musicians, Ms. Woodstock or Stockwood, whatever the hell your name is."

The woman lowly said, "It's Stockwood. I changed it for my career."

Julian, sounding as if he hadn't heard Ms. Stockwood's last statement, continued, "I loved her. Hell, I still love her." He paused. "I left her because she was planning out my life for me. Damn, I didn't even know who I was or what life was back then." She listened intensely. "I'm sure she thought I left because she wasn't good enough for me. The truth is...."

The woman on the other end of the phone interrupted. "Yes, the truth is what?" Anticipation was getting the best of her. She edged and prompted him for more information. He was silent for a moment, thinking how he had been pouring his heart out to this woman he didn't even know. Are you crazy or what? You're pouring out your heart to a freakin' stranger, thought Julian. He then lazily said, answering Bread's persistent question, "...The truth is that you should get you some business and stay out of mine!" He hung up.

The young woman on the other end of the line still held her receiver. She said low and tearfully, "Goodbye, Julian." Jarrod Charles came into his office. Brandie, his co-manager, said, "I'm glad you're doing this for Jewel, Daddy. You won't be sorry. Jewel's a good talent, a little wild and eccentric, but he's being himself." Jarrod looked at her strangely. "Isn't that the kind of company you wanted to build? Real musicians, making real music."

Jarrod caressed her cheek and said, "I don't know how I could have left you and your mom. You're my love, my life."

She replied sternly, "No...no, for a while, you're just my partner."

Jarrod shook his head, saying, "You know, I don't like this, but anything for you, baby." Brandie smiled. "I've worked hard for Dee's Records to be a success and if we start losing money or business because of your secrets, I'm letting the cat out of the bag." He raised his eyebrows. "You and my brother's crazy ideas...I must be crazy, too."

Brandie looked at him and said, "We won't lose anything, Dad. Just handle it my way for a while." She looked up at him with her big brown eyes, batting profusely.

Jarrod said, "You know I can't resist when you bat those loving eyes. This Jewel...must be a diamond."

Brandie said, "Oh...he is, he is. Jewel must never know who I am...until I tell you it's all right to tell him. He must only know that my name is Bread Stockwood and I am your partner...your co-manager." She frowned. "He will never see me, he can't! I just know how he would react."

She looked puzzled and thought back to her conversation with Julian. She thought about his statement about her trying to run his life when they were younger. She wondered if he would still feel the same way now if he knew she was the one responsible for Dee's Records contacting him.

Chapter Thirty-six

Later that night, Julian and Shelly were sitting on the couch. He had informed her of his good news. "I'm so glad you got a chance to sign with a second company, Julian," she said.

Julian yawned. "Yeah, now I can put some of those songs I have been writing to use."

Shelly said happily, "More millions in the bank, baby!"

Julian chuckled. "I write for the public, not for profit."

Shelly, giving in, said, "All right, baby, whatever you say." She put her arms around his neck. "I want you so much, baby. Make love to me tonight. We've been engaged for weeks now and you haven't even touched me."

Julian grabbed her and kissed her passionately and unexpectedly. Hungrily he moaned, "Oh baby, come on. I need you so much."

He and Shelly headed to her bedroom, the guestroom. She sat down on her bed as he quickly pulled off his shirt. His bare, hairy chest was exposed and inviting. She stood and ran her fingers through his chest hair wildly. "Oh God, I've wanted you for so long," she said. Her hand then lowered beneath his waistband.

"Oh yes, Shelly, yes," moaned Julian. He then pulled down her skirt, and it fell to the floor. She was now bare from the waist down. She stepped out of her skirt and kicked the skirt away as she continued to massage him. He heatedly kissed her neck. "Oh yeah, oh Shelly, more baby, more." He then caressed her curvaceous hips.

"Let's take these clothes off and get in bed," she said.

"Yeah...yeah," he said breathlessly. He then worked his hands up under her blouse, gently feeling her small, tempting breasts.

"Come on baby, let's get in bed," she said, prompting him.

Julian was licking and kissing Shelly's neck when his eyes widened. "No...oh no! We've got to stop this!" he shouted. He pulled his hands away from her body. "No, it's not right yet! I have to...I have to feel it."

Shelly seductively said, "I'm right here. You can feel me now, Jewel. I'm right here."

Julian sighed. "Don't get me wrong—you're exciting as hell, but I'm not in...." He again changed his approach in dealing with her. "I just want to wait until we're married before we have sex again." He added, "...In respect for you and for God."

Julian left her soon after their almost encounter. He went into his studio and wrote a new tune and played the tune on his guitar soon after writing it. Shelly just pouted and went back into the living room and sat on the couch. She had an angry look on her face.

The next morning, Julian walked into Dee's Records on O'Connor Street. It was eight o'clock on the dot. The receptionist, a thin brunette in her middle twenties, squealed, "Oh my God! Jewel, I'm your biggest fan! I've been looking forward to this meeting every since Mr. Chuck told me he had an appointment with you today." The receptionist ran her fingers through her straight, short, styled hair and looked at Julian, exclaiming, "Can I have your autograph?" Before Julian could answer, the star-struck receptionist said, "You look even better in person."

Julian, in his usual deep and seductive tone, said, picking up the pen on her desk, "I'd look even better if you...." He didn't finish his habitual and true to character flirtation. He looked at the receptionist with his big green eyes for a few moments, then began signing the scratch pad on her desk. Artie, who was standing by Jewel, chuckled slightly.

Carol, the receptionist, then pushed the desk intercom and excitedly said, "Mr. Chuck, Jewel is here."

Phillip Emery, who also was there with Jewel, said in a low voice, "What am I? A ghost?" Jewel laughed.

Jarrod Chuck said happily, "Thanks, Carol. Send him in, please."

Carol told Julian, "You can go in now."

Julian finished signing the receptionist's autograph. He had gotten her name from the name plate that was on her desk. He smiled at her, his big green eyes flickering shyly. He then said, "Thanks Carol," and dropped his gold-colored card on her desk. The three men left the receptionist's office and entered Jarrod's office.

Carol picked up the autograph and smiled at the inscription Julian had written: "To Carol, the cute fox behind the desk. May your life be enraptured in...Jewel!" She then noticed the medium-sized card he had dropped beside the autograph., She picked it up and read, "Let your conversation be without covetousness, and be content with such things as ye hath, for he has said, I will never leave thee or forsake thee."

Julian sat down in the chair on the right side of Phillip Emery. Both men were seated in front of Jarrod's desk. Jarrod cleared his throat and said properly, "So...you're Jewel." Jewel shook his head to the side, slinging his long black hair away from his face. He did not comment. Jarrod Chuck, being Jewel's agent's brother, looked at Phillip Emery. "The boy's got the look, Phil." He stood and walked around his desk, slapping Jewel on the shoulder. "He's got the look, definitely. He's just what Dee's Records needs."

Jewel's agent added, "He's the ticket, all right, for putting you guys on top."

Jarrod, looking calm, then said to Jewel, "I've heard your songs. I like your work. You're how old now?"

Jewel cleared his throat and said, "I'm twenty-four." His voice was deep and masculine as usual.

Mr. Chuck's eyes widened. He hit his desk with his fist and exclaimed excitedly, "This is what we're looking for! Hot damn! A young, open-minded man." Julian stared at him blankly. Phillip sat quietly, observing the collaboration of his client and Dee's Records. Jarrod then said, "Son, you're me twenty years ago."

Julian agreed. "Yeah."

Jarrod continued excitedly, "Sure, from what I've seen and heard of you, you've got spunk, guts." He paused. "And a damn good, open mind." Julian listened to the forty-three-year-old man intensely. Jarrod was a thin and slightly balding middle-aged man. He cupped his chin in his hand and frowned. He quickly said, "That's what we need, a different approach. It's just what Dee's

Records needs to take us to the top. We need a different sound...a spunky, I-don't-give-a-damn sound." Jarrod stood up from his chair. "We look at the screwed-up world and we write about it. Forget the stuck-ups who want to blame the music for corrupting their kids. In all actuality, it's really them, the parents' fault."

Julian nodded his head in agreement and said solemnly, "You're right."

Jarrod then said excitedly, "I know I'm right. The kids today aren't stupid. It's the parents wearing the rose-colored glasses who are the stupid ones."

Julian liked what Jarrod Chuck was saying, yet he still didn't comment.

Jarrod resumed, "Sure, sometimes a little discretion won't hurt, but sometimes maybe parents need to talk to their kids about what's really going on in the world. Instead of school...breakfast, lunch, and dinner."

Julian then said, changing the subject, "I want total control of the music that I create. And I only sing my music...my own songs."

Jarrod sat back in his swivel chair and said, "You know what you want, my boy. You're just like I was at that age. And I heard from Bran...." Mr. Chuck quickly changed the subject, knowing he almost blew Brandie's secret. "I, uh, head that you're quite the ladies man." Julian didn't comment. "So was I.... It almost cost me my marriage." Jarrod walked over to his desk and took out the contract papers. He handed them to Jewel, who in turn handed them to Phil.

Julian then said sternly, "We'll get back with you." He stood up, preparing to leave.

Phillip looked slightly at the contract, then at his brother. He winked his eye and said, "Uh...yeah Jarrod, you'll be hearing from us soon. Just give us time to look over the contract. We'll be in touch." Julian walked out of Jarrod's office. Phillip gave his brother the look of approval, then followed Julian out of the office.

"Goodbye, Jewel," said Carol. She was seated behind her desk typing as Jewel came out of Jarrod's office.

"Stay real," commented Jewel. Carol smiled briefly. Rock star Jewel, followed by Phillip Emery, then left the building. They got into the waiting limousine and drove off.

Brandie was parked down the street from Dee's Records. She saw Julian when he left the building and pulled off in his limousine. Excitedly, Brandie got out of her red car and ran into Dee's Records. "Hello, Carol!"

Carol shouted, "Hello, Bread! Mr. Chuck is in his office."

Brandie, before hearing all of Carol's statement, had already gone into her father's office and closed the door. Carol was a fairly new receptionist at Dee's Records and didn't know Brandie was Jarrod Chuck's daughter. She thought Brandie was just another employee, another idea of Brandie's to obtain annuity from Julian. She didn't want anyone to blow her cover until she was ready, or at least she knew how she truly felt about Julian Phalan Parr. "Hi Dad, how's it going?" asked Brandie as she entered Jarrod's office. She sat down in the chair in front of his desk.

"Fine...fine, Dee Dee. I think we've got a winner with your friend, Julian," said Jarrod. He then stood up from his chair. "Sorry honey, but I have a meeting with the band to get to." He added, "I'm gonna tell them about our, hopefully, new artist on the label, Jewel." He soon left Dee's Records.

Brandie stood up, then walked around her father's desk. She flopped down in his large swivel chair. She was looking over papers and neatening up the desk. She soon left Dee's Records for the day.

Chapter Thirty-seven

The next morning at 10:00 A.M. the phone rang at Dee's Records. Carol answered happily, "Hello, Dee's Records."

Phillip asked, "Yes, is Jarrod in?"

Carol replied, "No, I'm sorry he hasn't come in yet. However, his assistant is in."

Excitedly Phillip said, "Brand—I mean, Bread. Yes, let me speak to her."

"Yes sir," stated Carol. She then paged Bread's office.

Brandie answered, saying, "Yeah Carol, what is it?"

"You have a call on line one," replied Carol.

Bread hesitantly switched over to line one. "Hello, this is Bread."

Phillip shouted, "Don't sound so blue, child! Julian wants to sign with your record company!"

Brandie chuckled. "Oh...that's wonderful, Phil."

Phillip asked, "Well, when can we make arrangements? I just left his home and Jewel's ready to start jamming again."

"Well, Jarrod will be in at noon. Let's make it 1:30 today. Can you and Jewel be here then?" asked Brandie. She was sounding her most professional.

Phillip replied, "No problem, my niece. We'll see you then."

Brandie agitatedly said, "No...you won't see me here, Phillip! And remember, I'm not your niece. I'm Bread Stockwood, co-manager of Dee's Records."

"Don't get all bent out of shape, Brandie sugar. Wow! You must have it bad for Mr. Julian Parr."

Brandie angrily said, "Look! My name is not Brandie." Her voice lowered a little. "Call me Bread. And I don't have it bad for Jewel! I just don't want him to know that I'm responsible for him being with Dee's Records, you got it?"

Phillip chuckled, remembering. "Oh yeah...whatever. Julian must have laid you good." He again laughed.

Angrily, Brandie said, "Just make sure he's here at 1:30." She then hung up the phone. Phillip was still laughing as he hung up the phone as well.

Jarrod walked into the office. "What is going on?" he asked. "I could hear you shouting from my office."

Brandie was in the back office as she spoke to Phil. She stood up as Jarrod came into the office, then kissed him on the cheek, and said, "Nothing's going on, Dad. Jewel will be here at 1:30 to sign with our company."

"Hey! That's great!" shouted Jarrod.

Brandie then said, grabbing her purse, "Yeah, it's great, but I have to go." She walked over to the door, opened it, and said, "See ya!" then left.

Julian and Phillip arrived at Dee's Records at 1:25 P.M. They discussed legal formalities with Jarrod, copies of the contract were signed, and the collaboration between Julian Parr and Dee's Records was finally made. "I think we're in for an excellent venture, Jewel." Jarrod then shook Julian's hand. He also shook his brother, Phillip Emery's, hand.

Julian looked around the office. He then asked, "Where's your co-manager, Bread...Bread Stockwood? I talked to her on the phone the other day."

Jarrod had a strange look on his face. "Bread is rarely here. She's constantly going from here to there trying to recruit new talent."

Julian frowned slightly, then sighed. "Oh well, I guess I'll meet her one of these days.

Jarrod, avoiding speaking about Brandie, then said quickly, "Oh yeah, Jewel, I've got the perfect backup band for you, my boy." Julian was unaware that Phillip and Jarrod were brothers as Jarrod said, "I'll take you to meet with them tomorrow, say noonish?" A little while later, Jewel and Phil left Dee's Records.

That night at 9:00 P.M., Brandie called Jewel's home. He wasn't asleep yet, writing a song for a new album idea that he had. In his bedroom, he answered the phone after the third ring. He had thought Shelly was going to answer the phone in her room, but as usual she didn't

Brandie said, after Jewel answered the phone, "Hello, Jewel. Welcome aboard Dee's Record Company."

Julian replied, "Hello...Bread Woodstock—I mean Stockwood, right?"

She said, "Yes, it's me. Jarrod told me you were now signed with Dee's Records."

"Yeah, why weren't you there? I was looking forward to meeting you," said Jewel.

Brandie quickly stated, "I'm sure we will meet eventually."

Julian added, "Maybe it's for the best that we didn't meet Bread. I am an engaged man." Julian laughed slightly.

Brandie also laughed. "Yeah right, Julian. This is a first—you're engaged?"

Julian, ignoring Bread's last statement, said, "Jarrod told me he knew a cool backup band for me. Have you heard them? Are they any good?"

Brandie said excitedly, "Yes, I know the band he's referring to. They're very good. Their name is Granite.

Julian went on, "I get to meet them tomorrow. Why don't you and I meet there?"

Brandie nervously replied, "I...I don't know Julian. I'll try to make it." She added, "Phil told me about your receiving death threats. Now that you're with Dee's Records, we'll see what we can do about it."

Julian chuckled. "I wish you luck. This sick bastard wants me dead."

"Oh don't say that, you'll be fine," she said.

Julian then asked, in his deep voice, "What do you care, anyway? You're afraid to meet me. I can't seem to take my mind off of those threatening letters." Brandie was silent. "Are you just afraid to meet me or is it people in general?"

Brandie replied, "No...no, it's not that, Julian. It's just...it's...I can't."

Julian then said, getting frustrated, "Goodbye, stranger. And I do mean strange."

Brandie chuckled. "Goodbye, Jewel."

The next day at noon Brandie walked into Dee's Records. As soon as she walked into the door, Carol said, "Hi, Bread. Mr. Chuck will be out of the office all day. He and Jewel went down to the Cobb Stadium to see the rock band, Granite." Brandie stared at the girl blankly, who then said snidely, "I didn't think you knew that since you're hardly ever here, Bread."

Brandie frowned. "Yes, yes, I knew they were going to see the band. I spoke to my fa...." She quickly corrected her sentence. "To my...to Mr. Chuck this morning."

Carol placed a stack of typed letters in her desk drawer and said sarcastically, "Well, since you're hardly ever here, I didn't think you knew." Brandie, getting fed up with Carol, rolled her eyes. The receptionist continued, "I guess now you'll finally get to use that adjoining office of yours." She added snidely, "I always thought that one day I would be...should be the one to get that office. I don't see why Jarrod needs a co-manager when I am the one who does all of the extra work for him."

Brandie angrily retorted, "I talked to Mr. Chuck this morning Carol. He doesn't need you...today, so why don't you go home."

Carol chuckled. "Well, I guess I could use a day off."

Brandie breathed deeply and said calmly, "Fine, you can take the rest of the day off. I'll look after things around here.

Carol giddily said, "What a job! First I get to meet rock star Jewel, and now I'm getting half a day off."

Brandie headed back to her office and sat at her desk doing minor paperwork.

Carol walked back to Brandie's office and said, "I'm going to tidy up my desk, and then I'm outta here. Thanks for giving me the day off." She turned around and headed for the door. Brandie hadn't commented. Carol looked back at her and said, "You haven't met rock star Jewel yet, have you, Bread?"

Brandie then quietly said, "Uh...no, I don't know, Jewel." She quickly looked away. She knew that she wasn't a good liar and she didn't want Carol to suspect anything.

Carol opened the door to her office, then happily told her, 'Well, Bread, he's a real Jewel. You should stick around. Maybe you'll meet him." She chuckled. "I'm going home for the day." She left Brandie's office, closing the door behind her.

Brandie sighed. She then disgustedly said to herself, "Goodbye and good riddance," after Carol left her office. She continued to straighten up the papers on her desk, then heard voices coming from the front room.

"Hi, Miss...Jewel had an appointment today with Mr. Chuck. Is he finished yet? I was going to take him to lunch," said the giddy sounding female.

Brandie listened as Carol replied, "No, I'm about to leave. Jewel left with Mr. Chuck hours ago."

Brandie continued to listen intently as the other female said angrily, "Damn! I don't believe this. He told me his meeting was at eleven o'clock this morning. I'm Shelly, his finance.

Brandie, who was still listening gasped lowly, "Oh no, his fiancé. He was telling the truth."

Carol then said, "I'm sorry, but his meeting was at noon, down at the Cobb Arena.

Shelly rolled her eyes, then asked, "Well, may I use your phone?"

Carol thought about Bread being in the back office and said, "Yes, I'm sure that will be okay. I'm on my way out." She then left the building. She hadn't mentioned to Shelly that there was someone else in the building.

After Carol left, Shelly looked around the office, then picked up the phone receiver. "I need a private phone," she whispered to herself. She put the receiver back on the hook and called out, "Hello! Hello! Is any anybody here?" Brandie, who was seated at her desk, ducked down under the desk and didn't answer.

Shelly entered Jarrod Chuck's office. She looked around the room and gleefully murmured, "There's no one here." She then walked into the other door that joined Brandie's office to Jarrod's. She again shouted, "Is anybody here!" then looked around Brandie's office. Brandie stayed hidden under her desk, barely breathing. Shelly muttered, "That fool secretary left me here all by myself," then shouted excitedly, "All right!" She went back up to the front desk.

Brandie silently crawled into her father's office. She was clad in a two-piece silk suit, stockings, and high-heeled shoes. She whispered, "I'm gonna ruin my stockings," and crawled under her father's desk. She had moved closer so that she could hear what Shelly was up to.

Shelly was now seated at the receptionist's desk. She picked up the phone receiver and dialed her apartment. Ricky answered the phone, saying, "Yeah, what is it?"

"Hi, baby! It's Shelly. Jewel's back working again. We're gonna be rich!" shouted Shelly.

Brandie again frowned, then whispered, "Shelly—oh my God, it's Shelly Nohl from high school!"

Shelly continued her conversation with Ricky. "Yeah Rick, Dee's Records.... He signed a million dollar contract with Dee's Records." She then said excitedly, "I know baby, I know. We already have a joint bank account. Each time Jewel makes a deposit, I just go over and make a withdrawal." She chuckled. "Yeah Ricky, I know. I'm always careful. I send him a threatening letter every two weeks. If we don't make him lose his mind first, the murder's going to be easy."

Brandie's eyes widened. She whispered, "Oh my God, they're gonna kill him. I've got to do something." She forgot she was ducked under a desk. As she started to stand, she hit her head on the bottom part of the desk.

The thump alarmed Shelly, who nervously yelled, "Who's there?" Brandie was silent. The office building was eerily silent as well. Shelly then said to Ricky, after hearing no response, "It was nothing. I thought I heard a noise." She listened, then said, "Don't worry, I told you I'm not sleeping with the guy. I just accepted his marriage proposal so that I could have access to his money." Brandie was getting angrier as she heard Shelly's phone conversation. Shelly went on, "Don't worry, Ricky. He's trying to be noble, you know, sort of spiritual. I can take him for everything he's worth." She laughed while relaxing in Carol's leather chair. "The guy is real emotional. Many more of these threats and he'll be in the looney farm, anyway."

Jarrod pulled up outside of the building. Shelly, observing him through the window, said quickly, "I'll talk to you tomorrow, Rick...someone's coming." She hung up the phone and stood up.

Jarrod was approaching the building as she walked out of the door. He stopped her and said, "Is there something I can help you with?"

Shelly quickly said, "I...I was looking for my fiancé, Jewel. But your secretary told me that he'd left."

Jarrod looked at the voluptuous blonde. "Jewel didn't tell me he was engaged."

Shelly batted her eyes quickly and said, "Well, that's because he didn't want all the press people to find out. Well, I have to go." She walked to her car.

Jarrod yelled after her, "Nice meeting you, miss."

Shelly, standing at her car door, yelled, "Oh, of course it is." She then got in her car and drove off.

Jarrod entered Dee's Records. He frowned, noticing that no one was there. He had seen his daughter's car outside and so yelled, 'Dee! Are you still here?"

Brandie got up from under Jarrod's desk. "What...what's going on?" he asked. He had a puzzled look on his face.

Brandie, straightening out her skirt, approached him saying frantically, "They're trying to kill him, Dad! They're trying to kill him!" Tears suddenly came into her eyes.

Jarrod said, "Sit down honey." She sat in her father's chair. He asked her, "Now, who's trying to kill who?" He had an inquisitive look on his face.

Brandie jumped up and ran to the door. "I've got to stop her! I've got to stop them!" she yelled.

Jarrod grabbed his daughter, holding her wrists tightly. "Hold on—what the hell is it, Dee? What's the matter with you?"

Brandie breathed in deeply. She then cried hysterically, "She didn't know I was here. I heard her phone conversation. She wants to kill Julian."

Jarrod had a stunned look on his face as he said, "Oh my God! His fiancé?"

Brandie swallowed hard and said, "Yes, yes! She's the one who's been sending the threatening letters. She and some guy named Ricky. They're planning to swindle Julian out of all his money...and then they plan to kill him."

"My God, Dee Dee, we have to let him know!" shouted Jarrod. He then looked down at his watch. "Damn! I'm late. I have another meeting with the accountant. Honey, tell Jewel...tell him instantly. Call him or something. Just let him know! He's got practice tonight at the arena." Jarrod tapped her on the shoulder and left.

She sat down, preparing to call Jewel. "Oh, how can I do this?" she murmured breathlessly. She then picked up the receiver and dialed Jewel.

He picked up the phone on the first ring and said, "Yo!"

"Julian, this is Bread," she said.

Julian replied in his usual deep and sensuous tone, "Well, well. I thought you would never call. Did you dream about me last night? Are you ready to meet with me personally? You know, there's only so much we can do on the phone." Jewel chuckled.

Brandie, losing her temper, shouted, "Will you shut up! I don't want you anymore. Your fiancé's trying to kill you!"

Julian again laughed. "What are you smoking now? Or sniffing? It's a little early for that isn't it?" He then added curtly, "And when did you ever want me anyway?"

Brandie furiously growled, "Would you get serious? I heard her on the phone today. She...."

Julian's vain existence wouldn't listen to her. He cut off her comment, saying, "I can't believe you!" He slung his hair to his back. Disgustedly he continued, "You're crazy! I guess you're some introvert who doesn't like to deal with people face to face." He chuckled tiredly. "And now, because I told you that I was getting married, you want to tell me that she's trying to kill me! You don't even know her!"

Brandie nervously said, "No, no, that's not it. I saw the girl you told me about. She was in the office today looking for you."

Julian sarcastically and angrily said, "Yeah, I bet she was." He shouted, "How the hell do you know who was in the office! You never go to work anyway!"

Brandie breathed deeply. She was tying to control her temper. "Look, Jewel, I didn't call you to argue. I want to warn you...."

Julian interrupted Brandie and angrily shouted, "Yeah right! Warn me! I think you're some sick groupie manager, who doesn't want to see anyone happy...especially your so-called famous clients. I guess you're so miserable in your own little world that you don't want to see anybody else in love.

Brandie, on the verge of tears, said, 'Look, I just wanted to warn you. I overheard her and someone named...."

Julian again shouted, "So you're not only into lying, you're also into eavesdropping, huh?"

"No, Jewel, I was...." said Brandie.

Julian interrupted Brandie again and asked angrily, "You don't have a boyfriend do you, Ms. Woodstock? And I know you don't have a husband, Ms. fake-name-with-a-voice-to-match."

Brandie, disturbed said, "No...no, but my name is...."

Julian shouted, "Just what I thought! Some freakin' groupie psycho! That's what you are!"

"Jewel, please!" cried Brandie. "You have to listen to...."

Julian cut into her pleading. "I don't have to do shit, Ms. Woodstock. Or is it Ms. all-by-myself. Look, I'm under the management of Jarrod Chuck. That's who I listen to, that's who will be behind my comeback!" he shouted.

"Jewel! You don't understand! They are trying to kill you."

Julian paid no attention to her statement. He just said angrily, "When you've grown up...we can talk. Until then, have Jarrod call me. You're obviously wacked!"

Brandie then cried, "Julian, please! She's trying to kill you. I have to...."

Julian again interrupted her. "Listen, my fiancé has been in love with me since grade school. That woman worships the ground I walk on. So call up some of your other sucker clients and leave me alone! You must be one of those narrow-minded chicks who don't want to see a couple in love and happy." He then hung up the phone.

Brandie was still holding the receiver. "Hello, Jewel? Hello!" she shouted, then slammed the receiver down. "Fool! Julian, you're a fool!" She wiped the tears away. "And you'll soon be a dead fool," speaking to herself. She got up and walked out of Dee's Records, locking the door behind her.

Chapter Thirty-Eight

Shelly came back to Julian's home at 6:00 that evening. "Hello, love, I'm on my way to the Cobb Arena to rehearse with my new band," said Julian. He then kissed her on the cheek and went back to his room to continue dressing.

Shelly got a can of soda pop out of the refrigerator, then turned the TV on and flopped down on the leather couch. "Honey!" she yelled. "I'm just gonna stay around the house by myself tonight."

"Cool," yelled Julian from his bedroom.

"Yeah, with Artie gone, I'm gonna enjoy a private evening by myself," she yelled. Julian came out of the room dressed in jeans, boots, and a leather vest. His hairy chest was clearly visible. Shelly looked at him. "Ooh baby, you're looking hot tonight. I'm getting horny just watching you."

Julian laughed. "I'll be back around midnight," he said.

Shelly excitedly jumped up from the couch. "Honey, when are we gonna set a wedding date?" She looked down at the diamond ring he had given her. "I want to be your wife...have your baby."

Julian cleared his throat and took out a card from his jeans pocket, then said, "Don't worry, we'll set a date soon. Just keep on living with me and making me happy." He handed Shelly the card and said, "Later." Julian then left the house.

Shelly rolled her eyes in disgust and said, "Huh...you won't be living for too much longer. And I'll be rich!" She then went over to the phone. She dialed Ricky, saying, "Hey honey! He's gone now. Come on over. We have the house till midnight."

Ricky replied, "I'm on my way."

Shelly went and sat on the couch, then read the gold card Julian had given her. "My love be with you all in Christ Jesus. Amen." She rolled her eyes and said, "Ha! What a fool...A real sucker." She put the card in the side table drawer, then laid on the couch and waited for Ricky.

Brandie was still living with her mom in the small house on Reynolds Street. She laid on her bed thinking about Jewel. Corina was in the basement washing clothes. "I'm not an introvert!" shouted Brandie, speaking to herself. "He doesn't know who I am. He never has!" She jumped up from the bed, saying, "I'm not going to see him or his stupid band." She went over to the dresser and applied more make-up to her face. She grabbed her purse off of the dresser, went to the basement door, and called to her mother, "I'll be back shortly! I think I'm going to the office for a little while!"

"Sure honey, be careful. It's almost nine o'clock," said Corina.

Brandie shouted down the stairs, "I'll be back in about an hour. Dad should be coming home any minute!"

Corina said, "Sure honey, just take it easy."

Brandie walked to the front door, saying to herself, "I think I'll see if Julian's car is there." She got in her red Escort and drove to Belleville. She turned off the expressway and drove down Julian's street, Royal Street. She saw his car in the driveway and, frowning, parked a few feet away from his house. "Maybe he went in his limo," she said as she turned off her car lights.

Someone in a brown Chevrolet suddenly drove down the street and parked in front of Julian's house. The front porch light at Julian's house was on, and the security gate was unlocked. After Julian had left the house, Shelly had gone out to the gate and unlocked it for Ricky's entrance.

A tall white guy with blond, short hair got out of the brown Chevy. Brandie watched intently from her car. The man rang the bell on Julian's house. After a few minutes, Shelly opened the door. Brandie saw the grin on her face, and continued to watch as the blond guy embraced her passionately. "Oh my God," said a stunned Brandie. Her eyes and mouth widened with surprise. Next, Shelly and Ricky kissed very provocatively. Brandie continued to watch as he grabbed her around the waist and picked her up from the floor. Brandie then saw the door close on Julian's house. "Damn!" shouted Brandie. "That's your fiancé who's so in love with you, huh, Jewel?" she said speaking to herself.

Brandie sat there for another hour. She had the radio playing for company and her window was slightly rolled down. In a little while, Ricky opened the door. He kissed Shelly again and then left. As he headed for his car, he turned and shouted to Shelly, "Tonight's the night, baby! You said the Cobb Arena on Jeffers Road, right? I have to find a gas station first and then I'll head for the arena."

Shelly yelled, "Right baby, Jeffers Road, and I'll be here waiting for you." He got in the car and drove off.

Brandie, looking puzzled, said, "I have to warn Jewel." She called the police on her car phone and reported that a disturbance may be happening at the Cobb Arena tonight. She told the police to look out for a guy in a brown Cutlass. She hung up the phone and thought about the blond guy's words. "If that dumb-looking guy is Ricky, I don't have anything to worry about. He'll never find a gas station around here or the Cobb Arena." She then grabbed her vial of Mace out of her glove compartment. She dropped it in her purse and jumped out of her car.

She then ran up to Jewel's house and knocked on the door. "Ricky what's...?" said Shelly as she opened the door.

Brandie stepped in front of the open screen door. "The last time I looked, your man's name is Jewel," said Brandie. She then pushed her way past Shelly and walked into Julian's living room.

"What the hell is this?" shouted Shelly. "If you don't get your ass out of my house, I'll call security." She frowned, disturbed as she thought about Artie being gone. She looked at Brandie and courageously said, "You freakin' groupies are all crazy! Now get out of here!" She looked at Brandie's designer attire and then glanced up into her face. Shelly again frowned, noticing that she didn't look like a teenage groupie. "Who the hell? Wait a minute—I know you." She closed the door.

Brandie replied, "Yeah, Shelly, you know me. And I don't think you want to call security...not with the little game you're playing."

Shelly said nastily, "It's you! You freak. What happened—someone finally taught you how to walk!"

"This isn't about me, bitch!" said Brandie. "You and your boyfriend are trying to kill Julian, aren't you?"

Shelly replied coyly, "You don't know what you're talking about. Julian and I are..." she then flashed a large diamond in front of Brandie's face, "engaged. We're getting married."

Brandie sighed and said, "Beautiful. It's beautiful, you gold-digging tramp."

"Ha ha ha, you're still as crazy as when we were in school" snapped Shelly. She cut the laugh off abruptly. "Now get the hell out of our house."

"You're not going to get away with this, Shelly." Brandie folded her arms. "He doesn't love you anyway. You know it."

Shelly rolled her eyes. "Oh yeah...I'll get away with it all right. And you want to know why?" Brandie just stared at her. "Because, you stupid naïve fool, no one knows except you. I don't give a damn how you found out and I really don't care. You're just another love forlorn groupie." Shelly slung her blond hair away from her face. "No! Julian doesn't love you and you know it. You're still following him around, just like in high school." Brandie laughed and headed for the door. Shelly looked at her and said snidely, "Yeah, so what—you went to college and learned how to dress, thank God. Julian still isn't going to want you." Shelly chuckled, then looked at Brandie. "Well, to tell the truth, he isn't going to want anyone...dead. Bang bang; good night, sweet prince."

Brandie then yelled, "Oh my God! You're some kind of sick psycho nut case!"

Shelly laughed. "The guy is a creep. He used me. He took my boyfriend's job and he doesn't deserve to live."

Brandie's breathing increased. She then yelled, "I...I called the police on your boyfriend! He's probably in police custody now."

Shelly said coolly, "Dream on, nerd. Do you think this is the first time we've done this? We got away with it before, and we will again." She then told Brandie, with a eerie look on her face, "I wouldn't make plans for tomorrow...you ruby-colored freak."

Brandie, feeling ill at ease, reached in her purse. She felt the Mace and was prepared to pull it out and use it on Shelly if she had to. Her eyes were wide, and she didn't know what to expect from the obviously deranged woman. After seeing that Shelly was still all talk, suddenly panic struck her and she ran out of the house frantically. Shelly stood in the doorway laughing.

Brandie stopped running and looked back at Shelly, who was still laughing hysterically and said, 'Oh yeah, Shelly. I'm the vice president of Dee's Records, Jewel's record company...so you can take your groupie idea and cram it!" Brandie then yelled as she was about to get into her car, "Have a good night!" Shelly's laughter ceased. Brandie got into her car and burnt rubber leaving. She had a satisfied feeling, but she also was worried sick about Julian.

She quickly drove to the Cobb Arena. The place was crowded with police and police cars. Brandie parked her car right outside of the front entrance and jumped out of her car and ran through the door. The band was scattered across the stage. The police were huddled over someone who was lying on the stage floor. Hysterically, Brandie shouted, "No! No! Please God, no!" She headed toward the stage.

An officer grabbed her and said, "Sorry, Miss. You can't go up there. We're clearing the stage."

Frantically Brandie shouted, "I've got to get to him! Please, he's a friend of mine!"

A shorter African-American officer then said, "We're sorry, Miss. We're waiting for the ambulance."

Jarrod then came from behind the stage. 'Daddy, Daddy!" shouted Brandie. 'Brandie, baby come here," he said.

"I won't go on stage, I promise," shouted Brandie. She jerked away harshly from the officers holding her and ran to her father. "Daddy, is he dead? What happened? I called the police. I knew he was going to kill him." Brandie broke down crying.

Her father replied, "Brandie, get a hold of yourself. He isn't dead. He was playing along with the band and that guy over there came in and shot him." Jarrod pointed over to the back corner. The police had Ricky handcuffed and were escorting him out of the arena. "He was shot on the side of his chest, but...."

"But what?" Brandie asked.

He continued, "Julian was talking. He doesn't want to go to the hospital."

Brandie, sounding surprised, said, "Really!" She looked stunned. "His fiancé—they have to get his fiancé." The paramedics came in with an emergency stretcher. She quickly said, "Dad, I got to go," and ran up on the stage. She stood behind the paramedics, watching Jewel.

Julian viciously said, "No! Leave me here, please!"

The paramedic replied, "Mr. Parr, you have to go to the hospital!" After countless pleads with Julian, one of the paramedics looked around the auditorium and asked, "Is there anyone here related to him? Maybe you can talk him into going to the hospital. The bullet wound next to his chest is pretty bad. He definitely needs a doctor."

Jarrod responded, "I'm his manager. I've contacted his agent. We're trying to reach his family now."

After hiding behind paramedics in order not to be seen, Brandie stepped up close to Julian lying on his back on the stage floor. The paramedics had bandaged the gunshot wound. "I...I think I may be able to talk to him," Brandie said shyly. She bent down beside Julian. He was in a lot of pain and sweating constantly. His eyes focused on Brandie as soon as she started talking.

"M...my God. Is...is it rea...really you?" he managed to say.

"Yes, it's me, Jewel, and you're hurt. I don't want to lose you again. So why don't you let them take you to the hospital? They'll fix you up and...and I'll tell you everything when you're well." Brandie's eyes watered. She managed to smile anyway. "Hey, it's a miracle that you're talking now. Now let them take you and get you completely well."

Thunder sounds and lightning filled the auditorium. A ferocious thunderstorm had begun outside. Julian frowned. "You...that voi...voice, you're h...her. You sounded a little different when we were on the phone. But...but it's...you."

Brandie held Julian's hand and said, "Julian, please. I don't want you to die. Would you go with them...please?" The other band members and paramedics were all looking at Julian and Brandie.

Julian murmured, "Br...Bread Woodstock...why you're Bread Woodstock."

Tears fell from Brandie's eyes. "Yes...yes, it's me...I'll explain as soon as you get well. Now let them take you to the hospital."

Julian slightly laughed. He then managed to say, "Brandie, you...know bet...better than that."

Brandie agitatedly asked, "What?"

Julian replied, "Tell them all to leave."

Brandie's eyes again widened. She said, "Jewel, I can't. You...."

Julian whispered, "Tell everybody in here to leave pl...please. I...I ne...need to be...be with you."

Tears streamed down Brandie's face. She stood up and turned, facing the others in the auditorium. "Uh...he would like you all to leave." There was murmuring from the band.

The paramedics argued, "No, absolutely not! He will surely die!"

"Leave...tell them to...to leave," whispered Julian weakly.

Tears again ran down Brandie's cheeks. "I want you all to go! I don't know why, but it's what he wants. So will everyone leave. Maybe then he'll have me call his doctor." She looked at the paramedics and said, "I...I don't know. Just go, please. He doesn't want help with all of you here. So leave now!"

Everyone cleared the auditorium, murmuring as they left. But finally the auditorium was cleared. Brandie then said to Julian, when the auditorium was finally clear, "We're alone now, silly. But you still need a doctor."

Julian coughed. "Wh...why did yo...you pre...tend to be...s...someone...else?" he said incoherently.

Brandie's eyes again filled with tears. "Julian, you've been shot. I'll tell you later. Now let me call you a doctor!"

Julian replied, "No! Tell me, pl...please tell me."

Brandie sighed, giving in. "Okay, Julian. I saw you last year in a gift shop in California. You didn't look happy. Anyway, I left before you could see me because I was mad at you for leaving me after we made love years ago." Brandie sighed again. "Well, to make a long story short, I went to a lot of doctors and had a lot of physical therapy. They somewhat cured my polio condition, or at least they made it not so noticeable.

Julian smiled. 'Gl...glad for you," he managed to say.

Brandie replied, "Thanks. Well, anyway I never forgot how sad you looked in that gift shop. For the next few years I read how Bazaar Records had fired you and all, and how you had practically given up your music." Julian moaned. Brandie then said, "That's it! I'm calling you a doctor!"

"No...no, go...on. Tell me what hap...happened. H...how did you...you get to be at Dee's Records?"

Brandie rolled her eyes in fear. "Oh Julian, I really should get you to a hospital. But okay...I tried to hate you, I really did. But I couldn't." She took a napkin from her purse and wiped the perspiration from his forehead. "I went to one of your concerts in California and I fell for you all over again." He chuckled, then frowned from the pain. "I wanted to go backstage and see you, Julian, but I was afraid you'd only laugh at me and say, 'Look, the fool is still in love with me'". Julian again frowned, from pain and Brandie's words. "Well, anyway, I graduated with a degree in business and music theory. My father came to my graduation. I hadn't seen him since I was eight years old. He and my mom are trying to reconcile." She paused. "Well, anyway, Julian, he gave me an out-of-this-world college graduation present."

Julian breathed out the words, "Wh...what was it?"

"It was a record company. He bought a record company and said it will be mine when he retires!" Julian stared at her as she continued to speak. "Isn't that great Julian?" Julian, still staring at her, just listened. "Well, Julian, he named it after me. Well, not exactly after me. You see, my parents used to always call me Dee Dee as a child. My dad named the company Dee's Records." She took a deep breath in anticipation of what he would say and looked at him curiously.

Julian then said, "Congra...ulations." He had a slight smile on his face as he still observed Brandie.

She went on, "He named the company after me. I knew you would hate it if you knew I had anything to do with them getting in touch with you. So I let my dad, well, I asked my dad not to tell you who he was or that I was his daughter." Julian frowned as he heard Brandie's omission. "I thought you hated me. I knew you wouldn't sign with the company if you knew I had anything to do with it."

Julian licked his lips and smiled. He then said lowly, "And you called me silly. Go...go on, tell me the rest."

Brandie continued, "So I thought of an even better idea. We could change our names or use our nicknames and you would never have to know...well, not soon anyway." Julian croaked out a laugh. "So you see, Jarrod Chuck's name is really Jarrod Charles. He's my father. And Bread is a name I gained in college when I went on a bread and water fast. So, Bread is the name I used so that you wouldn't know who I was." She ran her fingers through her long red hair and said, "And the Woodstock thing is just symbolic of the music, the freedom in music."

Julian again laughed. he then said, "All...all that for me? I...I'm flattered."

Brandie didn't comment. She suddenly said, "Oh yeah—how we got in touch with you."

Julian sighed. "Now what?" he said breathlessly.

Brandie added, "Your agent, Phillip Emery."

Julian nodded his head.

Brandie continued, "He's my Uncle Everett. Remember I told you about him? His real name is Phillip Everett Emery Charles. That's how we got in touch with you. We asked him if you were worth signing onto our company. Phillip, being an agent, has a list of rock star hots and nots."

Julian guessed, "And...he told y...you I was hot."

Brandie chuckled. "Actually, he told us that you were a client of his. And that you were going though a dry spell. But you were definitely hot." Julian chuckled, then yelled out in pain. Brandie, panicking, said, 'That's it, Julian, I have to get you some help!" Brandie then ran her fingers through her hair.

"Wait...no" shouted Jewel. "I...I'm sorry I didn't believe you about...about Shelly. The...guy th...that shot me, Ricky...yelled to me before he blasted a ho...hole in me that this is...is for...t...taking his job and using his woman, Shelly." Julian again shouted in pain. "I...I guess I'm a fo...fool, huh?"

Brandie replied, looking concerned, "No, you were just lonely, and that blonde bimbo was just there." Julian laughed and again yelled out in pain.

Brandie stood up and frustratedly shouted, "Uhn-uhn, that's it! I'm not going to just let you lay there and die!"

Julian said calmly, "Then come lay wi...with me."

Brandie again shouted, "What!"

Julian replied solemnly, "I'm not afraid to die, Brandie."

She then shouted angrily, "You self-righteous son-of-a...." She rolled her eyes and folded her arms in disgust. "This is crazy. I'm just not going to stay here without doing anything and let you die on me!"

"Jesus said, I am th...the resurrection...and the light. He that believeth in me, though ye dead, yet shall ye live." Julian quoted the scripture and then chuckled. "I got that verse out without to much pain. Oh! Oh God! Help me!" he then yelled. "The pain! The...pain!"

Brandie nervously shouted, "Oh Julian, I'm going to call an ambulance. I'm glad you started believing, but this is crazy!" She ran down the stage steps.

Julian faintly shouted, No, Br...Brandie, no co...come back." He was losing more blood and his breath was leaving him.

Brandie stopped on the steps. She frowned and ran back up on the stage. "You may want to die, but I love you. I won't just stay here and let you leave me again!" shouted Brandie angrily.

The lightning from outside of the auditorium lit up the room. The rain that was falling fiercely hit the auditorium roof, sounding like footsteps. Julian then said, "I...I love you, Brandie.... I...I ne...never stopped."

Brandie's eyes again filled with tears. She bent down beside Julian and said, "Wh...why are you doing this to me? You're dying, and now you tell me that you love me."

Tears fell onto Julian's open leather vest where there was a large bloody cloth over the hole in his chest. He whispered, "Hel...help me."

Brandie again cried angrily, "How...how can I help you, Julian, when you won't let me!"

Julian interrupted her. "Hel...help me outside."

Brandie, confused by Julian's words, said, "What?"

Julian's voice was now barely audible. He managed to croak out, "Take me out...outside. God...God will help...help you and help me...me get better."

"Julian, it's a thunderstorm. I can't...."

Julian again interrupted, saying, "Please, I'm...I'm be...begging...you."

Brandie hesitantly took off her jacket. "I must be crazy, Julian. You need a doctor, not to be going out in this weather." She struggled to put her jacket around his shoulders.

Julian then said, "God...God cured yo...you from po...polio and h...he cured me of epi...epilepsy." He then whispered, "He'll hea...heal me now."

Brandie was now helping Julian to stand. Panicking, she said, "It's lightning, Julian. I don't know about this."

She then walked slowly, side by side with Julian, out of the auditorium. He was leaning against her for support as they headed toward the back door of the arena. With each step, he moaned and groaned. She nervously said, "I...I must be crazy, Julian."

She opened the back door of the Cobb Arena and walked him out to the adjoining field. She was still crying and struggling as she led him onto the field.

When they were a few feet into the field, he said, "There...lay...lay me down over there." She helped him over to the spot on the ground that he was referring to and sat beside him. Rain was falling hard. They could barely see in front of them. The thunder was loud and the lightning lit up the field.

It was now 11:30 at night, but the lightning lit up the atmosphere, making it look like daytime. Brandie's hair was now curless and hung limp on her shoulders. Julian just lay there on the ground as if in deep meditation. She took her hand and pushed her hair back so that it rested on her upper back. She shouted, "Julian! I'm putting you and me both in jeopardy.... You won't need a bullet hole to kill you—you'll die from being struck by lightning if we stay out here."

Julian opened his eyes and looked over at a still confused looking and feeling Brandie. He replied, "My...my parents had be...been trying f...for years to ha...have another baby." He breathed deeply. "One day, I su...suppose, it was just like...like this. My dad went outside to our shed to ge...get his guitar." He again moaned. She just shook her head sorrowfully. He then continued, "My dad told my mo...mother he had an idea fo...for a so...song." With every sentence, it seemed his pain got worse. "As my dad was br...bringing the guitar back to the house, he...he was struck by light...lightning."

Brandie shouted, "Oh no! What happened to him?" She was now drenched from the rain, as was Julian. He slowly rubbed the now almost nonexistent scar on his forehead.

He then said, "He w...was fine. That night, I was conceived."

Fascinated, her eyes widened. "Oh Julian, that's a beautiful story, the making of a rock star." They both laughed.

Julian then said, "Yea, may...maybe one day I'll write a book."

Brandie excitedly said, "You know, you really cou...."

Lightning lit up their surroundings again. A loud thunder sound filled the atmosphere. Electricity all of a sudden seemed to shoot across the sky. She covered her head and screamed.

Julian had started coughing uncontrollably. He seemed unable to stop. In a hysterical panic, she yelled, 'Oh no, Julian!" She crawled closer to him and grabbed his hand. His face seemed to be turning a pale bluish shade. She was now kneeling as she looked down at his face. He was still lying flat on his back as she held onto his hand in fear. She was trembling as she looked at his drawn and pale looking face.

She shouted hysterically, "No!...I'm going to call emergency. I won't let you die!" She stood up. She didn't want to leave him outside in the dreadful storm. But she knew he would surely die by the time he walked back to the arena. He was coughing harshly as an undecided Brandie teetered from foot to foot nervously, not knowing what to do. She then quickly yelled, looking at a helpless Julian, "Baby I...I'll be right back. I'm calling an ambulance!" She took off running through the muddy field.

It was still lightning profusely and the sound of thunder echoed their surroundings. Running through the muddy field, she slipped several times before reaching the arena. Finally however, she made it to the back door of the Cobb Arena. She quickly opened the door and ran inside. Her jeans were stained with mud from her numerous falls. She went over to the pay phone to dial emergency. When she put the quarter she had taken out of her jeans pocket into the phone slot, she didn't receive a dial tone. The phone didn't work; it was out of order due to the storm. "Damn! Damn! Damn!" she shouted, angry and disgusted. She headed back outside to Julian.

A crowd had gathered out front, trying to get a glance of the famed rock star. The medics again entered the arena. After searching and not finding him anywhere, they assumed that Brandie had called his personal physician. "They must have left out of the back," said one of the paramedics after observing the slightly open back door. Shortly after the paramedics left. Jarrod locked up the place and left as well.

Chapter Thirty-nine

Julian was still coughing profusely as he laid on the muddy outside ground. Flashes of lightning still lit up the atmosphere. Flashes of his mother also came into Julian's view. "Well, my son the rock star," said a younger and sober Rachel Parr. She was in their backyard at the Memorial Day barbeque.

Julian then saw himself at five years old at the Memorial Day barbeque. Rachel patted him on the back and said, "Go get your sister. It's time for you to eat." Julian was still coughing and trying to catch his breath.

He next saw visions of his dad, a younger Steven Parr, winking an approving eye at him. He then heard Steven yelling to him over the phone, "You shook your ass right out of a job!

Julian saw his sister Tracy at a young age, throwing him a ball. He was also younger. Julian then saw an older, more mature and drunk Tracy in his bedroom. "Come on, baby brother, I can make you feel real good. No one has to know," said a drunken Tracy. Julian then saw himself kick Tracy to the floor as he ran to the door in an attempt to get away.

As Julian opened the bedroom door, he saw Jolelle standing outside of the room door. He saw himself run past Jolelle and out of the house, vowing never to return.

As he went to the shed to get his ten speed bike, the members of his former rock band Wild were standing in front of the shed. They were blocking his entrance. "Go on pretty boy, get away from here," said Ricky. He was standing by Shelly with his arms around her waist. She said, "You're kinda religious, huh?" The whole band started laughing. Julian was blinking his eyes wildly trying to escape the images of his past. He was still coughing and choking.

Brandie was running toward him. "Julian! We've got to get you inside!"

Julian lifted his head slightly and saw her making her way toward him. He breathlessly whispered, "Brandie...love you...please co...come." A bolt of lightning, as if from out of nowhere, then struck the large tree that was next to Julian. Ricocheting off of the tree, the bolt then struck Julian. He died instantly.

"Jul...ian!" screamed Brandie, who was observing the incident from afar as she quickly approached. "No, God, no, please don't let him be dead," she said as she was again crying tears of devastation.

As she finally reached him she fell to his side. "No! Julian, no!" she cried. She put her ear to his chest, listening for a heartbeat, but heard nothing. She quickly lifted his wrist, trying to feel for a pulse, but there was again nothing. Julian was dead.

Brandie was now half-crazed and in shock. She cried loudly, "No! Julian, no! Why, God! Why?" Tears were streaming down her face. "He's not dead!" She looked up toward the heavens, then looked down at Julian and yelled, "You can't leave me dammit! You can't leave me!" She began beating on his lifeless chest.

Finally after receiving no response, she gave up. She lifted his body slightly by the shoulders and cradled his head in her arms. She cried for what seemed like hours holding Julian. She then said, taking a deep breath, "Pull yourself together, Brandie. You're going to have to tell people what happened."

She caressed his cheek gently. "Well, at least he died like he wanted to, on God's earth, under God's sky." As she caressed his cheek, he reached up and touched her hand. She jumped. "Oh Jesus!" she yelled.

Julian then opened his eyes. "Red...stick to managing stars because you're a lousy nurse."

Brandie happily said, "Julian! Oh Julian, you're not dead! Thank God! Thank God! You're not dead!"

Julian then sat up slightly on the ground. He kissed Brandie on the cheek and said, "I died, Red. I guess it just wasn't my time yet, though."

Brandie's eyes widened as she gasped. He continued, "I don't think I have a bullet in me either."

Brandie frowned. In astonishment, she said, "What?" He reached up on his chest and pulled the bloodstained cloth off of him. His skin was as clear and perfect as it ever was.

Brandie's face looked pale. "Oh my God, Julian, I think I'm going to faint."

Julian chuckled. "Don't faint, baby. This is just one more miracle."

Brandie slowly touched his chest, then said, "Yeah Julian...but you got shot a few hours ago. I saw the bullet wound...the blood." She swallowed hard. "Other people saw you get shot as well." She stood up, looking puzzled. The rain was now stopping. "And that guy who shot you is probably in jail now." She frowned. "Oh Julian, what happened here? What will we tell everyone?"

Julian pulled her back to the ground. He looked at her and smiled. "Red, this is our bond. The day the man upstairs decides to take us away, you'll know and I'll know that I died. I got shot, struck by lightning, and died."

"Oh my God!" she said, flabbergasted.

Julian laughed. "I saw the light. I've always had my own evil lightning rod, or at least I thought it was evil." He caressed her cheek. "I never allowed myself to look at the light. I was afraid to look. I thought that because it hurt and it was blinding, it was something evil."

Brandie, amazed by his words, said, "You...you mean you have seen this light before?"

Julian claimed, "Yes...ever since I was a kid. Ever since I used to have seizures." He chuckled. "I thought it was my doom. But now I know that it's a guiding light to my salvation. I saw it when I died and it led me back to life."

Brandie sighed. "Fascinating."

Julian continued, "I know it may sound crazy, but I actually died. All the people I know flashed before my eyes and I died. It was like...like this bright light brought me back to life, brought me back to you." Brandie was silent and just stared at him. "I saw the light the morning I left your house, years ago. I knew it was something...I knew I was different. I had to find out who I was, Brandie, that's why I left."

Brandie looked down at the ground shyly. She slowly gazed up at Julian. "You mean...you just didn't use me like you did all those other girls who were after you?"

Julian put his hands under her chin and tilted her head up slightly. Now facing her, he said, "You weren't like all those other girls then, Red. And you aren't like other women now. I loved you then, even though I couldn't admit it to you or myself." He looked into her eyes and said, "And I love you even more now. I'm telling you, me, and God above that I'll always love you."

Tears filled Brandie's eyes again. "I love you too, Julian. I always have and I always will." They kissed long and very erotically.

Afterwards Brandie breathlessly said, "What will we tell people when they ask about your gunshot wound?"

Julian laughed. "That was the last thing on my mind, to tell you the truth." He again tried to kiss her.

She avoided his advances, this time saying, "Come on, Julian. I'm serious."

Julian, giving in, replied, "Okay...okay. I'll tell them it wasn't that serious and that my doctor took care of me." He again kissed Brandie. "Overnight, at that. Since, I don't want to become a tabloid topic, we'll just keep what happened to me to ourselves. The public will never know that my doctor is the lord." Brandie agreed and they laughed again. Julian noted, "Well, it's probably one o'clock in the morning."

Brandie breathed deeply and said, "Oh I forgot, I told my mom I'd be back in an hour."

Julian stood up and grabbed Brandie's hand. She stood as well. He looked at her and said, "I know a beautiful, elegant hotel. It's one of the advantages of being rich and famous." Brandie kept a placid look on her face, even though her heart was breaking uncontrollably. He then said, "I want to make love to you Brandie."

Brandie shyly agreed. "Me, too. I want to make love to you."

Julian remarked, "I'm sure my limo driver has gone by now. We'll have to take your car."

They headed back into the Cobb Arena. She grabbed her purse and threw him the keys to her Escort. They then walked to the front door of the Cobb Arena. Brandie said, "You can throw that bloody rag in the garbage over there, Julian." She pointed out the trash bag in the corner.

Julian remarked, 'I think I'll keep it, tape it on for appearance's sake. I still have to look like I was wounded." He stuffed the rag in his back pocket.

Dee's Records owned part of the Cobb Arena, so Brandie had the keys to it, which she took from her purse. She and Julian then left the auditorium, and Brandie locked up.

Chapter Forty

Julian and Brandie walked into their hotel room at the Rest Inn Hotel. "Oh Julian, this is beautiful," she said. They ordered dinner, Julian getting shrimp, salad, and a non-alcoholic drink. Brandie ordered the same. They laid on the full-size bed awaiting room service as soft music played on the radio. "It's so weird being here with you, Julian," she said.

Julian turned toward her and said, "You don't know how many nights I dreamed of you and I together." He then kissed her luscious lips. As their eyes met, he slid his tongue into her mouth. As their tongues met, he gently grabbed the top of her hair, then slightly jerked her head back. He kissed her deeply, passionately, and completely. "Mmm," they both moaned.

As they kissed, he disrobed her and caressed her hips. Shortly after, her stone-washed jeans and satin blue panties were on the floor. She wrapped her legs around his waist. He lifted her sleeveless black tee-shirt off, exposing her medium-sized pouty breasts. She hurriedly unzipped his jeans, unbuttoned them, and then slid the black leather vest that he was wearing off of his taunt masculine shoulders. She began sliding his jeans over his hips as he continued to kiss her.

Someone knocked at the door. "Room service!" yelled the man.

Brandie disappointedly sighed, "Oh no." He then got up off of her, looking equally as disappointed.

He stood and rebuttoned and zipped his pants. "Coming! he shouted.

"Not quite," she said to Julian.

He laughed. "Honey, uh...I think you'd better go in the bathroom. You're a little underdressed." He had a joking smirk on his face.

Brandie got up from the bed, saying jokingly, "I shouldn't go anywhere. I was getting ready to make love to my man...how dare he interrupt!"

Julian chuckled. "Oh, I'm sure he'd love to see you like that.... Saves him from renting a dirty movie." He again chuckled.

Brandie rolled her eyes and said, "Okay, okay, I'm going." She walked into the bathroom.

Julian opened the door and the guy rolled their food in. He placed their plates on the table, along with the trays of food. A shirtless Julian said, "Thanks, man." He then tipped the delivery guy and the man then left.

Brandie came out the bathroom, grabbed her jacket, and put it on, zipping it up. He was observing her, and said, "Mmm, you look sort of cute in only your jacket."

Brandie giddily replied, "Yeah well, I hope you'll be taking it off of me soon."

"Let's eat, first, honey. You'll need the energy," said Julian, looking at Brandie as if he was turned on."

"Hmm, I can't wait," she replied. They ate and listened to the radio.

The deejay on the radio said as they were having their meal, "Today the music world may have lost one of their best performers. Rock star Jewel was shot by...listen to this now...his fiancé's boyfriend." Julian and Brandie stopped eating and stared at each other. The announcer continued, "It seems that Jewel was the target of an extortion attempt."

"You don't have to listen to this, Julian," said Brandie. She stood and walked over toward the radio. As she passed by Julian, he wrapped his arms around her waist and sat her on his lap. "Hey!" she shouted.

Julian said nonchalantly, "Let's hear what they have to say."

The announcer went on, "It seems our lone rock star has been shacking with his girlfriend. Or, at least he thought it was his girlfriend. Come to find out, the girl went to high school with Jewel. They had a fling and he dropped her. The girl swore revenge."

Julian said, "Damn, my whole life is on the radio." Brandie ran her fingers through his hair.

The announcer continued, "Wait, it gets better. It seems a few year ago, a rock band fired their lead singer and hired Jewel. Wait, it gets even better. It seems the guy also planned revenge on Jewel. Wait! Wait! Wait! It gets even better! The jilted girlfriend and the fired lead singer fell in love. They then become like amateur Bonnie and Clyde's. They went around swindling money from rich men, using the beautiful girl as bait. Well, you guessed it! The two swindlers finally got around to rock star Jewel. They had promised revenge on him anyway, and last night, the guy, named Ricky Hogan, shot Jewel at the Cobb Arena. Jewel was practicing for his comeback concert. That's when Ricky came inside the arena and shot him. We have no further information on Jewel's condition. All we know is that he refused to go to the hospital last night after being wounded. We'll keep you informed on this mysterious case in further updates."

Julian then said, "Now you can cut it off." The music again played on the radio. Julian said, "Naw...Don't worry about it."

He then picked her up and took her over to the bed. His eyes were wide and looked wildly seductive as he gently placed her shapely body, only clad in a semi see-through jacket, on the bed. The bedsheets were already neatly pulled back from their earlier encounter. She had a slight and seductive smile on her face as she lay on the plush bed. He looked at her curvaceous body with a wanton desire.

He then got in bed. Bending his arm and resting it on the feathered pillow with his cheek rested in his hand, he smiled and looked into her eyes. She was laying next to him, breathing deeply in anticipation. Noticing the rapid rise and fall motion of her jacket covered chest, he smiled. His big green eyes stared into her brown eyes. He spoke deeply and sensuously, saying, "You are so beautiful, Brandie. I don't know how I made it through the years without you." She caressed his cheek as he spoke to her. "I was blessed with my own personal cheerleader...my very own bodyguard. I was so fortunate and didn't even realize it." He ran his fingers through her long hair.

Brandie looked at him, then asked softly, "What? What do you mean?"

Julian caressed her cheek and said, "You believed in me, baby. When we were in school, you encouraged me to write poetry and you complimented me on the lousy songs that I wrote."

Brandie smiled. Shyly caressing his hairy chest, she said, "You were...I mean, you are gifted...special...precious...so precious."

Julian kissed her on the forehead, then said confirmingly, "See...you're still doing it. You're still my own personal cheerleader."

Brandie chuckled. "I guess you're right. I loved you then and I love you even more now."

Julian breathed in deeply and gazed down at her, still laying beside him. "You took a lot of heat for me, Red...and from me. When that kid, Shelly's old boyfriend...what was his name?" he asked.

Brandie, snuggled under the bedsheets, said, "Lance...that loser creep."

Julian laughed. "Yeah, Lance.... He really hated my ass, didn't he?"

Brandie quickly said, looking up at him, "He was jealous of you. All of those guys at that stupid school were."

Julian closed his eyes and said, "Yeah baby, but you would take up for me." He opened his eyes. "You were my bodyguard even then...even when those fools treated you like shit, and you're still protecting me now."

Brandie smiled, feeling his love. "What are words when you don't have an I.Q. no higher than one."

Julian laughed. "God sent me an angel...my own angel."

Brandie licked her lips, not exactly knowing how to respond to Julian's numerous compliments. She just said coolly, changing the subject, "Well...Shelly seemed to have been attracted to all of the guys who hated your guts." He again laughed. Brandie continued angrily, "Just give me five minutes alone with that dumb jerk, Ricky. I'll make him wish he never knew the name Jewel!" She reached over and playfully punched him in the stomach.

Julian grabbed her fist and planted a kiss on her knuckles and laughed. "Yeah, watch out world! My bodyguard's ballistic!" Lowering his voice, he then said as she laughed, "And I love every ballistic bone in her body."

Brandie slowly gazed up into his eyes. He looked seriously seductive and grabbed the zipper on her jacket. He unzipped it slowly, down to her belly button. She impulsively breathed in deep. He then caressed her right breast. Looking as if he was trying to stay controlled, he noticed the tattoo of a sparkling diamond on her right breast. He read aloud the words that were inscribed above the diamond. "Jewel's?" he said in a deep voice.

Brandie bit down on her bottom lip without commenting. He smiled, then rolled on top of her. Looking into her eyes he said, "Add forever." He kissed her lightly rouge-colored red lips. They held each other, kissing for hours. She could feel his apparent excitement increasing. He kissed her neck, then his lips lowered to her breast, then to her nipples, longingly and lovingly.

Brandie moaned as he kissed her body. She caressed his broad shoulders and back in ecstasy. "Oh Julian...you know how much I've wanted...this, I've wanted you," she said a breathlessly. She caressed his jean-covered buttocks, grabbing hold tightly. He then completely unzipped her jacket. She wiggled out of it and was again totally nude. He caressed her shapely thighs and hips and he moaned in satisfaction as did Brandie.

Julian looked into her eyes and said, "Take my jeans off.... Undress me!"

Brandie breathed in deeply, then sensuously said, "I thought you'd never ask." She unbuttoned his jeans as he tongued her neck and ears, ultimately ending up at her lips. She moaned in pure blissful ecstasy as she lowered his jeans off of his hips and thighs. He kicked his jeans off of his body, as he continued to caress her body. He couldn't seem to get enough of her and she, the same of him.

Julian whispered, "I want you to be with me always, to have my babies, to seduce me like you're doing now, forever." He kissed her shoulders.

She then said, "Hold up...hold up, Mr. I-can't-get-enough-of-you Parr."

Julian chuckled. "What? What is it, baby? What is it? I can't get enough of you, I never could."

Brandie chuckled. "You had me on your side about the babies and all. But...." He continued to kiss and caress her soft body. Hardly containing, she said jokingly, "I didn't seduce you! As I remember it, you're the one who carried me over here."

Julian was now licking her nipple. He stopped and looked into her eyes and said humorously, "And...?"

"And, you seduced me," she said.

Julian rolled off of her and said, "Aw man...now you're telling me that I coaxed you into making hot love with me...that I coaxed you into rubbing my ass so much that it's probably as red as your hair." His face held a slight smirk.

Brandie pulled the covers up to her neck, covering her entire nude body. She then batted her eyes playfully and shyly said, "Yes...Mr. Julian Phalan Parr. You knew I was innocent and you died, came back, and seduced me." She then licked her lips and chuckled.

Julian held up his hands in surrender. He said jokingly, "Guilty...I plead guilty. I brought you here against your will and made you screw the hell out of me."

Brandie laughed. "Well...you haven't exactly done that yet."

Julian, frowning, said, "What?"

Brandie said, looking seductively at him, "Made me screw the hell out of you!" She chuckled again.

Julian looked at her, then rolled again on top of her saying, "Oh...I will, sweetheart."

Brandie then swallowed hard and said, "I can't wait." She kissed his soft sensuous lips.

They made steamy, earth-shattering love. His thrusts were firm but gentle. They were energetic but everlasting. She still, wildly and harmoniously, matched her lover's thrusts. Running her fingers through her hair and then his, she was satisfied more than she ever had known she could be. He still continued to please her wholeheartedly.

"Oh yes baby!" she shouted as she pushed him on his side. She then forced him flat on his back. She was now on top of him. She made love to him as only a woman in love could.

They kissed and caressed each other, while thrusting quickly and fervently.

"Oh baby, yes! Don't stop! I love you so much," moaned Julian.

They made love for hours in happy euphoria. He quickly rolled her on her back again and made love to her until they both spasmed uncontrollably, with him moaning loudly and her letting out an operatic but enticing scream. They held each other tightly.

Julian huskily said, as he ran his fingers through her hair, "You're all I want and need. Stay with me...have my children, Brandie." She was silent. "I love you."

Brandie then said, with a sarcastic chuckle, "Oh, wouldn't that be great. I'll be hated worse than I was in high school, if I tie down the world's love God...their eligible bachelor, Jewel."

Julian then said, "I don't need the world's love, Red. I need your love."

Brandie was feeling uneasy and unsure of what he was actually getting at. She purposely ignored his comment and said happily. "Well baby...the world awaits you. We better get out of here and back to the real world."

Brandie and Julian then showered together and again made love in the shower. They then prepared to go to Dee's Records. They both dressed, with him putting on the sunglasses he had purchased in the hotel gift shop, and they left the Rest Inn Hotel.

Chapter Forty-one

Brandie and Julian arrived at Dee's Records at 12:30 P.M. the following day, after his unfortunate incident. "Jewel, you're all right!" shouted Carol, the receptionist. She didn't say anything to Brandie, who held on tightly to his hand.

Jewel chuckled, then said dryly, "Yeah Carol, it was just a flesh wound."

Carol excitedly said, "But...but they said...."

Brandie interrupted. "Come on, Julian." She opened Jarrod's office door. He was seated at his desk. "Hi, Dad," she exclaimed.

Julian then said, "Hello, Mr. Chuck...I mean...Mr. Charles."

"What the hell is going on! You were near death last night!" yelled Jarrod. "Your parents and I were worried sick. We couldn't find out where you were or what hospital you were in."

Julian then said calmly, 'Mr. Charles, boss, it was just a flesh wound. It wasn't serious at all."

"That's right, Dad. After you guys left the arena, I took him to his doctor. He said it was just a flesh wound, Dad."

Julian looked over at her and then back at Jarrod. "That's right...uh...he took care of me right there in his office." He again looked at Brandie. Jarrod looked at the both of them with a puzzled frown on his face.

Brandie then said, "You know, Dad, Jewel had epilepsy when he was a child. I guess that's why the gunshot graze affected him so badly."

Julian added, "A few more days and I'll be good as new.... Don't worry."

Jarrod stood. "Well, it's good to hear that, son." There was a moment of eerie silence in the office. "The police went into your house last night, Jewel. They arrested your fiancé."

Julian chuckled. Rolling his eyes, he said, "My fiancé, huh, yeah right. I want to get back in the studio as soon as possible. I have a few songs that'll really hit."

Jarrod agreed. "I can arrange for you to be in the studio Friday, all right?"

Julian smiled. He looked at Brandie and said, "Cool."

Jarrod sat back down. "I see you two have become pals."

Julian said, "Yeah...Brandie told me about all the name changes, and now we're cool."

Brandie laughed. "Yes, Dad, we're friends again. And I told him everything."

"Well, thank goodness for that," said a relieved Jarrod. "Oh...and Jewel, I contacted your father last night. He was worried sick. I think you should give him a call." He stood, looked at Brandie, and said, "Call your mother, young lady. She waited up for you practically all night. I have to go. I want to check in on Granite. They're practicing today." He headed for the door, then looked at Jewel. "Oh, and Jewel, I want you to start practicing. I'm scheduling your comeback concert for next month. Remember, you go in the studio Friday!" He chuckled. "Welcome back. Time to get to work." He then left Dee's Records.

Jewel looked at Brandie and shrugged his shoulders, saying, "I'm heading for home, Red. I've got to call my dad...let him know I'm okay."

Brandie then went into her office and called Jewel's limo driver for him. An hour later, he was in his limousine and headed for home.

Julian ran up the walkway and inside the house. Artie was sitting in the living room when he came in. "Hey boss! What happened to you? I thought you were in the hospital after that guy shot you yesterday." Julian went over and sat down on the couch. "I heard all these rumors about Shelly. They can't be true, can they?

Julian replied, "Shelly's boyfriend shot me last night. She's been playing me for a sucker all this time."

Artie frowned, saying, "I can't believe that. Are you sure?"

"Yeah Art, she's the one who's been sending me the letters. My manager overheard her planning to kill me with her boyfriend."

Artie said, "Oh God...I'm so sorry. But at least you're okay now. The radio and TV had you half-dead."

Julian got up from the couch and said, "Just a flesh wound, no need to worry." He then went over to the phone.

Artie remarked, "But you look happy. You aren't to sad about losing Shelly, are you?"

Julian replied, "I never loved her, Artie. You know that. But last night I also was reconciled with the one woman I truly love. She's my co-manager and all this time she didn't let me know."

Artie got up. "I'm happy for you, Jewel. I won't matchmake for you anymore, that's for sure."

Julian laughed. "That's for sure." Artie then went downstairs to his quarters. Julian picked up the receiver on the phone and dialed his dad's home.

"Hello...Parr residence," a female voice answered.

"Uh...yeah, is my father home? This is Julian."

"Julian!" shouted the young woman. "Ma! Dad! Come quick, Jewel's on the phone, he's all right!"

Julian stammered, "Tracy? Is that you?"

"Yes, yes...it's me, Julian. We were worried about you. Are you all right?" she asked.

He replied, "Yeah, I just had a flesh wound. I'm fine."

"Thank God," she said.

"And how are you doing, Tracy?" he asked.

She replied, "I'm fine, and I've been alcohol free since the year you left home."

Julian happily said, "That's great, Trace! You sound well!"

She then reflected, "Julian, I'm so sorry about that incident. I was drunk. I would never take advantage of my own brother."

"Yeah Trace, I know. I forgive you. Anyway, it was time for me to leave...find out who I was and what I wanted out of life."

Tracy remarked, "Man...you're a big star! That's what you are. Mom and I buy all your records and we brag about you to everyone."

Julian replied, "Yeah...that's nice, but I haven't been the model brother or son. I should have sent you and Mom some money when I got my first hit."

"Mom and I are fine, Julian. She doesn't drink anymore and she teaches music back at the elementary school." Tracy commented, "I hate my job, though. A salesperson in a woman's boutique wasn't my life's ambition."

"Oh yeah," replied Julian. "What is your life's ambition, Trace?"

"I've always wanted to design clothes. You know...like Kline or Gloria."

Julian excitedly said, "Oh yeah, you sure can make clothes, can't you?"

Tracy replied, "Uh-huh."

He then asked, "What's Dad doing? Maybe I'll call back later."

"No! Actually...," Tracy laughed and said, "he and Mom just woke up."

Julian's eyes widened. He asked, "Are you serious?"

Tracy answered joyously, "Yes, they've been going out together ever since he invited Mom and I to move in here two months ago. I think they may get back together." She handed the phone to Steven, who had just come down the stairs.

"Hello son, is that you?" he asked.

"Yeah dad...How are you doing?"

Steven didn't answer, instead asking, "How are you doing, son?"

"I'm okay, I only had a flesh wound. It was nothing serious."

"Thank goodness," said Steven. He breathed in deeply, relieved. "So, son...how's your music coming along?"

"It's coming along fine, Dad. Friday I'm going to the studio, and next month I'm starting my comeback concert."

"That's wonderful, son. Save us some tickets," said Steven.

"Julian?" asked Rachel after snatching the phone from Steven. "Julian! Baby, are you all right?"

"Yes, Mom, How are you?"

Rachel said, "Thank the Lord. Honey, I'm fine and I'm so glad you're okay."

Julian repeated, "It was just a flesh wound, Ma. I'm okay."

Rachel asked, "Honey...when will we get to see you? I'm really proud of you, Julian. I brag to all my co-workers about my famous son."

Julian's eyes filled with tears. "Mom, I'll see you all soon. I promise. I'll be recording a new album Friday, and I'll be doing some touring next month. But, I'll see you soon, all of you."

Rachel then said, "Okay, son, I'll be waiting. Goodbye now."

Julian said, "Bye Mom," and hung up the phone.

For the next few weeks, Julian was busy writing and going into the studio to record. Occasionally he and Brandie would go out. But most of the time, he would see her when he had a meeting at Dee's Records. They talked on the phone and she was content with that, as was he. The life of a rockstar.

Chapter Forty-two

It was a sunny, hot Monday. Julian went to practice at 4:00 P.M. at the Cobb Arena and played the new material that would be coming out on his next album. All right!" said one of the background band members. They had just finished a song Julian wrote titled "Brandie."

Brandie walked into the auditorium soon after they finished the song. "Hi, guys. You sounded wonderful from outside. I loved that song," she said.

Julian gazed at her and said, "Break time, fellas." He then walked off the stage. "Hey baby, good to see you." He kissed her.

She replied, "I just came to see you rehearse. Is anything wrong with that?"

He paused and said, "No, love...as a matter of fact, I'm glad you're here."

She asked, "Oh yeah? What's up?" She knew that usually Julian rehearsed without an audience. He didn't want anyone to see his act until it was absolute perfection and that included Brandie.

"I want you to help me choose something when I finish rehearsing."

Brandie's eyes widened. Her curiosity was overflowing as to what Julian wanted her to choose. She said excitedly, "What...what do you want me to help you choose?"

Julian yelled to the band, "Okay, guys, break's over."

He then told Brandie, who was still waiting for an answer, "I'll tell you later." He went back on stage and rehearsed vigorously. Brandie watched as he sang, did splits and spins, and played the piano. She cheered. She enjoyed watching the man she loved on stage doing the one thing he loved more than her.

At nine o'clock, Julian finished rehearsing. He sent the limo on its way and got into Brandie's car. He drove once again as they headed into Southfield, Michigan. "I'm looking for a house for my mom. Will you help me?"

Brandie happily agreed. "Of course, baby."

They drove around for an hour. Neither Brandie nor Julian saw a house they liked. "We'll go back out tomorrow," he said. "Can you come by for a while?"

Brandie unsurely said, "Well...it is Monday. I have to work tomorrow."

Julian replied, "Oh...okay, I understand."

Brandie caressed his cheek, seeing the disappointment on his face. "Yes, let's go to your house. I'm almost the boss at work anyway, right?"

Julian coolly replied, "You're right!" They headed to Belleville.

Julian pulled up in front of his house. She saw a fairly large and charming brick ranch-style house across the street from his house. It had a "For Sale" sign out front. "That's it!" she shouted. She had moved forward on the car seat excitedly and was staring at the house across from Julian's.

Julian looked across the street, too. He frowned and said, "Maybe you're right. That is a fairly nice house. I...I just never thought of my mother living across the street from me."

Brandie playfully hit him on the arm and said, "Julian!" He chuckled. She then said, "It's more than a fairly nice house...it's beautiful."

Julian and Brandie talked for a little while longer while sitting in her car. Shortly after, they headed up to his house. Artie was in the kitchen making himself a snack, when they entered the house. When Artie heard the front door close, he walked out of the kitchen and said, "Hey Jewel!" He then saw the shapely beauty standing beside him.

Julian smiled and said, "Artie, this is Brandie. Brandie...this is my bodyguard and chauffeur, Artie."

Artie exclaimed, "You're the chick at the gift shop!"

Julian asked, What?"

Artie continued, "She's the one I told you looked like she would make a good wife for you. The one I saw in California at the gift shop."

Brandie chucked, as Julian stood with a puzzled look on his face. "Yes, I went into the shop when Julian was there.

Artie clapped his hands together excitedly. "I knew it!"

Brandie continued, "I left before he saw me, though. I guess I was a little nervous about seeing him again." Brandie smiled. "Hello, Artie, I'm Brandie Charles. It's nice to meet you."

"Same here, Ms. Charles. I'll leave you two alone, now." He looked at Julian and walked back to the kitchen doorway. He looked back at Brandie and said, "You sure are pretty. If I was twenty years younger, Jewel would have some trouble." Brandie laughed.

"Good night, Artie," said Julian sternly. He slightly chuckled. Artie went into the kitchen again. He got his plate off the counter and headed downstairs to his furnished quarters.

Julian and Brandie sat on the couch and kissed each other passionately. As he kissed her neck, she glanced at the large living room. "This place is lovely, Julian."

Julian, sensuously planting kisses on her neck, said, "It's okay. I'm thinking of moving, myself."

Brandie was going to ask why, but she thought of Shelly Nohl. "I guess there are too many memories here, huh?" said Brandie.

Julian then said huskily, as he continued to kiss her, "Yeah something like that."

Brandie then asked, "I know it's none of my business, but did you two share the same bedroom?"

Julian laughed. "No, baby, she slept in the guest room. And no, I never made love to her here. I was tempted once, but I didn't love her. She wasn't you."

Brandie hugged him saying, "Oh baby, I love you."

Julian carried her to his bedroom and made hot steamy love to her. A few hours later, she left for home.

Chapter Forty-three

The Cobb Arena was filled with people. It was 7:45 P.M. and the show was to start in fifteen minutes. The curtains were closed on the stage, and the band was behind the curtain tuning up. Jewel was in his dressing room along with Brandie. She was applying his stage make-up.

The hysterical crowd chanted, "We want Jewel! We want Jewel!" After Brandie had finished applying his make-up, she said, "I have your guitar."

"My guitar?" asked Julian, looking puzzled. He slung his hair back.

She replied, "Yeah, the one you left over my house, you know, the night we...well, the night you left me." She went over to the closet.

Julian said, "I didn't leave you, Red. I told you, I had to go and...find out just who Julian Phalan Parr is."

Brandie took the worn-looking lavender guitar out of the closet and handed it to him. "I got it repaired in California," she said. "The guy said that it was old, that they didn't make them like that anymore."

Julian exclaimed, "Damned right!" He played a few chords on the guitar.

Brandie declared, "I took it with me to UCLA, Jewel. It was kind of...I guess, like having you with me."

Julian said, "Brandie, you don't know how much this means to me. It was my father's." He played a few more chords on the guitar.

The audience's cheers and stomps were getting louder. He chuckled. She kissed him on the cheek and said, "You better get out there."

Jewell handed the guitar to her and said, "It's ours now, Red. I might show it to Steven, but he thinks that thing is dead and buried." He again heard his fans call for him.

"I gotta go, Brandie."

She said quickly, "Break a leg, sweetheart."

Julian headed out onto the stage. The crowd went wild. He was dressed in gold satin tight fitting pants and no shirt. His gold suspenders accented his hairy muscular chest. He had on gold super-high boots. His hair hung long with a few waves in it.

Julian said, "Hello, Detroit! I'm back!" The crowd roared. They were standing up whistling. Some of them were jumping up and down and dancing. Julian shouted, "One, two, three, hit it!" His background band Granite played a pop song from his new album called "Rise." Julian sang the song like a heavenly being. He danced and played guitar like a man possessed. The audience's cheers were deafening.

Steven shouted, "Yeah! That's my son!" as did Rachel. They and Tracy were seated midway on the ground floor of the arena. Jewel belted out tunes from his past albums and a few from the soon to be released new album.

Brandie at first was watching from his dressing room behind the stage. Jewel's performance was extraordinary. Overcome with excitement, she was screaming and dancing like the audience. She ran down the hall and entered the arena also. The concert was sold out, so there were no more seats available. Brandie shoved her way through the cheering mob. She was looking for a vacant seat so she could check out the show.

Julian was on stage jamming the house like only Jewel could jam it. He was now singing a rock tune titled, "My Pebble, Your Rock."

Brandie finally ran into Tracy, whose boyfriend was out of town and was unable to attend the concert. She was standing and enjoying the show. Steven and Rachel were one seat over from Corina Charles and her husband, Jarrod. "Yes!" shouted Brandie as she saw the vacant seat. She again shoved her way over to where Tracy was standing. "Hi!" shouted Brandie over the loud music.

Tracy looked over at the petite young woman and yelled, "Hi! Brandie, isn't it?"

Brandie yelled, "Yeah! Is the seat next to you taken!"

Tracy shouted, "No, come on in!" She stepped back, allowing Brandie to enter. The whole audience was still standing, so in order to see Jewel, Brandie stood with the rest of the audience.

Rachel looked at the lovely girl who was now standing next to her. Brandie smiled. "Hello!" she shouted. Rachel nodded. She knew the girl wouldn't hear her if she spoke.

On stage, Jewel said, "I'm going to play you a love song, so sit back and enjoy!" He added, "It's called 'Precious Jewel.' It's the name of my new album...I hope you enjoy." He sat at the piano. The audience then sat down as well. They clapped as Julian started to play the piano.

Brandie touched Rachel softly on the arm. "Hi, I'm one of Jewel's managers. I'm the one who called you about the tickets."

"Yes, this is Jewel's father and my husband, Steven," said Rachel. She touched Steven on the shoulder. "Steven, this cute young woman is Jewel's manager."

Steven looked over at Brandie and said, "Hi." He then smiled. Looking over at Tracy and then Rachel, he said, "Don't tell me you two don't know who she is?"

Tracy said, "Yeah, I know who she is. She use to live in our neighborhood."

Rachel then said, looking strangely at Brandie, "No...no I don't remember her." Brandie laughed.

Steven said, "Rachel...it's Brandie, Brandie Charles—Corina's daughter."

Rachel's eyes widened. Astonished, Rachel said, "My God, child. I haven't seen you since you were in grade school." She looked at Brandie again. "You're beautiful. You're not that slightly plump tomboy hippie anymore, are you?"

Brandie shyly said, "No...Mrs. Parr, I guess not."

Rachel, in amazement looked at Steven. "I knew it was her, dear. Corina's husband owns the company. That had to be Brandie. It certainly isn't Corina," said Steven.

Rachel hit Steven's hand and said, "Shush."

Steven then laughed. "Face it, dear, Corina's a lovely woman, but the last few years...it looks like her only love has been the refrigerator." Steven laughed again.

"Shh," again said Rachel. "Like you said, Corina's a lovely woman, so let's just leave it at that."

Jewel was finally finished playing the piano solo to "Precious Jewel." The silent crowd whistled and clapped for him in the dark arena. Rachel still couldn't get over how wonderful Brandie now looked. Rachel looked over at her again and smiled. Brandie smiled back.

Jewel was still seated at his piano. He then said, "My family is here tonight, somewhere out there." The crowd cheered and clapped. He got up from the piano and said, "I'll be right back." The band played while he took a break.

A few minutes later, he returned to the stage with the lavender guitar. Steven stood up in shock. He looked up at Jewel, holding his old guitar, and shouted, "All right, son! All right!"

Rachel stood up also, looking astonished. She then said, "Where on earth did he find that thing!" She frowned.

Steven kissed her on the cheek and said, "It's his now, he deserves it." She smiled in satisfaction.

Julian played the guitar like the pro he was. The crowd stood again and cheered. He then said, "We're coming to the end of our show." The audience booed in disappointment and said, "Aw!"

"I don't want to go either," said Jewel. "This is my comeback concert and you all make me want to keep on coming."

The audience cheered and whistled. "Yeah! Yeah!" the audience shouted.

Jewel said, "This guitar belongs to my dad. I haven't really been close to my father or any of my family for the last few years." The audience was now silent. He laughed. "But that's okay. All that's gonna change." He added, "I just bought my family a house right across the street from mine."

The crowd again cheered and whistled. "Jewel! Jewel! Jewel!" they chanted.

Julian had a sad look on his face as he said solemnly, "Just to give them back a little of what they've given me." The crowd was still cheering.

Rachel said, "Oh my God!" She then cried.

Steven said, "What's wrong with you, woman?"

"I...I'm just so overjoyed," she said.

Tracy laughed and said, "That brother of mine is terrific!" She turned to Brandie. "He called me today and gave me a job as his wardrobe designer."

Brandie smiled. "He's the best."

The crowd was still in an uproar. Julian shouted, "This is the last song of the night, and I'm going to play it on Lavender Lightning, my father's guitar. He knows why I named it Lavender Lightning." He chuckled and then played the guitar.

He started singing the words to his final song of the night. "I've been holding back for so long, waiting for you to come to me. Still it's only you I see. That's why I pour myself a brandie...Brandie always soothes my soul, and now I'm never alone. So when this crazy world, it gets to me, I can count on my Brandie. My Brandie...ooh wheee I love you girl. You know...you know I do. If you come back it won't hurt so much and I won't keep drinking like a fool...drinking like a fool. But now I need Brandie, my Brandie helps me sleep at night. Someone's holding me tight, when I got my Brandie. Yeah! Yeah! Yeah! My Brandie." Julian continued to sing.

Lisa Chablis Gardner

Brandie's eyes were filled with tears, knowing that the song was just for her. But she had to share Jewel with the world. Brandie sighed. Part of loving a rock star, she thought to herself.

Epilogue

The crowd was cheering as Jewel finished his final song. "Wait a damn minute! You're engaged to me!" Shelly ran through the crowd and up on stage. "I don't care how much you love that red-haired weirdo. You're engaged to me! Do you hear me, Jewel!" shouted Shelly.

The guards ran up on stage and grabbed her arms. She was struggling wildly. Julian sighed. He blew a kiss to the audience. They were now oohing and ahhing at Shelly's scene.

Brandie just sat watching the frightening incident. She was thinking as she gazed at Julian, I love you, Julian. Julian, who was over by his piano and out of the way of Shelly, walked over to the microphone. He then said, "I love you too, baby." He blew another kiss to the audience and left the stage.

Brandie was now halfway to his dressing room. "He heard me! He heard my thoughts," said Brandie as she headed quickly to Jewel's dressing room.

Two officers were now handcuffing Shelly. "Back to the women's correctional for you," said the chubby one.

The other one said, "Women are always trying to run away from that place. You'd think they'd know by now that when they jump that fence, we can track them down wherever they are."

Shelly angrily said, "Go to hell, both of you!"

The officers laughed and took her to the car. "Back to the pen for you," said the chubby officer. They drove off.

Jewel's comeback concert was definitely an event to be remembered in more ways than one.

Brandie entered Jewel's dressing room. She was breathing hard from her swift run. "You...you heard me," said Brandie.

Julian was looking out of the window. He turned to Brandie and said, "I've been able to do strange things all my life, Red. Yeah, I heard you, like you were whispering in my ear."

Brandie's eyes again widened. "Oh my God!" she gasped. Brandie ran over and hugged Julian. "You're wonderful. I love you so much. Do you know that, huh?" she said excitedly. "I always knew there was somebody out there for me. Someone different, special...magical!"

Julian then pulled back away from Brandie's hold. He had a strange look on his face. He reached in his pocket and pulled out a small velvet box. "Abracadabra," said Julian. He then handed the box to Brandie.

"Oh Julian, you shouldn't have," exclaimed Brandie.

Julian then said, "Yes I should have, a long time ago. Open it."

Brandie sighed and said, "Okay, here goes." She then opened the box. Her eyes sparkled as she looked at the contents in the box. "Oh my Lord, Julian," cried Brandie. "No, you shouldn't have," she said, looking half in shock. "It's the most beautiful ring I ever laid my eyes on."

Julian took the ring out of the box, then held Brandie's left hand. He slid the ring on her finger. Tears again started to fill Brandie's eyes. Julian then said, "I want you with me always. Will you marry me?"

Brandie swallowed hard and said, "Yes...yes, there isn't anything more that I want to do than be your wife, Julian."

"December 24, 1994," said Julian. He looked into Brandie's eyes.

Tears rolled down Brandie's face as she said, "On Christmas Eve...baby, that's so romantic."

"Yeah baby, you'll be my Christmas bride," said Jewel. "Come on." Julian held Brandie's hand as he led her outside in the back of the Cobb Arena.

"It's raining, Julian. What are you doing?" asked Brandie.

Julian, looking devastatingly sexy, said, "Aren't you the redhead who wanted the man who fell in love with you to make love to you...." She and Julian both said, "In the rain."

Brandie caressed Julian's cheek. "You remembered."

"Everything about you. I even remember your scream," said Julian in a deep husky tone. "I want to make you scream, now baby." Brandie chuckled. Julian grabbed Brandie, holding her hungrily. He stared into Brandie's eyes sensuously. "Let me make love to you, baby." He again led Brandie toward the back door of the arena.

Brandie said, "I...I don't know about this Jewel. This is crazy! It's muddy out here. And I just bought this outfit. See...it's gold. It matched your stage wardrobe tonight."

Jewel said, "Stand back." He looked at Brandie from head to toe. "You look very sexy. Gold lace leggings, gold pumps, and a gold lace teddy. Yeah, you look very sexy." Brandie didn't comment. "But you'll look even sexier without it on."

Brandie laughed and said, "Jewel! Just take a cold shower, okay?"

"Uhn-uhn. I want you in the rain." He went over and kissed Brandie passionately and said, "I need it in the mud." He undressed Brandie and then himself. He threw the clothes on the ground, saying, "I'll buy you some more."

Julian and Brandie laid in the muddy field of the Cobb Arena and made wild passionate love. As he made love to Brandie, he hummed in her ear and began singing, "I've been a fool, my love. Breaking the hearts of many, I even broke yours, too. But, my love, forgive me for being cruel. I am yours—and you're my...Precious Jewel."

This was the love song Jewel had opened his concert with. It was the title song on his upcoming album, titled Precious Jewel.

Brandie moaned in ecstasy as Julian performed his magic. She could never seem to get enough his hard and large masculinity. His gyrations and thrusts overwhelmed her, resulting in Brandie's screams of passion. The light of dawn had shone miraculously from out of nowhere on the two lovers, directing and guiding their every move.